W9-AHY-374

STAR TREK
LOG TEN

Alan Dean Foster

Based on the Popular Animated Series Created
by Gene Roddenberry

A Del Rey Book

BALLANTINE BOOKS • NEW YORK

For EYTON G. MITCHELL, good friend,
doctor to the sick, minister to the helpless,
who realizes that the only difference between
a hand and a paw is a little fur

A Del Rey Book
Published by Ballantine Books

Copyright © 1978 by Paramount Pictures Corporation

All rights reserved under International and Pan-American
Copyright Conventions. Published in the United States by Ballantine Books, a division of Random House, Inc., New York,
and simultaneously in Canada by Ballantine Books of Canada,
Ltd., Toronto, Canada.

This book is based in part on the short story "The Soft
Weapon," by Larry Niven. Copyright © 1967 by Galaxy Pub-
lishing Corporation.

Library of Congress Catalog Card Number: 74-8477

ISBN 0-345-27212-9

Manufactured in the United States of America

First Edition: January 1978

Cover art by Stanislaw Fernandes

SIC TRANSPORT . . .

"Mr. Scott, Doctor McCoy . . . what happened?" There was an odd lilt to Kirk's otherwise normal voice. But after the disturbing experience of being frozen in a transporter field for an abnormal length of time, a few side effects were to be expected.

"There was a malfunction in the transporter, Captain. Maybe due to damage received from that pulsar we encountered. We had to put you in limbo for a while until I could get it fixed," Scott said. "You gave us all a bad scare."

Then Sulu's eyes widened, and he extended both arms out in front of him, rotated them over and back. His hands went to his face, felt his features.

"Oh my God. What's happened to us? What's happened to *me*?" He gestured shakily toward the body of the Captain. "If I'm Kirk in Sulu's body, then who are you?"

"I'm Lieutenant Uhura, of course," Kirk replied!

Also by Alan Dean Foster
available now from Ballantine Books:

STAR TREK LOG TEN

Log of the Starship *Enterprise*

Stardates 5538.6–5539.2 Inclusive

James T. Kirk, Capt., USSC, FC, ret.,

Commanding

transcribed by
Alan Dean Foster

At the Galactic Historical Archives
Ursa Major Lacus
stardated 6111.3

For the Curator: JLR

SLAVER WEAPON

(Adapted from a script by Larry Niven)

Stardate 5538.6. Transmission/private-personal. Code to officer annual allotment #C-5539, personnel budget U.S.S. *Enterprise,* on patrol in sector (censored) to: Mr./Mrs. Alhamisi Uhura, rural route 5, Kitui province, Kenya state, Africa, Earth 100643.
Begin transmission:

Dear Mom and Dad:
   Not much new from out here, since the scenery doesn't change too quickly. By the time this letter reaches you, Dad, the harvest should be in. I hope the corn has done well, because I understand that hog prices are fairly high and are expected to go higher, so you and Mom ought to be able to do very good business this year.
   How is everyone else back home? I am fine, thanks, and so is everyone else on board. We are enjoying a little routine, quiet patrolling for a change. Quite a relief after all the trouble we had with the Pandronians. I'm sure you read about that business in the local news. While I'm not at liberty to discuss details, take my word for it that there's more to that story than you've heard. We almost lost Mr. Spock to a (details deleted, ship compucensor).
   Dr. McCoy has promised to send brother David some interesting information on the multiple-community Pandronian life systems (at least, anything which Star Fleet doesn't censor). It's purely biological material and should be passable for communication. David could get a paper or two out of it, I think. Dr. McCoy will send it to David's office at Makere University Hospital in Kampala instead of to the house there, so it can be transmitted as official business.
   I'm still enjoying my work tremendously and am doing what I really always wanted to do—help to

push back the frontiers of knowledge just a little bit. I've never been sorry for going into Star Fleet or for having specialized in communications.

Do you realize, Mom, that when I'm on duty on the bridge I'm the only one who knows what's going on all over the ship? That's because I'm constantly monitoring interlevel and interdepartmental communications as well as deep-space transmissions. What other career could offer me anything to compare in excitement with what I'm doing right now?

Well, got to go now. This letter will use up all my personal communication's allowance for the next month, so you won't be hearing from me again before then.

Your loving daughter,

Uhura signed the message, punched it into the ship's computer for deep-space transmission, and drifted off into a daydream. She remembered killing the lion.

It was the day after her sixteenth birthday. The midsummer East African sun turned the soil to dust. Motionless regiments of hybrid corn grew higher than a man, hiding any glimpse of the towers of now-distant Kitui or the parched veldt ahead.

Uhura sat pouting beside her father as he guided the car over the lightly traveled roadway. She held the elaborately decorated spear indifferently, though she was careful not to let the sharp point scratch the transparent bubble-dome of the car. There was a certain boy she could have been picnicking with, and she would have far rather been there than here.

"I still don't see why I have to kill a lion, Dad."

Her father looked over at her, smiled through his neatly trimmed beard. "It is traditional. Once upon a time the tradition applied only to manchildren. But"—and his grin grew wider—"you women changed that a couple of hundred years ago. So now the ritual applies to you as well."

"*I* didn't change it." She folded her arms, looked exquisitely bored. The air-conditioning was crawly on her body. The short skirt she wore provided little warmth.

"Besides, it's cold in here. Can't I put my shorts and halter back on?"

"Tradition should be upheld, Uhura. Sometimes that's all one has to remind one of the past. Tradition says that to prove you have become a woman, you must kill a lion with a single spear, by yourself. Since you must do this in the manner of your ancestors, that means you must do it wearing their archaic attire also."

She fingered the heavy metal and bead necklaces which hung awkwardly from her neck. "Can I at least take these off? How could anyone fight while wearing five kilos of jewelry?"

Her father tried to soothe her. "Come now, it's not that bad. This will all be over with soon enough. You will do well, too. Your grandfather has foretold it in the bones."

"Chicken bones don't indicate the future." The lithe young girl snorted derisively. "They only indicate the former presence of an unlucky chicken."

"Your grandfather has more respect for ancient lore than most of his contemporaries, and certainly more than you children today! One day you'll admire him for it. Besides, he does no worse with his bones than the computer does when it comes to forecasting long-range weather."

"*He* loads the tapes," she said, but unconvincingly. Grandfather Uchawi was a lovable but peculiar old man.

Her father turned his attention back to the road. "Besides, you've always been a straight-A student in physical education. I trust in that even more than in your grandfather's bones."

Humming silently, the electric vheicle turned off the main roadway and moved down a much narrower path. Traffic here was infrequent. They had emerged from the yellow-green ocean of corn and were traveling over undulating, grassy plains: cattle country. Shining like milk quartz in the noonday sun, the benign crown of white-capped Kilimanjaro gazed down on them. Soon they would leave private land and cross force barriers into the Serengeti.

Uhura regarded her spear again, wishing the ceremonial feathers tied just below the blade were sewn to one of her summer dresses. Matching feathers were tied behind her, to the base of the oval shield and to the second spear she was permitted. This extra spear was a concession to the times. Since the ancient skills were so rarely practiced, she would be permitted two chances instead of the traditional one. Both weapons, however, looked much too fragile to challenge the tawny king of the veldt.

Her father reached the Serengeti force barrier and turned down a road paralleling it, until they reached a game-park gate. The path beyond was not paved. None of the paths in the vast parkland were.

He exchanged greetings with the automatic gate. It confirmed their names and appointment time and admitted them. For another hour they drove on, passing through rugged brushland. The area looked no different from pictures Uhura had seen of this country as it had been a thousand years ago.

Eventually the land cruiser slowed to a halt, settled gently to the ground. Her father slipped out, helping her with the bulky shield and second spear. Slinging one spear across her back, Uhura, by then resigned to her fate, hefted the shield in her left hand, the other spear in her right, and faced the high thornbrush across the way.

"How will I find the lion?"

"Don't worry, my daughter. The lion will find you. Be ready at all times, don't panic, and remember what you were taught in school."

With that he bestowed a brief, affectionate kiss on her forehead and returned to the land cruiser. She watched it rise, turn, and disappear down the path they'd come.

She stood alone, listening to the warbling of secretive birds.

Her nose itched, and she rubbed it with the hand holding the spear. Clear of the land cruiser's air-conditioning, she was no longer cold. If anything, she was rapidly becoming hot standing in the sun. Then she began to understand the appropriateness of her dress—or rather the lack of it.

With the disappearance of the vehicle, more birds sang freely in the surrounding trees and brush. Sounds of larger creatures moving about reached her. Monkeys, most likely. The sun was beginning to bother her, but she remembered what her lore instructor had told her, and hesitated before retreating into the shade. If there were lions about, the shade was a likely place for them to be resting.

Something brushed a bush on her right. She turned to stare at it, saw only branches. It was probably another monkey. If so, then this would be a safe place to escape from the sun. No monkey would move close to the ground in the vicinity of a lion. But it wouldn't take much to make sure. Finding a suitable rock nearby, she cleared it of ants, aimed it, and threw it into the rustling copse.

Something that sounded like a demolished building crumpling to the earth shook her ears. Though she had heard that thunder on many tapes, the real thing still paralyzed her. A shape the size of a small land cruiser erupted from the brush, an umber nimbus framing a vast mouth full of flashing white fangs.

In place of coherent thought, months of practice at school took over. Instantly Uhura dropped to her right knee. The shield stood braced against her left foreleg as she wrapped both hands tightly around the shaft of the spear, left hand over right as she ground the spear-butt sharply into the dirt.

The lion leaped.

A terrific concussion traveled along her arms and shoulders as the lion came down on the blade of the spear.

A killing strike first time was as much a combination of luck as skill. Uhura had been lucky. She wouldn't need to use the second spear. The point of the first had missed the ribs, slid between them to pierce the heart.

Even so, her posture was not quite perfect and the lion's trailing leg caught her, knocked her over backward, and sent the shield tumbling. But as she rolled to her feet and fumbled for the second spear she saw that the great cat was already lying still on its side. Her first spear protruded brokenly from its chest.

So fast had the attack come that she had the remainder of her allotted hour free. She was sitting in the shade enjoying her sparse lunch when her father finally arrived to pick her up. He emerged from the land cruiser as it settled to the earth. Curious, he inspected the motionless form of the lion, then came over to greet her. Pride glistened in his eyes and she felt a little embarrassed.

"You did very well, child."

"Thanks," she replied. "I'm glad it's over, though." She checked her wrist chronometer. "If we hurry I might still make the end of the picnic."

"That boy again?" He smiled. "All right, we'll hurry."

She pointed to the corpse as they walked toward the vehicle. "I hope I didn't break anything. It hit pretty hard on the spearpoint."

"Don't worry." Her father put an arm around her and playfully tugged the traditional Masai braids that hung from her head. "The operative motors, the generator, and the controlling elements are well protected in the head and legs. I've seen the insides and they're beautifully put together. Made to take a lot of punishment, too. See? The hour's up and they're starting it up again."

Sure enough, the lion rose as they watched. It used one paw to pull the spear free. There was no blood. Just a few shreds of torn plastic. The simulacrum walked over, politely handed Uhura her spear, and loped easily back into the brush.

"What happens, Dad, if somebody misses a kill with both spears?"

"In that case, sugar, the lion comes over, pats you on the head, and goes back into the forest to wait for the next tester like yourself. If you fail, you get to try again in six months."

He regarded the veldt silently for a moment, then added, "In the old days, if you missed with your spears, you never got a second chance."

Another land cruiser had pulled up alongside theirs. Two sixteen-year-old boys jumped out, accompanied by an older man and woman.

"We'd better leave. We're running into someone else's testing hour, and the simulacrum won't begin its stalk until both cars have left."

Uhura trotted alongside her father as they returned to their land cruiser. Both boys eyed her curiously but said nothing. The one nearest her was pretty good-looking, but their minds were elsewhere and she couldn't say anything to them anyhow. That was against the rules.

As she climbed back into the chilled cab of the land cruiser and reached gratefully for her everyday clothes, it struck her that according to modern tribal tradition she was now a fully adult woman. Probably she was supposed to feel different—excited or something. All she felt was relief that the ordeal was over.

The ritual hadn't been as boring as she had expected, however. The simulacrum of the lion had been *very* real, much more so than the ones she had practiced against in school. But her primary emotion was impatience to return to town.

As the land cruiser hummed smoothly toward the park gate, she wondered for an instant what it must have been like hundreds of years ago, when Masai youths had to go out on their own and confront real lions, not a composite of fluids and metals and circuitry. Ones with real teeth, which could cut through a shoulder in a single snap or crush a skull like an eggshell. She shuddered a little, and this time it wasn't an effect of the air-conditioning.

She had often gazed on the wild lions hunting out in the Serengeti. What made her queasy wasn't the thought of being eaten by one, but the concept of slaughtering one of the magnificent creatures simply to prove a point about aging which she found upsetting. Thank goodness she didn't live in such superstitious times, although her grandfather would have chided her for such disrespect.

II

Something beeped in her ear. Uhura woke with a start and activated the incoming call.

"Message from Starfleet headquarters, relayed, priority coded, Captain."

Kirk turned in the command chair to face her. "Restricted access, Lieutenant Uhura?"

She checked the signal code. "It doesn't say here, sir."

"Put it on the main screen then, Lieutenant."

Uhura complied, and a portrait took shape on the main viewscreen forward. The uniform beneath was not that of a military man but of a United Federation of Planets diplomat. Spock's brows lifted slightly in puzzlement. It was highly unusual for diplomatic information to come directly to them without being shuttled through Starfleet channels. Then the scene enlarged slightly to reveal a commodore sitting alongside. Spock relaxed. The situation had changed from unusual to simply curious.

"Captain Kirk," said the man in the diplomatic attire, "I am Joseph Laiguer, personal envoy and ambassador plenipotentiary to the systems of Briamos. I suggest a moment to familiarize yourself with the basic details of Briamos as supplied to all Starfleet vessels."

"Well, Mr. Spock?" Kirk glanced across at his science officer, who replied softly.

"A fairly recent Federation contact, Captain, on the fringe of explored territory. There are three closely aligned solar systems containing five inhabited worlds comprising the government of Briamos. The Briamosites are technologically advanced and possess their own modest space fleet. They are humanoid, though they average a third of a meter taller than human or Vulcan norm and are reputed to be a polite but suspicious people."

"That matches what I can recall about them. Thank you, Spock."

"You have now had time to discuss Briamos with your officers," the ambassador continued as if no pause in their conversation had taken place. "You may already have asked yourself why I am contacting you directly; also why I am calling from Starfleet headquarters if I am ambassador to these worlds. The answer to both is that I was called back for consultation, unfortunately."

"Why unfortunately?" Kirk asked.

"Because," the ambassador said, leaning forward intently, "it seems that the Briamosites abruptly decided the other day to hold a conference on their homeworld during which they will decide whether or not they will enter into a preliminary alliance—social, cultural, and military—with either the Federation . . . or the Klingon Empire."

What had thus far been a fairly ordinary communication was one no longer. Although no one on the bridge neglected his assignment duties, everyone delegated a portion of his attention to the figure speaking from the viewscreen.

"Observers and representatives of both the Federation and Klingon Empire have been invited to participate in the conference and to present their respective positions regarding the Briamosites' intentions."

"And you can't be there," said Kirk, filling in blanks. "Why not?"

"Among other things," the ambassador explained, "the Briamosites are noted for their impatience." He named a date. "As you can see, it would be impossible for me to reach Briamos from Starfleet headquarters anywhere near the time set for the opening of the conference."

"Are the Briamosites so impatient they wouldn't delay the start of such an important conference until you could arrive?" Impatience was one thing, Kirk thought, but this bordered on downright rudeness.

The ambassador was slowly shaking his head. "It is important to them, Captain Kirk. According to the Briamosite way of thinking, we will be the ones guilty of an insult if we do not arrive in time for the beginning of their conference. Therefore," and he rustled some papers before him officiously, "since the *Enterprise* is patrolling in the Federation sector nearest to Briamos, you are directed to proceed there, Captain, empowered to act as ambassador-at-large for the Federation with all due powers and rights in my absence and to act for and in the name of the United Federation of Planets." He dropped the papers, regarded the viewscreen pickup solemnly.

Kirk shifted uneasily in his chair. He would far rather have been informed he could expect to deal with a rapacious alien life form than with the intricacies of diplomacy.

As the ambassador concluded his talk, Spock turned and began speaking softly to his computer pickup. There were important preparations to be made, and he was commencing such activities already.

"That's all I have to say." The ambassador looked to his right. As he did so, the view widened to include the officer sitting next to him. "But Commodore Musashi has a few comments to add, I believe."

Kirk had never met the diminutive commodore now gazing out at him, but he knew of him by reputation: an old-line officer famed for directness and the brilliance of his tactical solutions to logistical problems. With the Romulans on one side and the Klingons on the other, plus assorted bellicose organizations in between, the United Federation of Planets had special need of men with Musashi's particular analytical talents. So, while the older officer would no doubt have preferred a ship command to a desk job, the requirements of the Federation kept him tied to Starfleet headquarters.

Kirk could sympathize with what he had heard. Only loyalty kept Musashi active. In Musashi's position, having to battle figures and charts and petty bureaucratic interference, Kirk probably would have resigned. The fact that the commodore remained to serve the Fleet despite personal feelings only made Kirk pay particular attention to what the man was about to say.

"I cannot overemphasize the importance of this assignment to you, Captain Kirk," the commodore began earnestly. "You must keep in mind at all times that these Briamosites are not only not just your average cluster of primitive aborigines, but are one of the most advanced races we have contacted in a hundred years." Spock turned his attention from various science readouts to pay attention as the commodore paused for effect, then continued.

"Starfleet intelligence has estimated that the five worlds of Briamos have a combined population of well over seven billion. In terms of natural resources these five worlds and the uninhabited satellite worlds of their three systems are quite wealthy. Here at Starfleet the impression of the Briamosites themselves is one of a competent, highly industrious people. It goes without saying that they would be a welcome addition even on a limited-alliance basis to the United Federation."

Musashi leaned back in his seat, sighed deeply. "Unfortunately, they could also become a powerful ally of the Klingons. From what we know of their natural temperament, which borders on brusqueness at times, they could blend in as well with the Klingons as with us.

"Should the Briamosites decide to link themselves with the Klingon Empire and should that relationship be cemented in the future, it would do much more than simply gain the Klingons a powerful friend. Because of their position on the flank of the Empire, the Briamosites could be counted on by the Klingons to anchor that portion of their empire and protect it from attack. Doing so would free their ships immediately to create considerably more mischief elsewhere."

"The term 'mischief' is imprecise, but I have no doubt as to the commodore's true meaning." Spock glanced over at Kirk as he spoke.

"I don't think anyone would, Mr. Spock," Kirk agreed.

Once again the pickup concentrated on the ambassador. "There you have the situation, Captain Kirk. We of the Federation Diplomatic Corps wish you luck and know you'll carry out your assignment to the credit of us all. I wish only that I could be there in person to assist you, but space and time preclude it." He paused, obviously trying to think if he'd forgotten anything.

"Again, keep in mind always the Briamosites' natural impatience. We've already contacted them and informed them that our representative—meaning you—will arrive in time for the conference. What else could we say?" He shrugged slightly. "They replied in their gruffly polite fashion that our representatives would be most welcome—indeed, would be anxiously awaited—but that the conference date is set and will proceed whether or not the *Enterprise* arrives on time." Another pause, and when he resumed it was in a low, almost warning tone.

"I need hardly tell you, Captain, that the absence of the Federation representative at the conference would be tantamount to an expression of disinterest on our part, if not an outright insult. Nothing could be better calculated to drive the Briamosites into the orbit of the Klingon Empire than for the *Enterprise* to arrive after the conference is scheduled to begin."

Kirk bridled at being so openly chided, but held his silence.

"You will proceed to Briamos by way of Starbase Twenty-Five. There you will receive additional briefings and more detailed information on what you can expect upon arriving at Briamos. You should have ample time to attend all the scheduled briefings and still reach Briamos well before the conference begins." The ambassador thought for a moment, glanced briefly over at the commodore, then said almost absently to the pickup at his end, "That's all, then, Captain Kirk. We of the Diplomatic Corps are with you in spirit if not in the flesh."

The picture faded. As it did so, Kirk thought he detected the barest hint of a reassuring grin on Commodore Musashi's face. It was a smile that said, Don't-mind-the-ambassador-he's-upset-because-he-can't-be-there-for-his-moment-of-glory-so-just-ignore-him-and-do-your-job.

"End transmission, Captain," Uhura announced formally as the last vestiges of image faded from the screen.

Kirk considered all he had just seen and heard, then swiveled to regard his first officer. "Well, Mr. Spock, I'd just as soon *not* engage in any professional word fighting, but we don't seem to have any choice. We're prisoners of our spatial position. At least we'll get to meet the Briamosites. They sound like an interesting people. I only wish we didn't have to be civil to a bunch of Klingons at the same time."

"I also have been intrigued by the little I have heard of Briamos and its inhabitants, Captain," replied Spock. "I am looking forward to the starbase sessions we will be attending."

Kirk nodded in reply, turned to face the helm. "Mr. Sulu, set a course for Starbase Twenty-Five."

"Yes, sir," Sulu responded, turning to his console.

"Standard cruising speed, Mr. Sulu." Kirk hesitated, then asked, "By the way, do we have coordinates for Briamos? In the event we run into trouble, we might have to bypass the starbase and proceed directly to Briamos."

Sulu made a rapid check of the navigation computer. "Coordinates for Briamos were entered last input session, sir. If we have to, we can get there from here."

Kirk relaxed a little at that information.

"Anticipating difficulties, sir?" Lieutenant Arex inquired from his position at the navigation station.

"Lieutenant, given the importance of this conference to both the Federation and Klingon, I'd be surprised if we *didn't* run into a little interference."

"Yes, sir," the Edoan acknowledged in his quiet way. "Dense of me not to see that, sir."

"Excuse me, Captain."

Kirk frowned slightly, glanced over a shoulder toward communications.

"What is it, Lieutenant Uhura?"

"Sir, I have"—she sounded a bit uncertain, which was unusual in itself—"another priority message coming in."

It was Spock who voiced the most obvious objection. "Are you certain it's not a ghost of the first message, Lieutenant?"

Uhura was rapidly checking several readouts. "No

sir, absolutely not. I haven't quite traced the place of origin, but it's definitely not coming from Starfleet coordinates."

There was silence on the bridge while Uhura fought with abstract math. As usual, she won. "The signal is very weak, Captain." Again delicate hands moved in an attempt to coax the incoming message to greater clarity. "Odd." She was staring at a single readout now. "According to my instrumentation the signal is emanating from a system known as Gruyakin."

"Mr. Spock?" But Kirk needn't have urged his first officer, who was already reading the requisite information from the science computer screen.

"The Gruyakin system consists of twelve planets circling a K-6 star, Captain," he reported. "Two of the dozen worlds are reported to be marginally habitable, but there are no settlements of any kind. The only item of interest stems from reports of a vanished civilization on one of the two inhabitable worlds."

"Then who," Kirk wondered aloud, "is broadcasting a message strong enough to reach this far?"

"I don't know, sir, but I have an acceptable signal now."

"Let's see it then, Lieutenant." Kirk turned his attention once again to the main screen.

Despite Uhura's best efforts and some heroic image enhancing by the communication computers, the picture that appeared there was fuzzy and distorted. But amid the interference everyone could make out a tired and none-too-clean, middle-aged human woman. They could also discern a few details, including prematurely gray hair, deep-set blue eyes, and an expression awash with worry and grave concern.

"Does anybody . . ." she said, obviously in the middle of repeating a by-now-old message. Abruptly she noticed an unseen control on her left and looked into her own pickup out onto the bridge of the *Enterprise*. Kirk wondered if her view of him was as weak as his own was of her.

"Sorry if we've startled you," he said, "but you were broadcasting on a priority Starfleet frequency."

"I know what we're doing!" she replied, a mite testily. Then it was her turn to apologize as she ran a hand over her forehead to brush aside several trailing hairs. "Excuse me, whoever you are. We've all been under a lot of pressure here. We still are.

"My name is Shannon Masid. I'm in charge of this expedition to Gruyakin Six." She used a thumb to gesture sharply over one coverall-clad shoulder.

"One of the two inhabitable worlds in the Gruyakin system, Captain," Spock whispered to him.

Despite the poor quality of the transmission, Kirk could just make out the curving wall of a transparent dome behind the woman and a very little bit of the landscape beyond. A few hardy, thin plants showed against the dome, as tired and beaten as the topography they grew upon. A lake so dull and black it might have been the source of the Styx lay in the distance.

"What expedition is that?" Kirk wanted to know. "According to our information there are no outposts in the Gruyakin system."

"Not so fast, sir. Who might you be?"

Kirk was a little peeved at what sounded almost like an accusation. This was evident in his reply, which was a touch sharper than he meant it to be. "I'm Captain James T. Kirk, commanding the U.S.S. *Enterprise*, en route to Starbase Twenty-Five."

"*Enterprise* . . . Starbase Twenty-Five." The woman appeared relieved, then said importantly, "Captain, I'm afraid I'm going to have to ask you to alter your course."

"Alter our—?" Kirk was speechless.

"I am sure Ms. Masid has a reason, sir," Spock said gently.

"I'm sure she does, Mr. Spock," Kirk replied firmly, "and I'm sure it's valid—to her." He directed his voice to the command-chair pickup.

"Ms. Masid, the *Enterprise* is on a mission of vital importance to the Federation. I can't imagine any circumstances under which we could alter our course. If you're in some difficulty, please explain its nature and we'll see that relief is sent to you promptly. But I'm afraid we cannot—"

"How do I know you're who and what you say you are?"

For a second Kirk's outrage threatened to overpower his reason. Then he considered the suspicion and fear in the woman's tone. His exasperation gave way to curiosity. This Masid did not look or sound like a fool. Then it came to him, something he had noticed as soon as she'd appeared on the screen but had only placed just now.

She wasn't just frightened. She was terrified. That had not been immediately obvious because she was fighting to keep her emotions under control.

"How do I know," she continued anxiously, "that you're not in some kind of disguise, that your appearance isn't meant to fool us?"

"Mr. Spock, play the visual pickup around the bridge," Kirk directed.

Spock did so, and the woman's darting eyes on the screen showed that she was following everything intently.

"Satisfied?" Kirk asked when the pickup had completed a circuit of the bridge.

"Almost. If this is a ruse, it's an elaborate one. Just one question," she went on rapidly. "Who won the Federation tridimensional hockey championship three years ago in the double-overtime final game, and who was named most valuable player?"

"Really, Ms. Masid!"

"I'm dead serious, Captain," she replied. "That information isn't likely to be in an enemy's computer banks."

"Her seriousness appears genuine, Captain." Spock was convinced of the woman's sincerity. "If you'll wait a moment I'll check the computer files in the recreation section and—"

Sulu interrupted him as he prepared to recover the necessary information.

"That's not necessary, Mr. Spock." The helmsman put himself on the pickup. "The Eridani Gryfalcons," he said. "Most valuable player was center-forward-up Shawn Ge-Yrmis."

"Thank you, whoever you are. That's right." The

woman on the screen smiled gratefully. Sulu glanced at the science station, and Spock nodded approvingly in return.

"That's as conclusive a test as I can think of," the figure on the screen declared. She folded her hands on the battered worktable before her. "I've got to accept that you're who you say you are.

"Our expedition isn't large or permanent enough to qualify for outpost status," she explained. "That's why we're not listed in your computer. I'm in charge of Federation Archeological Expedition Four-Six-Two, investigating the remnants of a dead civilization on Gruyakin's sixth planet."

"That matches the information we have, Captain," Spock declared.

"The civilization of this world," and she gestured again at the desolate, unimpressive landscape barely visible through the dome behind her, "was not particularly important, nor does it seem to us to have been especially impressive. Nevertheless, it was a civilization and all such are deemed worthy of study and investigation."

"I'm familiar with the motives of the Federation Science League," Kirk commented drily. "You still haven't explained your reason for utilizing a priority distress frequency."

"We've found something here which *is* impressive, Captain. It's the reason for our signal, for my unfriendly attitude, and for my caution in dealing with you. We couldn't risk having an unfriendly power learn what we've unearthed here. Captain, we've found a sealed Slaver stasis box."

Silence on the bridge.

Kirk turned to his first officer. "Mr. Spock, what are the odds of finding a Slaver stasis box on . . ." He stopped, waved diffidently. "No, never mind. All that matters is that such a box exists."

"We've been broadcasting our priority call ever since we found the box, Captain." The reasons for the archeologist's tenseness became clear. "Going on two weeks now. We haven't much of a transmitter here. Your ship is the first that's passed within hailing distance." She smiled slightly again. "This isn't a heavily funded expedition. As I said, Gruyakin's not thought to be very important.

"You see now, Captain Kirk, why you must change course. As far from developed Federation worlds as we are, I've been frightened that some unfriendly power or unprincipled group of humans might stumble on our discovery. A sealed Slaver stasis box, of course, is beyond price."

"I understand now, Ms. Masid." Kirk regarded her sympathetically. "You were right to be so cautious. The temptation would be enormous even for an honest man. We'll be there as soon as possible and we'll relieve you of that box."

"Thank you." She was so obviously happy that it was embarrassing. "I can handle responsibility, but this is a bit too much for me, Captain. We'll be anxiously awaiting your arrival here."

"Your pardon, Captain," Spock began urgently, but Kirk hushed him.

"I'll be glad to see the damn thing gone," Shannon Masid was saying. "So we can all get back to some simple, uncomplicated excavating. We'll have our beacon set to provide you with beam-down or landing coordinates. Gruyakin Six out . . ."

"Captain, you cannot afford to miss the orientation sessions at Starbase Twenty-Five and still expect to make credible and accurate ambassadorial decisions." Spock regarded the captain expectantly. The hoped-for suggestion was not long in coming.

"No, I can't, Mr. Spock. But _you_ can."

"That was my thought as well, Captain."

Kirk completed a mental outline. "You, Lieutenant Uhura, and Lieutanant Sulu will travel via shuttlecraft to Gruyakin Six and take custody of the stasis box. While you are doing that, I'll be undergoing briefing sessions on Briamos at Starbase Twenty-Five. We'll depart from Briamos upon completion of those sessions or immediately on your arrival from Gruyakin, whichever falls nearest to the time set for the beginning of the conference." He paused thoughtfully, added, "I'd rather have you undergo those same sessions, Mr.

Spock, but I'm confident that as long as one of us attends them, he can fill in the other on Briamosite protocol and such with the aid of tapes."

"I believe I can cope with the material sufficiently, prior to our arrival at Briamos, Captain."

Kirk smiled imperceptibly. "I'm sure you can, Spock." The smile vanished. "I wouldn't consider sending you three," and he gazed in turn at each of the three designated officers, "prior to so vital a conference if an unopened stasis box wasn't of nearly equal importance."

"Captain?"

"Yes, Spock?"

"Rather than have Lieutenant Commander Scott substitute in my place, Captain, and have someone take over in turn for him, I request permission to have Lieutenant Vedama of Sciences handle my duties in my temporary absence. I'll have little time to brief him, but he's a highly competent officer who deserves the opportunity to gain some experience in a command position. He has served as chief science officer on smaller Starfleet vessels. For him to take over for me on short notice, even for a week or so, will be excellent training."

Kirk nodded approvingly. It was like Spock to have the interests of a younger officer in mind even as he was about to embark on a serious mission of his own.

"I haven't heard anyone speak ill of the officer you mention, Mr. Spock. Request approved. You'll detail the lieutenant personally before you depart."

"Of course, Captain."

Rising from the command chair, Kirk met with the three department officers near the turbolift doors. "You'll leave as soon as possible. If you reach Gruyakin and have even a suspicion that another vessel might be in your spatial vicinity, get in touch with us immediately."

"What could you do in such a situation, Captain?" Spock wanted to know. "You still cannot deviate from your appointment with the briefers at Starbase Twenty-Five."

"One crisis at a time, Mr. Spock." He went on more seriously. "I really don't know. Much would depend on our exact position relative to Gruyakin and the base, and the position of the other ship, its markings, and so on. The difficulty stems from the fact that the contents of a Slaver box might be worth more than an alliance with Briamos, or they might be worthless. Let's hope no such problems arise. Just pick up the box and get out of the Gruyakin system as fast as you're able."

All three officers acknowledged the captain's orders, then hurried to their cabins. Only the minimum of personal effects would be taken. A shuttlecraft had very little spare room. But they wouldn't be gone very long and nothing beyond the basics was required.

Not long after leaving the bridge, they were clustered in the shuttlecraft bay. Engineer Scott was waiting to greet them, having just finished a personal checkout of the little shuttlecraft *Copernicus*.

"Have a nice trip, Mr. Spock, Sulu, Uhura," he said. "Bring back lots of pictures."

"From what I've seen of Gruyakin Six, Mr. Scott," Spock replied perfectly deadpan, "visual mementos would not be of much interest. However, I'm certain you'll find what we're going after of considerably more interest."

"And what might that be? I was only told to make the shuttle ready for a fast flight."

"Everything's been happening all at once, Mr. Scott," Sulu explained. "An archeological expedition on Gruyakin Six has found a Slaver stasis box."

"A Slaver—" Scott let out a long whistle, looked impressed. "No wonder the captain's in such a hurry. Why isna the ship goin'?"

"The *Enterprise* must reach Starbase Twenty-Five by a certain date, Mr. Scott." Spock was making his own, inevitable fast inspection of the shuttle. "Sending out a shuttle to Gruyakin is the only way everything can be properly accomplished in the time remaining to us. The sooner the stasis box is aboard the *Enterprise*, the better it will be for the Federation."

"Aye, Mr. Spock. Here to Gruyakin to Starbase Twenty-Five. I dinna think I'd care to be makin' that trip myself."

"I share your concern, but we have, as I've explained, no choice."

Scott gestured at the shuttle. "Well, there's no need to worry about the *Copernicus*. I've triple-checked everything myself and you've got long-range supplies bulging every storage locker. If you have to stay out longer than you plan, you're equipped for it."

"I hope not." Uhura looked anxious. "I'm curious to see what these controversial Briamosites are like. I've never heard of Starfleet speaking so highly of a new civilization or potential new ally. They must be something special."

"They can hardly be more special than a sealed stasis box," said Sulu fervently. "I've heard about them all my life, read about them on tapes, seen pictures of them, but I never expected to see one in person."

"In appearance," Spock commented as they entered the shuttle, "a stasis box is not particularly impressive. The knowledge of what lies inside more than makes up for any abstract esthetic deficiencies, however." He turned in the doorway, looked back out into the shuttle bay.

"Good-bye, Mr. Scott. We'll be seeing you again very soon."

Scott waited until the shuttle door had sealed itself, murmured a heartfelt, "Amen to that, Mr. Spock." Then he jogged to the near wall and punched an intercom switch.

"Attention, attention! Chief Engineer Scott speaking. All personnel are directed to clear the shuttlecraft bay. Clear the shuttle bay for launch." He thumbed another switch, was rewarded by the clamor of the bay alarm, then hit the communications nub once more.

"Bridge . . . Shuttle bay."

"Kirk here. That you, Scotty?"

"Aye, Captain. Clearing the bay. I'll be out myself in a second."

"Thanks, Scotty. We'll take it from here. Bridge out." He turned to the communications station, now manned by Lieutenant M'ress. "Communications check, *Copernicus,* Lieutenant."

"Checking, sirr," The Caitian officer purred back at him as she studied her console. "Channel open."

Kirk spoke into his chair pickup. "Mr. Spock, this is the captain speaking."

"Communications check good, Captain," came the clear reply. "All shuttle systems check out normal. Ready for departure."

"Stand by." Kirk turned to face the slight, nut-brown little man seated at the science station. "Open the shuttle-bay doors, Lieutenant, Vedama."

"Opening shuttle-bay doors, sir." The science officer's voice was almost as gentle as Lieutenant Arex's, but clipped at the end of heavily consonanted words. Vedama's ancestors had fought for a subsistence existence outside a bloated city on Earth named Bombay. Now the great-great-grandson of those struggling peasants commanded more knowledge at his fingertips than had all his ancestors combined.

At the stern of the *Enterprise* vast metal panels slid ponderously aside. There was no one in the chamber, now open to space, to see the few wisps of unreclaimed atmosphere puff out into emptiness. Several lights flashed on and then off, were matched by smaller tell-tales on the ship's bridge.

"Shuttlecraft away, Captain," Vedama reported.

"Close bay doors."

"Closing doors, sir."

Kirk turned his attention to the main viewscreen. "Lieutenant M'ress, give me shuttle channel and the view from aft scanners." M'ress nudged certain controls and a picture of the *Copernicus*, floating behind the *Enterprise*, appeared on the screen.

"Mr. Spock?"

"All shuttle systems continue to function normally, Captain," came the instant reply. "Preparing course to Gruyakin."

"Mr. Spock," Kirk continued more softly, "I meant what I said earlier. If you encounter another ship in the Gruyakin system, notify me immediately. Don't try to save time by coping with an intruder yourselves. You're not equipped for it."

"I understand, Captain. Hopefully we will see nothing but subsolar shuttles at our destination. We will rendezvous with the *Enterprise* at Starbase Twenty-Five at the appropriate time. *Copernicus* out."

"*Enterprise* . . . out." Reluctantly, convinced he had forgotten something, Kirk switched off.

After a while he considered beaming the shuttle again, but he had really nothing more to add. Spock was not the reckless type, but— Then it struck him what was actually bothering him. He wanted to be on board the *Copernicus*, racing to Gruyakin. Not on his way to sit like a schoolboy again before a set of repetitive lectures.

There were no such things as adults, he mused idly. Only older children . . .

III

From the time it left the *Enterprise*, the *Copernicus* was traveling at maximum shuttle speed. Spock intended to retrieve the Slaver stasis box as fast as possible, both to insure its safety and to make sure that they would reach Starbase Twenty-Five in time for them to sit in on the last of the Briamos briefings. Consequently, it wasn't too long before they had entered the Gruyakin system and taken up orbit around its sixth planet.

That world was no more impressive from orbit than it had been when seen on the main screen of the *Enterprise*. It was clearly a tired, worn globe, an old world with no high mountain ranges and only shallow oceans. Yet at one time in the distant past it had been home to a hopeful civilization. Perhaps the people of Gruyakin had also yearned to reach the stars, only to fall back in failure. Galactic archeology had long ago proven one thing: Those races who reached the stars expanded, advanced, and grew. Those who did not often fell to squabbling among themselves over petty tribal differences, only to disappear long before their natural time.

The same thing might have happened to Vulcan. It had come very near to happening on Earth.

Yet down there among the dead cities and forgotten memories lay one of the most valuable single objects in the galaxy, a Slaver stasis box. How and why it had come to be in this unimportant place was a question the archeological expedition might answer in the future. For now, it was important to place that box and its as-yet-unknown contents under more protection than a group of scientists and researchers could offer.

"I've located their beacon, Mr. Spock." Uhura glanced up from the *Copernicus*'s modest console.

"Homing in," reported Sulu, as he angled the shuttlecraft in the direction provided by the beacon.

Uhura made adjustments to another section of the console, then announced with satisfaction: "Audio contact."

"Identify yourselves," a strident voice demanded in the small cabin of the shuttle. "Our main phaser batteries are trained on you! Identify yourselves."

Sulu chuckled, but Spock spoke normally into the pickup. "You can drop the subterfuge, Gruyakin Six. This is the shuttlecraft *Copernicus* from the U.S.S. *Enterprise*, here to pick up . . . cargo. Commander Spock speaking. Is that you, Director Masid?"

An audible sigh reached them over the speaker. "Yes, it is, Commander. Excuse our bluff. It's not much, but it's the best we could think of." A pause, then: "We're mighty glad you're here. The *Enterprise* isn't with you?"

"No. This is the only way we could satisfy two vital commitments within a limited time."

"What difference does it make?" Uhura looked askance at Sulu, who shrugged.

"You have our beacon?" the director asked.

"Yes. With your permission, we will land immediately."

"The sooner the better. Gruyakin out."

Spock thought to ask a question, but decided not to call back. They would be down on the surface soon enough and he could ask it in person. He was feeling some of the same concern as Uhura. There was something going on down on the blighted surface of this world . . .

It wasn't often Sulu had the chance to pilot a shuttlecraft, much less to make a planetary landing. The transporter was a far simpler and faster device. But one couldn't have told this from the smoothness of their touchdown, which was a silent, safe tribute to the lieutenant's training and natural ability.

He brought the shuttle to a halt alongside the dark lake they had first observed during the initial transmission from Gruyakin to the *Enterprise*. Black volcanic sand along the narrow beach extended out indefinitely into the water and explained the lake's grim coloration. Ruined buildings, testaments to a forgotten alien architecture, lined the far shore of the lake.

Immediately to their left and slightly farther from the shoreline shone the familiar bubbles of pressurized domes. In the bleak setting they provided a comforting, if spartan, reminder of civilization. The expedition's quarters were far from luxurious. Love of science and the quest for knowledge could often enable people to endure hardships no sensible person would otherwise willingly submit to.

"Peculiar," commented Spock as he regarded the horizon near the domes. "They knew we were coming right down. I'd think there'd be someone here to meet us."

Sulu frowned as he studied the terrain. "Not a pretty world." He checked instruments, gazed at readouts. "Atmosphere is breathable, which is to be expected, but thin. Altitude equivalent of roughly three thousand meters on Earth. That might explain why no one's running to greet us." He peered closer at an isolated dial. "Judging from the content of certain trace gases, I don't think this world's going to smell very good, either."

Uhura squinted and then raised a hand to point. "Here they come. There's a vehicle of some kind."

A small, oval-bodied crawler was speeding toward them from the general region of the domes.

"Driver's a little reckless," Uhura observed disapprovingly.

Covering the intervening ground at high speed, the vehicle whined to a stop before the shuttle as Sulu let down the ramp. The atmosphere which now filled the shuttle had a faint flavor of overripe vegetation tinged with sulfur. Sulu tried not to look pained as they moved to meet their greeters.

Spock recognized the woman getting out of the far side of the crawler as expedition director Masid. Two men followed her toward the shuttle.

"They appear worried," he said speculatively. "I'd have thought they would be relieved by our arrival. I'm anxious to learn why they're not."

Uhura's nose twisted as they started down the ramp. "Phew! I think I'd wear a life-support belt here, even if the air is considered fit for breathing."

"An injudicious waste of energy, Lieutenant," Spock chided her as they walked toward the approaching threesome. His own nostrils twitched as a particularly noxious odor brushed them. He had to confess privately that Uhura's idea was not without merit.

Masid noted his insignia, went straight up to him and extended a hand. "Commander Spock." Her grip was surprisingly firm.

"Director Masid." He took in the expressions of the two men who were accompanying her. All three humans wore expressions akin to those who had recently placed large bets on a sure thing, only to learn that it wasn't so sure and that they had three minutes to withdraw their bets.

More significantly, the taller of the two men had a recent phaser burn scarring the left side of his neck.

"You've had trouble," Spock said. It was not exactly a question.

The director was panting heavily, fighting for air and not because of Gruyakin Six's thinner atmosphere. It was clear she had been running hard. "It's the box," she said reluctantly. "It's been stolen."

"Stolen!" Sulu couldn't believe it. "Didn't you have it under guard? Something that valuable—"

"Please, Mr. . . . ?"

"Lieutenant Sulu," he replied.

"Lieutenant," she explained wearily, "try to understand my situation here. This is purely a scientific expedition. I'd thought that I could believe the psychological profiles in our records. Those profiles were accurate save for one man. Even given the possibility that one of my people might conceivably be tempted by the wealth the box could represent, I thought that our isolation here, with no way for anyone to get off-planet until the relief ship arrives, would prevent any criminal action toward the stasis box. Well, I was wrong. The psychologists were wrong."

"You had best fill us in on exactly what has taken place," Spock suggested gently.

"The man's name is Jaiao," she began tiredly. "One of our excavators. Just because he's not as bright as some of our scientists was no reason to suspect him of harboring dishonest thoughts. Jaiao's difficulty is not unique. He simply feels he's not as wealthy as he would like to be." Her face twisted into a sardonic grin. "That's the problem."

"He stole the box by himself, then?" inquired Spock. "He is acting alone?"

"As far as we can tell." Masid gestured toward the distant domes. "Leastwise, no one's rushed to help him so far."

The criminal bent of certain humans never ceased to perplex Spock, and the present situation appeared founded on less logic than most such incidents.

Masid shook her head. "Be stunned if I know what came over him." Again she gestured at the domes, taking care to indicate the bulge farthest from their right. "He's locked himself in a storage dome."

"Have you tried to reason with him?"

She eyed the first officer strangely. "For some five minutes, until it became clear the devil himself couldn't talk him out of his foolishness. We also tried exhausting the air in the dome, but he has a life-support belt and plenty of power packs for it, so *that* didn't work."

"What can he do against you, to keep you from simply rushing him?" Sulu asked.

"He has a weapon in there, a model 6BB displacer.

That's one of the portable tools we use for excavating the ruins. It's clumsy compared to a hand phaser, but in the hands of someone like Jaiao, who knows how to use it, it makes a pretty nasty weapon, as Charlie here can tell you."

The man with the ugly burn mark on his neck nodded. "He's not fooling with that thing. He didn't miss me by much—and I don't think he was trying to miss me at all."

"If you tried exhausting the air in his dome, he'd just cut his way out into thinner but still livable atmosphere," Sulu pointed out. "You must have *some* weapons, or at least other displacers and people who know how to run them. How many of you are there here at the station?"

"I know what you're thinking, Lieutenant." Masid nodded. "It won't work. I didn't mean to imply that Jaiao is stupid. He's not, he's just not as brilliant as some of our higher-ranking professionals here. But he knew what he was doing before he took the box, had his strategy pretty well planned out. He went straight for the storage dome, with its ample supply of water, power, and food.

"If we rush him," she finished somberly, "he's threatened to use the displacer to try and open the stasis box."

"If we could be certain there was nothing in the box for its mechanism to protect . . ."

"Oh, it's sealed all right, Commander," she told him.

"Isn't there some way we can neutralize the field without him knowing about it, Mr. Spock?" The helmsman looked hopefully at his superior.

"I fear not, Mr. Sulu. An unopened, sealed box maintains its stasis field by means we still do not understand. Inside that field, time stands still, perfectly preserving whatever its original owners wished to put inside.

"There are methods of safely opening a stasis box. It has been done a number of times. But if the opening is not carried out with the utmost care and proper instrumentation, the results can be disastrous. I personally know of one stasis box that was opened hastily and improperly. It contained a variety of disruptor bomb. It may also have contained many other things, but we will never know of them. When the box was tampered with in that sloppy fashion, the bomb went off.

"I have heard of other means, equally lethal, which the Slavers employed to assure the security of their boxes. This person's threat to open this one in a hasty, crude fashion is a very real threat to anyone nearby."

"Sorry. I apologize, Director Masid." Sulu looked contrite. "I should have guessed you had reasons for not having made a direct attack on him already."

She smiled back at him. "We're researchers here, not members of the military. We don't know how to proceed or what to do next. We do have one shuttlecraft, located far on the other side of the domes, for emergency use. Our main relief ship isn't due for another three months. There are several inhabited systems within the range of our own shuttle."

"I can imagine what he is demanding," said Spock knowledgeably.

She nodded, once. "Free access to the shuttle and a guarantee of noninterference until he reaches it. He won't get that from *me*. We'd sooner have him break the box seal and destroy the whole base rather than let him slip away to maybe sell the box to someone with belligerent intentions." There were murmurs of agreement from the two men flanking her.

"Of course," Spock pointed out, "the box may not contain anything that might be of use to such people. Neither weapon nor weapon-adaptable device."

"But we can't take that chance . . . of course." Masid eyed Spock approvingly. "We think alike, Commander."

"I will accept that to a certain point," Spock agreed cautiously. "I still believe our best attempt to, ah, defuse the situation is to reason with the man."

"It's hard to reason with someone who has most of his sense in his back, Commander," declared Masid firmly. "Maybe you can do better than we have, but I doubt it." She eyed him with suspicion.

"We must at least give the appearance of negotiating in good faith." Spock looked thoughtful as he glanced

toward the domes. "I want to see what the physical situation is, before deciding how to proceed. In order to
do that we must convince him to talk with us."

"All right," agreed the director. "The fact that
you're Federation military might have some effect on
him. I'm afraid he's convinced himself that he's gone
too far to back out now."

"I don't think so," Uhura disagreed. "So far he's
guilty of nothing worse than simple theft."

"And assault with intent to kill." That came from
the unforgiving-sounding man on Masid's left, the one
with the burn from the displacer.

"Perhaps he will talk to *you*." Masid appeared ready
to half persuade herself that something might be done
before someone was killed. "Just remember that Jaiao
has visions of endless wealth running through his head
and he figures this is his one chance in life to get it."

"All I require is that you tell him who we are and
aid us in getting to talk with him." Spock started
toward the car. "The sooner we begin, the better it will
be. We are on a tight schedule ourselves."

The cargo compartment of the battered little land
vehicle was spacious enough to hold them all without
crowding, if not in comfort. Once inside, Masid piloted
the vehicle over a circuitous course across the surprisingly rugged terrain. Lava had flowed here in the recent past and there were cracks and rills to be avoided.

On the way they passed other members of the expedition. All of them worked hard at being interested in
their assigned duties, but they glanced furtively and often in the direction of the car and the new arrivals
within. Sulu noticed several of the anxious faces. He
couldn't blame them. If the undoubtedly nervous man
in the storage dome tried to force open the stasis box,
everyone nearby might instantly vanish from existence.

The lock leading into the domes was simple in
design and fragile in execution, and heavy-duty seals
weren't necessary. The lock was present for con-
venience only, to permit the expedition to maintain the
slight comfort of normal atmosphere within its living
quarters. On dour Gruyakin, even the slightest luxury
was worth a little extra expense, the helmsman mused.

Inside, they followed a corridor to where a man and woman were crouching behind a tripod-mounted device of metal and plastic. Spock recognized it as a displacer of a type similar to the one Director Masid had already indicated was in the hands of the thief. Such a device was designed to move modest quantities of earth and stone with fair precision. His own small hand phaser contained more destructive power. The displacer could still neatly remove a man's head from his body, however.

As they approached, the woman rose, eyed the three officers speculatively, and addressed the expedition head. "He's still holed up in there, Director. He's been very quiet."

"Asleep?" Spock queried.

She looked up at him. "No. We heard some crates being opened. He's using the time to build up his easily accessible supplies, I think."

"We thought of that too, Commander," Masid said regretfully. "I told you Jaiao had this planned out. He says he's set up an alarm system to warn him if anyone gets within three meters of him. That's not much warning, but I don't want to risk the lives of any of my people finding out how fast his reaction time is. Anyhow, we can't tell when he's sleeping and when he's not. He blew out the visual monitors in the dome's roof, and he stays out of sight."

"Sounds like he's ready to settle down for a long stay," observed Sulu as he moved forward.

Masid took a couple of quick steps, cut him off. "Take it a little slower here, please, Lieutenant. Jaiao's shown a tendency to be a bit trigger-happy." She gestured upward and they saw the dark streaks on the tough dome material where blasts from the displacer had struck.

Keeping close to the near wall, they moved cautiously toward the storage dome. They reached a place where the corridor opened into a two-story-high single large chamber. In places, it was stacked almost to that curved ceiling with tubes, cylinders, and crates of all sizes and colors.

Sulu was in the lead and cautiously peeked around

the last bend in the corridor. "I can't see him," he whispered back to the others.

"A little to the left of room center," Masid advised him. "He's built himself a nice little barricade with a couple of big gas tanks in front."

Sulu shifted his gaze slightly, located the bulky metal cylinders. "Still can't see him . . . He's well hidden, all right." The helmsman kept an eye on the disconcerting arrangement of containers. One of the brightly colored shapes moved slightly. "I see him now. He's staying down low, Mr. Spock. I don't think we could get a phaser on him clean."

"What about reflective surfaces, Mr. Sulu?"

The helmsman stared long at the makeshift fortress in the center of the room. "No good, sir. Everything that's piled close to him is plastic, ceramic, or some other dulled material. Nothing polished enough to risk bouncing a beam off."

"I didn't think of that." Masid looked impressed. "But don't attribute it to Jaiao's intelligence. I don't think he's *that* smart. We just don't have much stored in metal or glass cases, that's all."

Spock started forward. "Let me have a look, Mr. Sulu."

The lieutenant hugged the wall as he edged back into the corridor, trading places with the first officer. Spock peered around the corner, immediately located the thief's makeshift ramparts.

"What is his last name, please?" he asked.

"Beguin," Masid told him.

Spock nodded, turned, and leaned as far into the room as he dared.

"Jaiao Beguin," he called sharply. No answer. He tried again. *"Jaiao Beguin!"*

A rustling sound reached them from the jumble of crates and cylinders, though no face appeared among them. "You know what I want! I'm getting impatient!" The voice was high-pitched, angry.

Sulu leaned over, whispered to Uhura. "Not even Mr. Spock's going to be able to reason with this one. The director's right: He's a little crazy."

Ignoring the byplay behind him, the first officer of

the *Enterprise* concentrated on analyzing the reply to his call, dissecting every nuance, building a temporary psychological profile of the speaker out of a couple of short, terse statements.

"This is Commander Spock of the Federation cruiser *Enterprise*. I am in command of a landing party from that ship. We are here to recover the Slaver stasis box, which is valuable property belonging to the Federation government and all its peoples.

"At this very moment, heavy phasers are trained on you both from my position and from outside this dome. You cannot escape. We can kill you if we have to, instantly, before you can damage the box—and the box and its contents will not be affected.

"Thus far you can only be charged with simple theft and assault. If you turn over the box and surrender, it will go much easier on you."

The reply to Spock's carefully worded combination of promise and threat was a peal of barking, none-too-stable laughter that bordered on the hysterical. "I don't believe you!" it declared imperiously. "If you could kill me and not damage the box you would have done so already, without giving me any warning. Who do you think you're fooling with?"

Spock could have answered the man's question, but it would do no good to antagonize him further. Besides, Spock hadn't expected the man to give in readily.

"Didn't you hear our shuttle land?" he called.

"Yeah, I heard it," Beguin admitted, his voice a bit softer and more speculative now. "You could have a cannon trained on my forehead for all I care. I've got the box right in front of me, between my legs. It's sitting on the workplate of a compacter. You know what that means?"

Masid looked startled, and whispered to Sulu and Uhura. "Our compacter is a device for crushing rocks and other material for detailed analysis of their constituent parts. It's got an idle control. If it's running and he trips the trigger for fast release, it'll throw about a thousand kilos of pressure onto the stasis box!"

Sulu looked worried. "Is that enough to crack the box, Mr. Spock?"

"It is possible," the first officer finally replied after considering the problem thoroughly, "depending on the strength of the field inside the box and how much of it shields the box material itself. I would prefer not to risk it."

The nervous, taunting voice of the thief interrupted them. "Go ahead and shoot, why don't you, Mr. Spock of the *Enterprise*? Why don't you shoot? You might kill me before the auto-release I've set on the compacter can trigger it . . . but I don't think so. In any case, I'm betting my life that you're not willing to take that gamble. I'm going to bet that you're not going to risk the lives of all the people in this station, including your own."

"You are quite correct," Spock shouted back at him, "but neither can you escape with the box. It is a stalemated situation you cannot win."

"I don't see why not." Bravado mixed with assurance in the man's voice. "I've planned this pretty careful. You can't do anything to me without having me throw the compacter pressure onto the box. And while you sit and make up your minds I can get along nice, thanks."

"What about sleep?" Spock countered. "All the food and water in the world won't help you when you need rest, nor will your imaginary warning device if we rush you from several sides simultaneously."

"I figure with the stimulants I've found," Beguin responded, "I can stay awake operating efficiently for another forty hours or so. But you're right, Commander Spock. You could make trouble for me if I fell asleep. So this is what we're going to do: If I don't hear something positive about my request for the shuttle in forty hours, and I find myself falling asleep, I'll just have to assume you've all outsmarted me. That'll mean all my work's been for nothing, won't it? I'll be very discouraged and depressed. I think," he concluded, his voice rising slightly, "that in that event I'll just let the compacter go on the box anyway, to see what happens."

Spock and the others ignored the laughter drifting

out of the room. "We now know how much time we have left to work in."

"What happens if the forty hours are up and we haven't figured out how to pry him loose from that box?" Uhura stared straight at Spock.

"We will deal with that eventuality in thirty-nine hours, Lieutenant," Spock informed her crisply.

"He's got it all planned out, all right," she observed. "He's smarter than I thought."

"There is a difference, Lieutenant, between true intelligence and animal cunning. The latter is the virtue our opponent possesses and it is that we must cope with."

"Whatever, it's *working* for him," she argued.

"True enough." Spock turned his gaze to the attentive director. "Are there any other entrances or exits to this storage dome?"

"No, none," Masid informed them.

Spock nodded knowingly. "Given the care with which this theft has been carried out thus far, I would not be surprised if that is yet another reason why he retreated here. Did you consider cutting another entrance?"

"We did," she confessed. "I decided there's no way we could do it without Beguin hearing or seeing us, or both, and the last thing I wanted to do was panic him."

"Quite right." Spock eyed his companions. "I have a thought . . . but I would prefer an idea with a better chance of success than I postulate for my own."

"What about inducing some kind of odorless, colorless gas into the dome's ventilation system?" Uhura proposed. "If it was seeped in gradually, it might knock him out before he knows what's happening."

"I would almost consider that, Lieutenant," Spock admitted, "save for one drawback. If he is staying as close to the compacter and the box as he insists he is, then I would be surprised if he is not keeping a hand close by the compacter trigger at all times. The danger of knocking him out without anyone else around is that his hand or body might fall on the compacter trigger." He glanced briefly back into the chamber.

"Somehow we must get someone close to him, so

that he cannot possibly throw the compacter switch in a last futile, defiant gesture." He paused. "I see one possibility. There is a very large container just to the left and rear of his likely resting place." He glanced backward. "What does it contain, Director Masid?"

She crawled forward, peered around the corner. "I see the one you mean, Commander, but I don't know what's inside. I can't keep track of everything that comes in in the way of supplies. Just a minute."

She retreated, climbed to her feet, and disappeared down the corridor. Several minutes passed before she returned with a tall man in tow, the one with the scar on his neck.

"Charlie's our quartermaster. It's his bailiwick that Beguin appropriated. That's how he got that burn." She gestured to him and they both managed to glance into the room. "The big crate on Beguin's left, Charlie . . . what's in it?"

"Give me a second." The man leaned farther into the room, squinted at the container in question. Just as he ducked back into the corridor, a faint but lethal bolt from the displacer scored the floor where he had been a moment before.

"That's just to let you know that I'm still watching!" a loud voice warned them. "Lucky for you I'm not asleep, or the whole place would go up!"

Leaning back against the corridor wall, Sulu eyed the smoking trench in the floor respectfully.

"I do not think we can reason further with him," Spock announced.

"I knew that in the first place." Uhura sniffed at the odor of burnt duraplastic.

"Nevertheless, it had to be tried. One is always hopeful—"

Charlie cut him off. "I remember now. I wanted to be sure. The crate holds bulk food rations, Commander. Should be mostly small containers of raw proteins, natural sealed meats and stuff."

"Nothing that would make much noise if it fell within the crate?" Spock asked.

"No . . . I wouldn't think so."

Masid's gaze narrowed. "What are you planning, Commander?"

Spock gestured just behind them, at the couple manning the makeshift weapon. "You have other displacers besides that one?"

"Sure," she said quickly. "They're all out at the various sites we're working but—"

"How long to bring two of your best ones in and set them up near here?"

She still didn't quite believe what Spock was indirectly proposing. "Within an hour, I guess. But I thought we already ruled out any attempt at cutting through—"

"Not to cut," Spock corrected her, "to *dig*. We will position the displacers precisely and tunnel beneath the dome. The tunnel will come up under the box very slowly and quietly. We'll make a little natural background noise, but the ground will muffle the sound of the displacer, which I understand is a relatively silent instrument when operated at low power."

"That's so," Masid admitted.

"Whoever goes through the tunnel can cut through the bottom of the container manually. A phaser set on low power should slice through the plastic container material quickly and with little noise. Then he can pass the contents of the container back through the tunnel. Simultaneously we will engage Mr. Beguin in conversation."

Masid gave him a very querulous look.

"I had not expected enthusiasm," Spock confessed. "It is far from an ideal plan. I am not pleased with it myself. But in the absence of any alternative . . ."

No one said anything for a long moment. Then the director nodded to Spock. "All right, Commander. This sort of work is more your job than mine. I don't like it, but we'll try anything."

The displacers were brought in. After careful calculating, they were set in place and turned on. Their efficient operators had muffled the already-quiet devices with insulating material and they dug in near silence. Nor was there any noticeable vibration.

Nonetheless, to be absolutely certain Beguin didn't grow suspicious—and to try to wear him down a little mentally—Masid and the three officers from the *Enterprise* took turns arguing, threatening and appealing to the barricaded thief. Helpfully, he argued back, seeming to enjoy their futile attempts to cajole him out of his hideaway. Occasionally he would fire a blast from his displacer in their direction, apparently for no other reason than because it kept him amused.

Spock had no illusions about what would happen when the drugs started to lose their effectiveness and Beguin found himself growing drowsy. His maniacal humor would fade concurrent with his alertness.

At the moment, the first officer was watching the dirt and rock emerge in buckets from the rapidly lengthening tunnel. It would take longer this way, but a conveyer would be dangerously noisy.

Uhura studied a small diagram, drew some lines on it, and compared them with calculations scribbled in the diagram's margin. "They should be in position any minute now, Mr. Spock."

"Yes. I'll want both you and Mr. Sulu to cover the area as best you can with your phasers. Don't fire unless you're certain he's clear of the stasis box and the compacter. Don't worry about hitting me. I'll try to get him away from the compacter trigger, and then—"

"Excuse me, sir." Sulu took the liberty of interrupting his superior. "I think I ought to be the one to go."

"This was my idea, Lieutenant, and I'll be the one to take the necessary risks, since I'll be the one responsible for this attempt's success or failure."

"Exactly, sir," pressed Sulu urgently, "and that's the very reason I should be the one to go."

"Explain yourself, Lieutenant."

"Mr. Spock, you can hold this man's attention better than any of us. That's the really critical part of the operation: not charging him from behind but distracting him from the front. If we can do that effectively, then anyone can jump him."

"He's right, Mr. Spock," Uhura agreed.

The first officer considered the objection only briefly. "I do not like the proposal but I cannot counter your arguments. Very well, Lieutenant Sulu. You will be the one to attack from inside the crate. Take special care with your phaser setting when you get ready to cut through the container bottom. It is imperative Mr. Beguin not hear you. As time passes without our meeting his demands, he grows progressively more unstable."

"Don't worry, sir," Sulu assured him. "I've seen what his displacer can do. I don't want it pointed in my face when I come out of there . . ."

IV

The displacers finished their work quickly. After a final conference with his companions and a wish of "Good luck" from Uhura, Sulu found himself crawling on hands and knees through the smooth passageway. Half-fused earth slid by under his palms.

Small lights had been placed at regular intervals in the tunnel by the excavators, so he had no trouble seeing his path. Nor did he have to be told when he was nearing his destination, since the tunnel floor and ceiling turned sharply upward. The excavators had used their displacers to cut long notches in the floor there. Otherwise the intermittently slick surface would have offered poor purchase for ascending.

Aware that he was under the storage dome now and that the highly excitable Beguin was somewhere above and just to his right, Sulu continued with greater caution. He passed the last emplaced light, which threw just enough illumination for him to make out a dark mass ahead: the bottom of the crate.

Edging close to it, he removed his pre-set phaser and trained it on the dark, thick material. Silently, the low-power beam cut through the dull-surfaced substance. Sulu had to move slightly, hugging the wall of the tunnel, to avoid drops of liquid, hot plastic dripping out of the steadily widening hole.

When he had enlarged the gap enough for a man to fit through, he turned off the phaser and replaced it at his waist. All was silent above, save for distant voices. Spock and the others were doing their part, arguing with Beguin and keeping his attention focused elsewhere.

Carefully, Sulu edged upward, began the dangerous task of removing the smaller packages from within the crate. Working fast and efficiently, he soon emptied the crate of a substantial portion of its contents, sliding them down into the tunnel. Then, a short pull—and he was on his knees inside.

For the last time he rehearsed his next moves in his mind. First, he rechecked his position. Beguin ought to be off to his right, through that wall of his crate container, there. Sulu shifted more containers, giving himself a clear path to the crate wall in the opposite direction from Beguin's position. Then he activated his phaser again.

Gently Sulu applied the soft, short beam to one of the crate walls, near the top. Once more the preformed material softened, ran down into the crate. Fortunately, the plastic melted without an odor, as Spock and Masid had assured him it would. He reminded himself that there was no reason for Beguin to go for a stroll and every reason for him not to, but he still worried that the thief might somehow notice what was going on behind him.

As the hole appeared and widened and lengthened, the distant voices became clearly audible. Spock was arguing with Beguin, using all the semantic forces at his command, trying to convince him to surrender the box. Chances of that were slim, but the critical thing was to keep the thief occupied long enough for Sulu to slip clear and make a good run at the compacter and its half-hysterical guardian.

With a top line cut through, Sulu started curving the phaser beam down along one side. That done, he switched to the opposite side, still straining for the sound of footsteps outside the crate. As the opening enlarged, he found he could follow the details of the conversation taking place behind him. Spock's steady, calm words alternated with the irregular, high-pitched retorts of Beguin.

Then the phaser began cutting across, parallel to the bottom of the container. Sulu slid his fingers slowly into the nearest vertical crack, gripped firmly. It wouldn't do to have the thick slab of plastic tumble outward to the dome floor. A final snick and the opening was complete. Steadying the cut section with his right hand, the helmsman switched off his phaser and set it down. Then both hands gripped the cutout and pushed. It slid neatly outward and he laid it quietly on the dome.

If his position had been properly gauged, Beguin should be on the exact opposite side of the crate from him. A cautious glance showed only stacks of cylinders and containers ahead.

After a minute had passed without a displacer beam abruptly roasting his container, Sulu crawled out and readjusted his phaser. A first glance around the tall black square revealed additional piles of material, containers of all sizes and shapes scattered about. There was a hint of motion and he drew back, still watching.

A head and gesturing arm appeared. "Why don't you quit trying to talk me out of here?" Beguin shouted warningly. "I'm not giving up the box."

"You are not leaving Gruyakin with the box in your possession," Spock's distant voice countered immediately.

Beguin was beginning to sound tired. "You already know what happens then. If I don't get what I want in"—there was a brief pause—"in twenty-one hours, I open the box with the compacter and we all die."

"Not necessarily," Spock objected. "We do not know for certain that this box contains a disrupter bomb or other destructive device. In that case, *you* will be the only one to die."

"Maybe you're right," Beguin conceded readily. "I've heard that some of the stasis boxes that were found were undefended. But it doesn't matter, because you can't take that chance, can you?" Beguin concluded with an unholy chuckle.

Everything indicated that the thief's attention was concentrated solely on the one entrance to the storage dome and that he suspected nothing. Sulu began his

approach, working his way patiently across the floor
using scattered crates and containers for cover. If anything he was being over-cautious. He would have been
difficult to spot even if Beguin had been looking for
him.

Very soon he was crouched directly behind the small
wall of piled crates and cylinders Beguin had shifted
for his own protection. Starting immediately he would
have to be extra careful. He wouldn't have any cover
inside the circle of containers.

He considered his options once again. At such close
quarters, it would be difficult to miss Beguin with a
phaser burst. But there was still the chance the thief's
limp body could fall across the compacter trigger, so
phaser fire remained a last resort. Somehow he had to
find a better way to get the man away from the compacter controls.

At first he had been glad of the jumble of cylinders
and crates. They had made his approach to this point
fairly easy. But they no longer served a useful function.
He hoped to find a gap in the container barricade that
he could rush through, but as he inspected the piled
boxes he could find no such break in the wall. Certainly he couldn't start pulling crates away. Beguin
wouldn't be so distracted by Spock that he would fail
to notice someone pulling his ramparts down behind
him.

There *had* to be an opening somewhere in the barricade. Moving on hands and knees and keeping as close
to the floor as possible, Sulu started off to his left. He
had circled almost the entire barricade and was dangerously close to Beguin himself before deciding that this
half of the wall was impenetrable. The ongoing dia-
logue between Spock and the thief formed a surreal ac-
companiment to his explorations.

Returning, Sulu repeated his search to the right of
his original position, with similar results.

One place, where the wall was rather low, was the
best he could find. As long as Beguin remained distracted, there was a chance Sulu could scale the wall there
and reach the compacter before the thief could trigger
it. Once he cleared Beguin from the controls, the com-

motion would bring Spock, Uhura, and the others running.

Returning to his chosen spot, Sulu leaned against the crates and started edging to a standing position, positioning his right leg for the jump he would have to make. The conversation had faded, but he would wait until the arguments resumed before making the leap.

Sulu's head meanwhile slowly came up and for the first time he glanced into the center of the circle of containers—straight into the startled eyes of the thief! Beguin was gobbling provisions from an opened storage crate. Both men were paralyzed for the briefest of seconds.

Then Beguin whirled, made a dive at the compacter. Desperately Sulu made a jump for him, but even the adrenaline suddenly surging through his body didn't provide him with enough lift to clear the barrier completely. His right foot caught on an upthrust cylinder and sent him sprawling to the floor in a clatter of dislodged crates.

"Wait," Sulu shouted frantically. *"Don't!"*

Beguin, his eyes wild, and perhaps temporarily not sane, was at the compacter. He threw himself onto the trigger. Voices yelled in the distance as Spock and the others, having heard Sulu's shout, began charging the barricade.

They could not outpace the compacter. With a whirr the sides of the device engaged, slammed into the stasis box. A peculiar bone-tingling screech resulted, like a thin metal point dragging across a piece of slate. The sound increased until Sulu's teeth hurt. One edge of the stasis box appeared to crumple slightly inward. Fascinated, Sulu could only stare at what might prove to be the cause of his imminent annihilation.

He had no place to run to, of course. Instinctively he threw an arm across his face to protect his eyes. But if a disruptor bomb were presently being engaged within the box, his arm would make no difference.

Out of the corner of an eye Sulu saw something rise from the surfaces of the box. He was certain the lid hadn't opened and no crack appeared in the smooth metal sides. There was no explosion, no sudden disintegration of matter within the storage dome. Instead, there was a short, soundless, actinic flash that temporarily blinded the helmsman.

The sound of running feet and anxious voices reached the barricade, people swarming over it. Someone bent over Sulu, helped him to his feet.

"Are you all right, Lieutenant?"

"Sulu! What happened?"

He blinked, and tiny suns faded as rods and cones adjusted to the normal light. Spock and Uhura were supporting him, one at each arm.

"I'm okay." He blinked again, rubbed at his eyes with both hands. "What did happen?" Then he was staring apologetically at Spock. "I'm sorry, sir. I couldn't stop him from throwing the trigger. He was standing right next to me when I looked inside for him."

Spock didn't appear angry. On the contrary, his reply was more curious than reproving. "It appears not to matter, Mr. Sulu." The helmsman noticed that the first officer was no longer looking at him, but instead was staring at something else nearby. "This stasis box is defended, but not by a disruptor bomb. It acts only upon those in its immediate vicinity who try improperly to open it. Look."

Sulu finally did so, turning to stare in the same direction as his superior. The stasis box, to all outward appearances unaffected, still rested in the paralyzed jaws of the compacter. One of the scientists was standing next to the device, which had been turned off, cautiously inspecting the tightly held box.

Jaiao Beguin stood nearby, a surprised expression on his face. He appeared to be completely encased in a softly glowing, silvery material like chrome paint.

"What happened to *him?*" Sulu asked, gaping at the statuelike figure of the thief.

"It would seem," Spock theorized, "that anyone who attempts to open this particular stasis box is promptly enveloped in a stasis box of his own."

"It's not a fatal method of defense, then," said Sulu, unable to keep from staring in fascination at the frozen silvery figure of the unfortunate Beguin.

"Not technically, no," Spock agreed. "Our thief will remain conveniently frozen in time, as would anything encased by a stasis field, until such a time as a stasis-field disruptor can be used to release him safely. It will be quite a useful method of restraining him until a Federation expedition can arrive here with a disruptor and release him from his own field." He added firmly, "At that point he will be transferred to a less exotic but equally confining place of imprisonment."

"If that's all the box does, Mr. Spock, why can't we try and open it ourselves? The worst that could happen would be that the opening device or its operator would also be encased in another stasis field." Uhura eyed the box excitedly.

"Not necessarily, Lieutenant," Spock hastened to correct her. "We do not know by what method the box's defense system decides on who is trying to open it improperly. This time it encased only the immediate operator of the opening device. We cannot assume that if we attempt the same thing the box will not decide to encase the entire station. We have no idea of its limits."

Uhura looked downcast. "We'll have to wait to see what's inside it, then."

Spock nodded. "At least until we rejoin the ship, Lieutenant. I am certain Engineer Scott can construct an adequate stasis-field disruptor." He walked over to the compacter, exchanged a few words with the scientist inspecting it. The woman threw a small switch and the sides of the compacter moved away from the box. Spock picked it up. It rested inert and innocent in his arms. He turned to his two companions.

"First, we must get to Starbase Twenty-Five and rendezvous with the ship. The captain and I allowed ample time for us to reach here, pick up the box, and make rendezvous, so I do not think our unexpected delay will be of any consequence. We still have plenty of time to reach the base before the *Enterprise* is required to depart for Briamos. Nevertheless, I wish to get there as quickly as possible."

Uhura concurred. "I've got to admit I'll feel a lot more comfortable back on board myself."

"And *I'll* feel comfortable," Sulu added fervently, "only when that"—he pointed at the quiescent cube resting in Spock's grasp—"is safely on board the *Enterprise* . . ."

"I want to thank you, Commander," Director Masid was saying as the three officers prepared to board their shuttlecraft, "for relieving us of responsibility for that," and she indicated the stasis box. "Its potential for causing trouble is too explosive for us, even if its defensive mechanism isn't."

"There is no need to thank us, Director Masid," Spock replied from his position atop the boarding ramp. "We were fortunate, and that is no substitute for being skilled. We were all lucky that the box contained something besides a disruptor bomb to defend itself with. Good-bye for now, and good luck with your digging."

"Thanks to you," she murmured as the shuttlecraft thundered into the dark sky, "I think I may be able to enjoy it for a change." She turned to the car waiting to take her back to her office in the administration dome.

It's amazing, she reflected, how a reprieve from expected death can make formerly ordinary work seem fresh and exciting . . .

V

"Captain? Captain Kirrk!"

Kirk swung the command chair and looked toward the communication station. "What is it, Lieutenant M'ress?"

The Caitian communications officer who had taken over for the absent Lieutenant Uhura had one paw pressed to the left side of her head. She was slightly bent over in her seat and it looked to Kirk as if she was wincing.

"What's the matter, Lieutenant? Are you in pain?" He was immediately concerned.

"No, not exactly, sirr. I . . . I'm not surre what's wrong, but something . . . is. I feel very peculiarr all of a sudden. Dizzy. It's almost familiarr, like something I've felt beforre, but . . . I can't place it." She rose unsteadily in her chair. "I'm afrraid I have to ask to be excused frrom duty, sirr."

"You don't have to ask and there's no need to apologize, Lieutenant. I only hope it's nothing more than a bad headache."

"It . . . doesn't feel like a headache, sirr."

"Report to Sick Bay immediately," Kirk ordered her. "Lieutenant Talliflores will take over for you."

"Yes, sirr." M'ress made a few adjustments to the controls on her console, her hands moving with unaccustomed awkwardness over the familiar instrumentation.

At that point Kirk was out of the chair and striding over to her. "Never mind contacting your relief," he said, worried. "I'll do that myself. Just get to Sick Bay. Think you can make it by yourself?"

"I believe so, sirr."

Despite her assurance, Kirk helped the lieutenant to the turbolift. He left her with a reassuring smile, which turned instantly to an expression of troubled concern when the doors closed behind her.

Back in the command chair, he activated the intercom. M'ress's relief was on recreation time now and probably wouldn't be in his cabin. He set for shipwide general broadcast.

"Lieutenant Talliflores, Lieutenant Talliflores. Report to the bridge immediately."

That task concluded, he leaned back and mused over M'ress's sudden ailment. Why it should trouble him so, he couldn't say. It was only natural that occasionally one of his bridge crew should take sick, despite their usual exemplary healthiness. Perhaps it was because M'ress was always so vibrant and alive. Try as he could, this was the first time he could recall the communications officer falling ill.

And yet . . . hadn't she indicated that her symptoms were akin to something she had suffered before?

He was still mulling over the incident when Lieutenant Talliflores arrived, worried and out of breath.

"I'm sorry, sir, if I—"

"Never mind. There's no problem." Thus assured, the swarthy officer relaxed. "I'm going to have to ask you to take over the remainder of Lieutenant M'ress's shift. You can do double duty until she returns, Talliflores. Your recreation time will be accredited accordingly."

"Yes, sir." Talliflores moved to take up station at communications. In the middle of his standard checkout of the instrumentation, it occurred to him to ask why he was taking M'ress's normal position. "If I may inquire, sir, is anything wrong? Lieutenant M'ress and I went sliding only yesterday. I didn't notice anything wrong with her."

"She complained of not feeling well, and of being dizzy." Kirk offered the officer reassurance he couldn't feel himself. "Probably just a headache. It didn't seem serious, Lieutenant. I expect her back before her shift is up."

"That's good to hear, sir." Talliflores looked relieved. He was a close friend of both M'ress and Uhura. That was only natural since they shared the same station, performed identical duties on different shifts.

But after several hours had passed without the reappearance of M'ress, Kirk felt compelled to check on her condition. He thumbed the intercom.

"Sick Bay, this is the captain speaking."

"Sick Bay, Nurse Chapel speaking."

"How is Lieutenant M'ress, Chapel?"

There was a brief pause before McCoy's assistant replied. "Fine, as far as I know, Captain. Why?"

Now it was Kirk's turn to hesitate. Something was wrong here. "What do you mean, 'As far as I know'?" he finally replied. "What was wrong with her? Or hasn't Bones made a diagnosis yet?"

"Diagnosis, sir? As far as I know Dr. McCoy hasn't seen Lieutenant M'ress except in the officers' mess or maybe in the recreation section." Chapel's tone turned abruptly from one of puzzlement to concern. "Why, is something wrong with her? If there is, this is the first I've heard of it."

Lieutenant Arex glanced back from his place at the navigation-helm. His quizzical stare was matched by that of lieutenant Vedama, who looked over from the science station.

"Chapel," Kirk finally asked, "didn't Lieutenant M'ress report for treatment of a mild cerebral disorder?" He checked his command-chair chronometer. She ought to have been in Sick Bay for several hours by now."

"Just one moment, sir. I haven't been here long. Let me check today's records." There was a pause while Kirk fidgeted impatiently at the delay.

"No, sir," Chapel eventually informed him. "I see no record of Lieutenant M'ress checking in for observation or any other reason. I believe I— Just a moment, sir."

A new voice sounded over the intercom. "Jim, what's this about Lieutenant M'ress?"

"Bones, M'ress left the bridge over three hours ago. She was complaining of dizziness and other unidentifiable difficulties. She was having difficulty operating her equipment, but she insisted she could make it down to Sick Bay on her own." He took a deep breath. "Apparently she couldn't."

"It doesn't look that way, Jim. I just came on duty myself. I haven't seen her and if Chapel says the records don't show her checking in, well, then she didn't check in."

"That's bad. Hang on a minute, Bones." Kirk turned to communications. "Lieutenant Talliflores, give me security in the officer's section, Deck Five." Talliflores did so.

"Security Deck Five, Ensign Atete speaking."

"Ensign, this is the captain. Lieutenant M'ress is missing. Check her cabin. You have permission to break the lock seal if necessary, to enter."

"Yes, sir," the ensign responded alertly. "A moment."

There was a wait, first while the lieutenant checked to make certain it was indeed Kirk who was speaking to him, and then a longer one while he performed the necessary check.

"No, sir," he finally reported back, "the lieutenant is not in her cabin."

"She may be ill," Kirk told him. "It's possible she fell behind something."

"I made a thorough check, sir. She's nowhere in her quarters."

"Thank you, Atete. Bridge out."

Kirk switched back to his chair communicator, where Sick Bay was waiting on hold. "Bones, she's not in her quarters."

"You said she complained of dizziness and that she had trouble with her instruments, Jim," McCoy repeated carefully. "Did she seem to be in pain?"

"I couldn't tell, but if she was she didn't complain about it," was the captain's reply. "She just said she was feeling peculiar, and that she thought it was familiar. I'd say she was as much confused as sick."

"It doesn't sound like a headache, Jim. I could be wrong. I hope I *am* wrong. I'll check our Caitian references. The important thing is to find her. If she's lying unconscious in a corridor somewhere . . . Let's hope she's just sitting somewhere in a daze."

"I'm going to find out, Bones. Stand by at your end." He faced communications. "Lieutenant Talliflores, give me shipwide broadcast."

"Aye, sir." Talliflores adjusted controls, then signaled to Kirk, who directed his voice to the command-chair pickup.

"Attention, all personnel. Lieutenant M'ress of communications was scheduled to report to Sick Bay some time ago. She did not do so. The lieutenant was suffering from dizziness and possibly more severe disorder as well. Lieutenant, if you hear this and can respond, please go immediately to the nearest communicator and check in with either the bridge or Sick Bay. If you are unable to respond verbally, try to make yourself visible.

"While not neglecting your assigned duties, all personnel are requested to keep an eye out for lieutenant

M'ress and to notify Sick Bay as to her location and condition upon seeing her."

He switched off general broadcast, spoke to Sick Bay again. "Unless she's hidden herself somewhere, Bones, that should find her for us quickly."

"I hope so, Jim," the *Enterprise*'s chief physician replied slowly. "It doesn't sound serious . . . yet. But it sure sounds peculiar. Sick Bay out."

"Funny," Kirk mused after McCoy had clicked off, "that's exactly how M'ress described it . . ."

In a quiet section of the small forest that formed part of the *Enterprise*'s recreational area on Deck Eight, a strolling off-duty food technician paused to listen to the Captain's urgent message even as he was curiously eyeing an indistinct form crouching behind a large shrub in front of him, slightly off the main pathway.

As soon as the message ended, he walked toward the bush. "Hey, you there!" The form didn't move out into the open. The technician continued walking toward the bush.

"Say, aren't you Lieutenant M'ress?" he inquired when he got near enough to make out the individual's outline. "Didn't you hear the captain?" Still the figure gave no sign of moving. "You're supposed to report in immediately." Uncertainty gave way to sudden concern. "They said you were supposed to report to Sick Bay. Are you all right, Lieutenant? Can I help?"

He reached out a hand toward the figure. "I said, do you need any—"

Rising in one motion, the figure spun violently on the startled crewman. Wide, glaring cat eyes blazed at him, nostrils flared widely, and the slim figure was puffed to more than normal size. It was not the appearance the technician expected from a ranking officer.

Slowly he took a step backward, away from the heavily breathing figure. "Now take it easy, just slow down a moment, ma'am. If you've got some kind of sickness or something . . . I don't think I'd better—"

The technician whirled, turned to run. His mouth opened as he framed a call for help. As it developed, he managed neither a shout nor retreat. Lieutenant M'ress fairly exploded off the grass. As she landed on the man's back her hands went around his neck and both squirming, struggling shapes fell hard to the ground.

VI

Like a dull white copepod swimming in some unimaginably vast ocean's black depths, the shuttlecraft *Copernicus* raced for Starbase Twenty-Five and its rendezvous with the *Enterprise*. Within the shuttle's control room the Slaver stasis box, fifty centimeters on each side but considerably larger in import, gleamed metallically in the center of the single rest table.

Spock was pacing back and forth near the table while Sulu manned the tiny craft's controls. Uhura stood near him, staring out the fore port at the slowly changing panorama spread out ahead of them.

They were back on schedule, which meant they had plenty of time to reach the Starbase before the *Enterprise* was required to leave for Briamos. But that was small comfort to Spock. He was regretting every hour of the learning sessions Kirk must be attending on Briamos and its inhabitants, sorry for every detail he was not present to absorb firsthand.

In addition, he was as anxious as Uhura and Sulu to learn what the enigmatic stasis box contained. Only on board the *Enterprise* could he and Engineer Scott assemble a proper stasis disruptor for safely opening the ancient container.

Bored with the view forward, Uhura turned to the less spectacular but more intriguing object resting on the table. She gazed speculatively at the box. With ample time to do nothing but reflect on what it might contain, she had managed to conjure any number of incredible wonders—though they were wonders no larger than fifty centimeters on a side.

Inside that unimpressive cube of metal time had

stood still for perhaps a billion years. Certainly whatever relics lay so magnificently preserved had to be valuable, as the contents of stasis boxes usually were. And maybe dangerous as well, as they often were. She no longer had any doubts about the value of whatever lay inside. The box's unique method of protecting itself all but stated that something inside was well worth defending from the casually curious.

Spock was making notations in his pocket recorder when he noticed Uhura's stare. "Speculation is no less intriguing for usually being inaccurate, Lieutenant."

"I *was* wondering what might be inside, Mr. Spock. I know a little about the Slaver Empire, but not enough to make an accurate guess."

"You have a great deal of company, Lieutenant," the first officer assured her. "Our entire store of information concerning the empire of the Slavers is sketchy at best. We know that they were masters of all the intelligent life in this part of the galaxy a billion years ago. That is a long time for anything in the way of reliable information to have survived. It's hardly surprising that so little has."

"Masters of the galaxy until a billion years ago . . ." Uhura murmured wonderingly. "Until one race finally mounted a successful revolt. It must have been a time of chaos." Her gaze went from Spock back to the stasis box. "Are these the only sources of information we have about their empire?"

Spock turned away, eyed the blaze of stars forward. "The only factual ones. Even rumors die in that length of time. But we have learned a little."

Uhura turned to listen, moved forward again. In doing so, she missed the sudden appearance of a slightly blue glow that materialized around the box. Its teardrop shape was silent. The tip of the azure halo pointed forward.

"The Slavers," Spock declared, ignorant of the mysterious aura which had enveloped the box behind him, "and all their subjects were exterminated in the war that followed that eons-old revolt. Intelligent life had to evolve all over again in this part of the galaxy." He fell silent, thoughtful. "So far," he eventually added, "the stasis boxes are the only remnants we've been able to find of those many lost and doubtless great civilizations."

He frowned, noticed Uhura staring as if mesmerized behind him. "Something wrong, Lieutenant."

By way of answer, she pointed. "Why is it glowing like that? It wasn't doing that before."

Spock whirled and saw for the first time the unmistakable aura which had encapsulated the box. Moving to his right, he noted its shape, let his gaze travel naturally from the point of the teardrop shape back out the front port. Ahead and drifting slowly to starboard was an impressively radiating spiral, a stellar object sufficiently spectacular that it had to be on the charts. He thought he recognized it.

His attention turned back to the no-longer-inert stasis box. The point of the teardrop, he was convinced, was not stable but instead was shifting slowly. Not unexpectedly, it was changing to a starboard direction.

"Mr. Sulu, what is our current position?"

Sulu executed a fast check of his instruments and glanced back over a shoulder as he spoke. "Passing Beta Lyrae, sir. One hundred and forty-two degrees northeast of the galactic plane." At this point he noticed the glowing blue cloud enveloping the box. "Where did that come from?"

The point of the blue aura was still moving steadily to starboard, tracking the changing position of Beta Lyrae as efficiently as any instrument.

"We do not know where it comes from or how the box produces it, Mr. Sulu, but it is not a unique phenomenon. I have heard of such a thing happening before. Most unexpected and most fortuitous."

"Fortuitous? I don't understand." The helmsman looked understandably confused.

"The motion of the blue aura surrounding our box," Spock explained, "would indicate that there is another stasis box orbiting Beta Lyrae."

Uhura was equally new to the phenomenon described by Spock. "Another one!"

Spock appeared baffled, almost hesitant to answer.

"It is, as I said, unexpected. Your surprise is well justified, Lieutenant Uhura. It seems most illogical for a stasis box to remain in this vicinity, undiscovered, for so long. Beta Lyrae is one of the most impressive sights and one of the rarest in the explored galaxy. Every ship that passes by would likely slow to observe and enjoy its spectacle at leisure.

"Still, the only known stasis-box detector is another stasis box. Detection is, obviously, by means of that blue aura. Perhaps none of the many vessels passing Beta Lyrae possessed a stasis box. But given the number of observers, both casual and scientific, who must have spent a good deal of time in this vicinity, I confess to being puzzled that a stasis box's peculiar characteristics have remained undiscovered for so long."

He broke off to take another look at the glowing box. By now the point of the teardrop had shifted around to a position facing forty-five degrees aft of the shuttle. Rapidly, he considered the time and date, made some hasty calculations. As important as it was for all three of them to attend the Briamosite briefings at Starbase 25, this was something that they could not ignore. While their presence at the pre-conference briefings was desirable, it was not critical.

"Mr. Sulu . . ." he began, reaching an inevitable decision once all the relevant facts had been considered.

Sulu glanced back at him hopefully. "Yes, sir?" That was all he said. No suggestions were offered, no arguments presented. They weren't necessary. Spock could tell by the expressions on their faces how the two other officers felt. Not that they influenced his decision. His new orders were based solely, as always, on logic.

"Bring us about," he directed the helmsman, fulfilling the latter's hopes. "We will investigate the Beta Lyrae system and attempt to locate the source of the activity affecting our own stasis box."

Sulu couldn't repress a pleased smile. "Aye, aye, sir."

Coming around in a tight arc, the *Copernicus* slowed and plunged deep into the double-star system of Beta Lyrae.

Under Spock's direction, made after a careful study of the shifting stasis box aura, Sulu brought the little ship close in. The closeup view of the unusual binary was as awesome and beautiful as anything in the galaxy. Their viewport was filled with the nebulous yellow giant star, which was the most obvious feature of the system. It was somewhat flattened by the force of gravity and rotation. A line of fiery red hydrogen joined it to its smaller companion, a brilliant dwarf star that shone like a sapphire cabochon. A whirlpool of thin crimson like a streamer of fringed crepe spread out from the blue star in an expanding spiral. The hydrogen faded from pigeon-blood red to dull maroon to a smoky blackness. Even the blackness announced its presence by blotting out the stars lying behind it.

"It's a beautiful universe," Uhura murmured as she drank in the overpowering sight, "and a varied one."

"The beauty's in the variety," Sulu added, equally entranced.

Spock was talking less poetically into his recorder and did not comment so blatantly on Beta Lyrae's attraction, though he admired it as well. Besides its obvious chromatic effects, there was an inherent attractiveness in the order and balance of gravitational and other forces, in the precision of the system's mathematics. Nor was that view exclusively Vulcan. Many human scientists would have found the physical construction of the binary more impressive than its mere visual appearance.

At the moment he was explaining their course into his recorder. "Stasis boxes and their contents are the only remnant of a species powerful enough to have ruled, once, an entire section of our galaxy," he dictated. "Their effect on our sciences has been incalculable. In one box was found the flying belt which was the key to the artificial gravity field presently employed on starships.

"Hence my decision to forgo the briefings preparatory to the conference on Briamos in favor of pursuing a positive lead to another such box in the Beta Lyrae system." He clicked off, put the recorder aside. They were moving near to the object that the *Copernicus*'s compact but efficient instrumentation had long since located.

It was a frozen, almost airless world, a dull white globe too far out to receive appreciable warmth from either of the twin suns. It was as ordinary and unimpressive as the binary was stupendous. In any case, they were not searching for life or a world to colonize but, instead, for another of the Slavers' valuable bequests, the box which was simultaneously inheritance and tombstone.

"Beginning final approach," Sulu announced mechanically, "preparatory to orbital insertion."

Soon they were circling the equator of the chill planet. Measurements indicated that in comparison to the surface rotating beneath them, Earth's most inhospitable tundra was a vision of Elysium and its South Pole a veritable paradise.

"Now, Mr. Sulu."

The helmsman didn't have to look behind him. He knew that the point of the teardrop aura must be stabbing straight down through the mess table.

"Commence landing approach," Spock continued formally. "Try to take us down in as tight a descending spiral as you can, Lieutenant."

"I'll do my best, sir," Sulu assured him, his attention riveted on his readouts and controls.

"That will minimize our searching," Spock informed them, "if we can keep the point of the aura perfectly perpendicular with the surface below us. The second stasis box should be directly under us when we land, or at the very least within walking distance." He moved to stand by the front port.

"If the box is out in the open, visual identification before we touch down is vital. We must take care in that event not to set down on top of the box. In addition to the inconvenience, the box mechanism might interpret our touchdown as an attempt at opening it improperly. We could conceivably find ourselves in the position of our boxed thief back on Gruyakin Six."

"Don't worry, sir," Sulu replied tersely. "I have no intention of standing around for the next billion years, no matter how healthy or well-preserved a stasis field keeps me."

They dropped through the thin, almost nonexistent atmosphere. Sulu brought the shuttle to a smooth stop on a jumbled, frozen plain. Spock assured him they had *not* set down on the box itself. At the last moment the point of the teardrop had shifted slightly to port, indicating that they would land clear of it.

Faint wisps of as-yet-unidentified gases drifted overhead, the only indication that anything lay between the roof of the shuttlecraft and the killing emptiness of interstellar space.

Spock walked back to the stasis box as the helmsman cut the engines. He studied it intently. "What would *you* say, Lieutenant Uhura?"

She bent over, stared beneath the table where the point of the blue aura penetrated. "It's certainly not pointing straight down. I'd say it's inclined slightly in . . . that direction." She rose and pointed.

"I agree." Spock moved forward and stared hard out the port in the direction the aura point indicated. "Yet . . . I see no sign of another box, at least not nearby. It is there, however. This is not surprising, in view of the unevenness of the terrain. Life-support belts."

They moved to the single large storage locker, slipped the belts around their waists. Spock checked Uhura's and Sulu's belt operation with a compact device taken from the locker. Then Sulu checked Spock and Uhura; and then it was Uhura's turn. Thus doublechecked and assured that all systems were functioning properly, the three officers entered the *Copernicus*'s airlock, each encased in a lime-yellow aura no denser than the mysterious blue one surrounding the stasis box they had taken with them.

Sulu and Uhura each had their phasers out and ready—a standard precaution. They had had little time for pre-inspection of this world and experience had shown that a planet which seemed devoid of life could often provide as many unpleasant surprises as a far more fertile and hospitable globe. Spock was carrying the stasis box, flanked on the right by Uhura and by Sulu on the left. The blue aura now pointed straight ahead. The lock cycled, and a brief puff of unreclaimed air escaped into the alienness beyond.

The three exited into a frozen hell. They saw no hint of any life, malignant or otherwise. Not a plant, not an insect, only an icy plain bordered by rippling, jagged hills and distant mountains of ice-bound stone that had likely never felt the weak warmth of the distant binary. It was difficult for any world orbiting a twin sun to support life, due to the often erratic nature of its planetary orbit. The frozen emptiness of Beta Lyrae I appeared to be no exception.

As they walked across the ice-covered ground the glow from the stasis box in Spock's arms intensified, turned almost azure. In contrast, the lime-yellow halos projected by their life-support belts remained constant. As always, Uhura reflected on how feebly inadequate these seemed, to be the only thing holding back the monstrous cold and airlessness pressing tight around them.

In many ways the stark, dead landscape they were crossing was more forbidding than empty space. The interstellar void was merely sterile, while the corpse of a world on which life could exist, given a few changes in atmosphere and location, was almost palpably threatening.

Uhura was not afraid to give voice to her feelings. Besides, it was reassuring to hear another voice in that desolation, even if Spock and Sulu were right next to her. "I never did like these barren little worlds. They always make me feel as if I'm walking on one huge grave."

"We're not tourists here, Lieutenant," Spock commented firmly. "Kindly keep your mind on the business at hand."

Uhura bristled at the harshness of the reprimand. However, Spock's intention had not been to reprimand her but only to take her mind off the depressing landscape surrounding them, which he succeeded efficiently in doing.

"Mr. Spock?" Sulu stepped lightly over a miniature crevasse. "If it takes one stasis box to find another stasis box, how did they find the very first one?"

"I would like to say that its presence was deduced, Lieutenant Sulu. I would like to relate that it was discovered after a great deal of study based on material carefully assimilated by a number of highly competent researchers utilizing the most modern technology. However," he continued drily, "that is not what happened.

"The first Slaver stasis box was discovered the same way as so many truly unique phenomena are—by accident." He turned slightly to his left, following the compass point of the blue aura toward a low rise topped with freshly cracked ice.

They mounted the rise. Spock halted, retraced his steps several meters, moved a little to his right. At that point the apex of the blue glow jabbed straight down. All that lay visible below their feet was hard-packed frozen gas and water vapor. Sulu pushed at the surface with a life-support, aura-shielded boot.

"The other box appears to be almost under us, or at least very close by," Spock announced. "If I recall correctly what is known about the inter–stasis box relationship, then judging from the hue and sharpness of the field this one is projecting," and he motioned with the stasis box in his hands, "I would guess that the other lies perhaps thirty meters below us. Considering," and he indicated the surrounding tortured topography, "the evidence of violent tectonic disturbances in this region, that is hardly surprising. We should be grateful the box is buried no deeper than it is."

Sulu was adjusting his phaser setting as he spoke. "In that case it shouldn't be too long before we can dig it out, especially if this is mostly ice beneath us." He finished setting the phaser, pointed it downward. "In this low pressure the ice should boil away as soon as our phasers melt it, and on this low a setting"—he indicated his own weapon—"we don't run any risk of damaging the box. We ought to be able to—"

He stumbled as the ground heaved. A violent explosion burst the surface behind them, sending ice fragments flying. Stunned, they turned as soon as they could recover their balance. Uhura remembered what

Spock had said about severe earth disturbances in this region.

But the explosion had been too localized for a quake, too modest for a volcano, and it was immediately apparent that the cause was artificial in nature. A concealed tunnel or cave had appeared in the ice. A half-dozen space-suited figures flew toward them from the opening, propulsive backpacks powering them toward the three shocked officers.

Sulu caught a glimpse of who wore those suits and knew instantly he would have preferred a volcano.

Each suited figure was a little over two and a half meters long. Their pressure suits were armored to withstand both phaser charges and solid-core weaponry. The bubble helmets topping the suits were fully transparent. The suits themselves could have been designed to accommodate human beings, save for their unusual size and the long, twisting segmented sections which extended from the base of the spine. They indicated tailed creatures.

Only one known race fitted those particular proportions.

"Kzinti!" Uhura, crouching and raising her phaser simultaneously, let go a blast. The energy charge glanced harmlessly off the armored suit of the nearest alien.

Another of the Kzinti fired at Sulu. There was a flare of darker light against his life-support aura.

The aliens had surrounded them. One landed just behind the helmsman, tried to lock massive arms around him. Sulu slipped partially clear, wrestling desperately with his much larger opponent.

Behind the helmet a startlingly feline face stared angrily down at him. The alien tried to pin Sulu's arms while keeping a grip on its phaser, a standard-issue Federation weapon which looked grotesquely tiny in an armored, four-digited paw that could easily have enclosed both of Sulu's hands. Bright pink ears that resembled the amputated wings of some tiny flying creature fluttered on the alien's head as it battled in frustration to secure a binding grip on its smaller but agile opponent.

Despite Sulu's agility, this was a fight which could have only one outcome, since the three Federation officers were both outsized and outnumbered by their alien attackers.

Two other Kzinti landed behind Sulu, and he was unable to avoid them all. They soon had him pinned between them.

Just before one phaser blast partially penetrated her life-support aura and knocked her unconscious to the chill surface, Uhura was certain she glimpsed Spock standing calmly nearby, watching the fight. He still held the stasis box in both hands, instead of a working phaser.

As she fell, she saw him handing the invaluable stasis box to one of the huge Kzinti. Her mind refused to accept the evidence of her eyes. The impossible thought that Spock could be a coward or worse occurred to her as the alien environment her life-support aura held at bay seemed to close in tight around and blot all thinking and speculation from her mind.

Sulu had been phaser-stunned when he refused an order to stop struggling. Now the Kzinti muttered among themselves, their attention shifting constantly from the stasis box to the two crumpled humans. They kept a watchful eye or two on Spock. The Vulcan made no move to resist when one of them asked gruffly over his helmet frequency for the phaser the officer still wore at his waist. Spock handed it over as docilely as he had the stasis box.

Once their last possible opponent had been rendered helpless, the aliens relaxed a little. Spock took the opportunity to study the motionless forms of his companions. Both Sulu and Uhura seemed to be breathing regularly. Their lime-yellow auras remained intact and strong, indicating that the belt mechanisms hadn't been damaged. That meant they were in no immediate danger. Their life-support belts would sense the change in their metabolisms and adjust accordingly, just as they would if the two officers had fallen asleep instead of having been stunned into unconsciousness.

Spock's thoughts were mixed but steady as always when, by gesturing, the Kzinti indicated he should move toward the tunnel they had appeared from so unexpectedly. Other Kzinti hefted the unconscious forms of Uhura and Sulu, while one more picked up the coveted stasis box. There was a good deal of recognizable chortling over the prize, which indicated the presence of something far more elaborate than a casual trap.

A short march down a phaser-cut tunnel brought the party to an open airlock. One Kzinti gave Spock an ungentle shove into the open chamber. The first officer made no protest, offered not even a hint of displeasure at the rough treatment.

It took three cycles for every member of the group to be transferred into the fresh air of the Kzinti ship. The design of the lock and numerous other aspects of construction immediately indicated to Spock that they were boarding a vessel, and not a totally unfamiliar one at that. But then, most of Kzinti technology was derivative of Federation or Klingon engineering.

Further marching through the powerfully scented air brought the party to what appeared to be a crew ready room. In keeping with the requirements of Kzinti physiology, the room was huge by Federation standards. An oddly shaped table large enough for several Kzinti to sit comfortably around dominated the center of the room. Lockers and instrument panels lined one entire wall. Again, nothing was remarkable about the instrumentation. Much of it looked familiar, although altered in some cases to accommodate the size of the Kzinti hand.

Gently, almost reverently, a Kzinti put the stasis box onto the massive central table. The rest of the group gathered around and began an animated discussion of their booty.

Spock watched them silently, occasionally glancing sideways at Uhura and Sulu to make certain their condition didn't suddenly take a change for the worse. In his own mind he had already taken full responsibility for the catastrophe. But that was unfair, as any outside observer would have insisted.

True, he had pointed out the unusual circumstance of another undiscovered stasis box lying within an oft-visited system like Beta Lyrae. He should have exercised greater caution in their search for the second box, should have seen the clues to the Kzinti presence even though they were concealed beyond the detecting ability of any mortal.

Kirk would have been the first to point out that Spock had no choice but to pursue the possible existence of the second box, and that he could not possibly have foreseen or guessed at the presence of the waiting Kzinti. But Spock was ever more critical of his actions than anyone else could be.

But an event detrimental to the interests of the Federation had occurred as a result of his decisions. He was guilty and condemned—unless the error could somehow, unlikely as that seemed, still be rectified before permanent damage was done. The Kzinti possessed the stasis box he and the others had traveled so fast and far to pick up. Its contents now became doubly important. Not only would they not be used to benefit the peoples of the Federation, but in the hands of the belligerent Kzinti they could be employed to bring only harm.

How much harm depended on the exact nature of those contents.

Spock was anxious to see inside. He had a perverse desire to know exactly how much damage his actions had caused the people of the Federation and the Federation itself.

A human experiencing the same thoughts might have screamed and damned himself, begging for his captors to shoot him in punishment for his mistake. Spock merely stood quietly. He faced the theft of the box as calmly as he had its acquisition. An observer would not be able to tell from his demeanor that the Kzinti had even arrived. Only his mind was operating much faster than before, and that was not visible.

Moans came from nearby. Sulu and Uhura were beginning to stir, recovering from the stun effects of the phasers. As soon as they were able to stand by themselves, a pair of Kzinti moved to assist them roughly in rising all the way. They escorted both groggy officers over to Spock and left them standing next to the first officer.

Spock had already noted the surface on which he had been directed to stand, and on which Sulu and Uhura now swayed unsteadily. Roughly five square meters of a thick metal mesh, it resembled a carpet woven of steel instead of fiber. He had recognized it as soon as they'd entered the large room. It was a police web, one identical to those used by Federation authorities for restraining prisoners without damaging them. The webs were portable and much simpler to maintain than an energy- or solid-barrier cubicle. When not needed, the jail "cell" could simply be rolled up and tucked away in a locker somewhere.

His observation was immediately confirmed. A Kzin nearby touched a wall control. Spock instantly felt himself paralyzed from the shoulders down. The force field generated by the mesh held him as firmly as any visibly bonds. The field was strong enough to retard perspiration in a prisoner, but given the cool climate of the ready room and the fact that their incarceration was likely to be brief, he didn't expect that would be a problem. As a bonus, the field kept the still unsteady Uhura and Sulu from falling over.

It took an effort, but Spock managed to turn his head enough to see his companions. They were beginning to regain full control of their nervous systems, including their minds. When they came around completely there would be questions, and Spock prepared himself for some awkward ones.

Uhura blinked, tried to take a step toward him, and found she was unable to move so much as a toe. Her head also came around slowly. "Mr. Spock . . . where are we?"

"Inside a Kzinti spacecraft, Lieutenant. Of what size and capability I have been unable to determine."

"Just a minute." Sulu was taking in their surroundings, eyeing the cluster of arguing Kzinti around the table. "Something doesn't make sense here— Wait, I remember now. Kzinti aren't supposed to have hand phasers, let alone space armor. Where did they get those weapons?" He gestured at the nearest Kzin and the pair of phasers slung at its hips.

"I don't know, Mr. Sulu, but you are quite right about their possession of weapons." Spock recited, "The Treaty of Sirius does not permit them any weapons capabilities at all, beyond the operation of a few police vessels. Obviously, the treaty has been broken."

The Kzinti left the room, still growling and grunting among themselves.

"This severe violation must be reported," Spock went on, "as soon as we reach Starbase Twenty-Five."

Sulu's expression was more eloquent than words, as if to say, *You mean,* if *we reach Starbase Twenty-Five.* But he didn't say that. Instead, his attention shifted to the grated surface they were standing on.

"Police web. We won't be able to do anything unless we can turn it off somehow."

They were left alone to discuss their plight for some time, before equipment-laden Kzinti re-entered the room. Under the direction of one Kzin with engineer's markings they deposited the equipment around the central table.

Devoid of their pressure suits they looked a lot like plump orange cats, save for their fanlike ears and the furless, pink, ratlike tail that twitched and moved restlessly behind each of them. Each was of considerable bulk, and an unmistakable, if feral, gleam of intelligence shone behind every pair of blazing yellow eyes.

As they chattered among themselves and moved equipment and instrumentation about, Spock concentrated on noting differences between individuals. For the most part these were slight. One Kzin had a bright patch of white on its nose. Another's fur was colored to form a pair of dark stripes over both eyes. These minor differences made the startling appearance of the last Kzin to enter the room all the more striking. In contrast to the healthy, robust girth of its companions, the newcomer was thin—downright scrawny. Instead of twitching restlessly about, its tail drooped to drag listlessly on the deck, and the pink batlike ears curled flat against the head as though soaked by a month's rain.

Along all of one flank, the dense orange fur was twisted and matted beyond combing, as if the Kzin slept exclusively on the same side and never moved. The fur resembled the gnarled hair of a dog, repeatedly washed and dried, who broke the cycle by rolling in mud. Nor was the expression of the newcomer normal. Instead of the other Kzinti's usual fierce or proud demeanor, this one wore a look of perpetual disillusionment.

Uhura decided that the scrawny arrival was either dreadfully unhappy or haunted by some as-yet-unknown affliction. "What are they up to now, Mr. Spock?" She gestured with her head at the compact but complex machine that was being erected alongside the central table. "What's that?"

"I cannot be positive." Spock had to raise his voice to make himself audible over the increasing yowls and grumblings of the orange-colored assembly. "But from the haste and excitement with which they are supervising the construction of the device, I would guess that despite differences in design and crudeness of engineering, it is a stasis-field nullifier."

"They're going to try to open the box, then, and there's nothing we can do to stop them." Sulu was simultaneously angry and downcast.

"It is the logical thing to do—and you needn't whisper, Lieutenant. At the moment they seem to have absolutely no interest in us. So we can talk normally, without much fear of being abused, although a certain amount of caution in what we discuss would be advisable."

He gestured with his head toward the far side of the room. "You see the lean, bedraggled Kzin, the last one to enter the chamber?"

"You mean the one back there in the corner?" Uhura asked.

"Yes. He is a reader of minds, a telepath."

"I thought I'd heard something about that." Uhura looked satisfied. "I remember reading that all Kzinti telepaths were unhappy neurotics who'd just as soon

not have their special talents." She nodded ruefully.
"That one sure fits the description. What a miserable-
looking creature." At her last words, the telepath
cringed. That also was typical of his condition. A normal Kzin so slighted would be on top of Uhura by
now, frothing at the mouth.

Spock warned them again. "There is no sure way to
guard our thoughts from him. Orally we can say what
we wish, but mentally we must be constantly on
guard." He paused a moment, thoughtful, then added,
"Lieutenant Sulu, the telepath is not likely to concentrate much on Lieutenant Uhura or myself. For different reasons, she and I are considered by the Kzinti to
be inferior beings.

"It will be helpful to keep in mind that the Kzinti
are meat-eaters. If you sense that ugly one probing
your thoughts, there are better things to concentrate on
besides visions of resistance or hate. I believe it would
be more effective if you were to concentrate at such
moments on enjoying a raw vegetable. The thought of
eating anything not-meat is repulsive in the extreme to
a Kzin. Even the most perceptive among them cannot
think rationally if afflicted with overpowering nausea,
and I expect that to hold true for telepaths as well."

"Yes, sir. I'll concentrate on wallowing in salad."
Sulu looked pleased at the thought. "Maybe I can goad
them into revealing something of their intentions, besides opening the stasis box, of course."

"There is one other things we should all keep in
mind." Spock fought his own neck muscles in order to
turn his head to look at the *Enterprise*'s chief communications officer. "Lieutenant Uhura, what I am about
to say may be critical, and it will be difficult to comply
with. While we are in the presence of the Kzinti, do
not say anything, do not suggest anything, do not do
anything inventive. You must strive to look harmless,
ignorant, virtually inanimate."

"Any special reason, sir?"

"Are you forgetting that Kzinti females are no more
than dumb animals?" Spock tried to tell whether or not
the scraggly Kzin telepath was concentrating on him,
then decided that if anything he was still wholly ab-

sorbed with monitoring his fellows and possibly also Sulu.

"In an emergency," he reminded Uhura, "the Kzinti may forget that a human female is an intelligent creature, capable of original thought and activities beyond the merely instinctive ones of eating and sleeping."

"Thanks," snapped Uhura. "Thanks a lot, *sir*."

Spock was patient. The lieutenant's gut reaction was only to be expected. "Lieutenant Uhura, I value your intelligence highly. So does Lieutenant Sulu, and everyone else on board the *Enterprise*. But we may be able to seize an opportunity to escape if the Kzinti believe you have none. This is not a time for emotional reactions. Let the Kzinti react emotionally, as they are inclined to do. Our chances lie in calculation and reason . . . and in being ready."

Uhura replied much more softly this time. "Yes sir . . . You're right, of course." She smiled a dangerous little smile. "Don't worry. I'll do my damnedest to convince our captors that I'm nothing more than an automaton."

VII

Kirk moved continually between the command chair, the science station, and the helm-navigation console. Under the guise of inspecting readouts and information, he was really disguising his nervousness. Having places to walk to concealed the fact that he was in a mood to pace the floor.

Another distraction was the *last* thing he needed. He should have been able to concentrate all his attention on the upcoming conference, save for wondering how Spock, Sulu, and Uhura were progressing in their expedition to pick up the Slaver stasis box. Now he had a fresh, utterly unexpected problem on his hands. There was still no word on the whereabouts of Lieutenant M'ress, and the Caitian communications officer hadn't reported herself in to Sick Bay.

He didn't know it, but his troubles were about to be complicated a dozenfold.

"Captain?"

Kirk slid heavily into the command chair, swung to face communications. "Yes, what is it?"

Lieutenant Talliflores looked confused and unhappy. "I have two reports just in, sir."

Kirk perked up a little. "They've found Lieutenant M'ress?"

"No, sir. One report is from Engineering. Commander Scott says that one of his warp-drive techs, an ensign M'viore, has disappeared." Talliflores checked his recorder readout. "The other report *is* from Security, but it has nothing to do with Lieutenant M'ress. One of their own ensigns engaged in the search, name of R'leez, has vanished and does not acknowledge her orders."

"Both Caitians," a concerned Kirk declared after a brief pause. "That makes three of them: M'ress, and now this R'leez and M'viore." Swiveling in the chair, he looked to the science station.

"Mr. Vedama, I don't believe we have any other Caitians in the crew, but would you check, please?"

"Aye, sir," Vedama responded in his soft, lilting voice. It took only a few seconds to run the check through the computer. "You're right, sir. Those three are the only representatives of the planet Cait listed in the personnel records."

"Obviously we're dealing with a Caitian racial malady, then," Kirk announced. "But what? Some kind of disease, maybe, but how could they all be affected so fast? None was near the others when they were stricken. How could a disease be communicated so quickly throughout the ship? Unless Caitians are subject to periodic attacks of madness. But I've never heard of anything like that affecting them."

"Neither have I, sir," his acting science chief added.

"Excuse me, sir." It was Talliflores again.

"Now what?"

"A report coming in from Sick Bay, Captain. Dr. McCoy wants to talk to you."

Kirk allowed himself a sigh of relief. "At least Lieutenant M'ress has made it safely to Sick Bay. Maybe Bones has some idea by now of what's causing the Caitians to act this way." He flipped on his chair intercom. "Bones, how is she?"

"How is who, Jim?" McCoy sounded unusually tense and irritated.

Kirk's spirits sank. "Didn't Lieutenant M'ress report in to you yet?"

"No, she hasn't, Jim. And now I desperately wish she would, because I have reason to believe she isn't going to."

"You sound awfully positive, Bones. What makes you so sure?"

"Jim, I've got a food technician here, an Ensign Sanchez. He insists that he found Lieutenant M'ress crouching under a bush in the recreation forest area. She didn't respond when he called out to her, so he walked over to see if he could help. He heard your broadcast and thought she might've been too sick to respond."

"Go on, Bones," urged Kirk tensely.

"Not only wasn't she too ill to respond, Jim, but when he approached her she attacked him."

Kirk felt dazed. He conjured up an image of the communications officer in his mind: calm, efficient, usually in complete control of herself . . . It didn't fit.

But neither did her not reporting to Sick Bay.

"Bones, is he certain it was M'ress?"

"Just a second, Jim. You can ask him yourself."

A shaky voice replaced that of Dr. McCoy. "Sir, Ensign Sanchez here. Yes, sir, I'm positive it was Lieutenant M'ress."

Even as he listened, Kirk found it hard to believe. He was even willing to go as far as to ascribe the incident to a delusion on the ensign's part, except that M'ress *was* missing. While Sanchez sounded upset, he was perfectly coherent. There was no reason to discount his description of the encounter.

But Kirk was still incredulous. He had to be certain M'ress's actions were the result of some aberration on her part. "You say she attacked you, Ensign? I've known Lieutenant M'ress ever since she was assigned to the *Enterprise*. She's a competent, responsible officer, hardly the type given to irrational acts and especially to an act of violence against another crew member. You're positive you did nothing to provoke her?"

"Provoke her, sir?" In spite of his condition, the ensign managed to sound suitably outraged. "Sir, all I did was repeat to her what she must have heard herself, that you'd directed her to report to Sick Bay. The moment I made a move to touch her she gave me this crazy look. I started to back off, intending to call for medical help, and that's when she jumped me. I swear, sir, all I did was offer to help her, and when she made it clear she didn't want any help, try to get away."

"I can verify Ensign Sanchez's story, Jim," said McCoy, cutting in. "He has a substantial number of pretty deep scratches. Even well-trimmed Caitian claws can inflict rugged damage if they're used in anger. They're much thicker than human fingernails."

"Captain." It was Sanchez again. He sounded almost defiant. "I'm sorry to have to say this about a superior officer, but I don't think the lieutenant is quite sane. She didn't respond to any of the things I said, either before I approached her or while we were fighting."

"Did she say anything at all, Ensign?" By now Kirk had reluctantly accepted Sanchez's story. The scratches detailed by McCoy were the final convincer.

"Only in Caitian, sir, a lot of yowling and screeching it seemed like to me. I don't know the language, but she *sounded* as angry as she was acting. Frankly, sir, from the look in her eyes I thought she was ready to kill me." Sanchez paused a moment, added emphatically, "It was raw emotion I saw in her face, sir. The kind of expression you expect on the face of a crazy animal, not a superior officer. That's only my impression, of course, and I couldn't get too analytical about things. I was too busy trying to keep from being cut up."

"I understand, Sanchez." The ensign could be forgiven, Kirk felt, for exaggerating his impressions in the hysteria of the moment. Kirk was about ready to give vent to some emotions of his own.

"Bones, you can finish treating the ensign and release him. Sanchez, just one last question for you."

"Yes, sir," said the ensign.

"You told me that you thought Lieutenant M'ress was ready to kill you. Why didn't she? Did you fight her off? I presume neither of you was armed."

"No, sir. At least, if she had a weapon, she didn't show it. But me, fight her off? On the contrary, sir. I'm about her size, maybe a little bigger, but it was like tangling with a small tornado. No, sir, I didn't fight her off. It was pretty funny, now that I think back on it. She just kind of stopped all at once, gave me this real peculiar look . . ."

"What kind of look, ensign?" This was McCoy speaking.

"It's hard to describe, sir. Like she was sorry for what she'd done and yet she'd do it again in a minute. Then she took off and disappeared into the landscaping."

"Do you think she's still down in the recreation area?" Kirk thought to ask.

"I couldn't say, sir." Sanchez sounded exhausted. "I didn't hang around to look for her. All I could think of was getting out of there with the rest of my skin intact."

"All right, Ensign. Thank you. Bridge out."

"Sick Bay out," McCoy responded.

Kirk turned to his science officer. "Lieutenant Vedama, what do you make of all this? First, Lieutenant M'ress disappears and then two Caitian ensigns, and now I learn that one of my most trusted officers is running around silently attacking other members of the crew."

"Sir," Vedama announced apologetically, "I'm no expert on the Caitians."

"My second in command of communications goes berserk, without any visible reason, and no one knows anything!" Kirk sounded understandably peeved. "Lieutenant Vedama, see what you can find on Caitian social patterns. Dr. McCoy will be researching possible medical causes. Maybe it's not a medical problem."

"Yes, sir." Vedama turned to the science computer, began his searching.

Kirk's attention shifted forward. "Mr. Arex, are we still on course schedule for arrival at Starbase Twenty-Five?"

"Slightly ahead of time, sir," the Edoan navigator replied. "Shall I change our speed?"

"No. We'll resolve this trouble before we arrive. Maintain heading and warp-speed." He glanced back at communications.

"Lieutenant Talliflores, relay a message to Security. Tell them I want search teams on every deck to hunt for Lieutenant M'ress and the two absent ensigns. Inform them that all three Caitians are probably dangerous, prone to violent response if approached, and possibly not responsible for their actions.

"Under no circumstances are any of the three to be assaulted with anything stronger than a phaser set for stun. Emphasize to all teams that the three crew members are likely to be suffering from a noncommunicable racial disease as yet unidentified, and that they haven't turned traitor or anything as ridiculously imaginative as that. When captured, all three are to be taken directly to Sick Bay for treatment."

"Yes, sir." Talliflores operated instruments. "Relaying, sir."

In the absence of further information, Kirk leaned back in the command chair and pondered what had happened so far. In the following silence he had ample time to consider and abandon at least a dozen theories concerning the Caitians' actions, none of which seemed even marginally probable.

His chair intercom buzzed for attention.

"Jim," the voice from the speaker announced, "McCoy here. I've received two more casualties."

"What?" Kirk sat up straight in the chair.

"That's right, two more. From different decks. One thinks he was attacked by Lieutenant M'ress. The other identifies his attacker as Ensign M'viore."

"M'viore, too." Kirk felt dazed. "Bones, what the hell's going on here?"

"I wish I knew, Jim. Caitians are normally a very

controlled people. This is the first incident of its kind that I can recall taking place aboard the *Enterprise* or for that matter any other ship I know of, in which Caitians were involved. It doesn't make any sense."

"I know that already, Bones. What about temporary insanity?"

"Occurring simultaneously in three different personalities? Highly unlikely, Jim. I've been checking their records in the medical computer. All three crew members have a history of perfectly normal health, both mental and physical. Not one of them has ever shown any tendency toward mental instability, let alone all three of them. Sorry, Jim, but it has to be something else."

"Anything we could have brought on board, Bones?" Kirk wondered. "Maybe something that could have contaminated their food, affecting them and no one else?"

"I'll check their diets as best I can, Jim, but it's impossible to know exactly what they've eaten lately, never mind for the past few weeks or months. If it's something they did eat, the responsible substance might have been ingested long ago and is only now manifesting itself. There's only one way to check that out and that's to submit all three of them to a detailed biochemical body analysis, to find out if there *is* a foreign substance affecting their stability."

"To do that, Bones, we have to catch them."

"And that's the immediate problem, Jim. In order to cure them, we've first got to find them."

There were three members in the search party. All had their phasers out and set for stun. Ordinarily that would be enough to give them a quiet confidence, but this situation was different from any in recent memory. Even when the quarry was a member of the ship's crew, at least one had some idea what to expect. This time, no one from the captain on down seemed to have any idea what was happening. All they knew was that they were searching for three Caitian crew members who had possibly gone crazy.

Presently they were combing the recreational forest

on Deck Eight, having started from the section where
the missing officer M'ress had last been seen. Other security parties were performing similar searches both on
this deck and elsewhere on the ship.

"Hasmid," whispered one of the security men to his
friend on his left, "I understand that Caitians are supposed to be able to move unheard and unseen through
this kind of terrain. Just because it's located in the
middle of a starship doesn't mean they can't function
as efficiently as they can on the surface of a planet."

"Quiet, Kasuki!" the other responded sharply.
"You're makin' me nervous. And this isn't any kind of
terrain. It's only the recreation area."

"Shut up, you two!" snapped the officer in charge of
the little group.

They were traveling in a line through a particularly
dense clump of vegetation. In spite of their attentiveness, they hardly had time to react when the three
Caitians hit them simultaneously.

Kirk's chair intercom yammered for attention again.
Kirk jabbed the acknowledge button almost viciously.
"Kirk here."

"Jim, McCoy again," came the concerned response.
"One of our patrolling security details got beaten up. It
looks like our three fugitives have joined together
somewhere down on Deck Eight."

"One minute, Bones." Kirk switched over to
shipwide frequency. "Attention, all security personnel.
All security personnel, this is the captain speaking. Seal
off Deck Eight. Shut down all turbolift service to Deck
Eight. Personnel on Deck Eight are instructed to continue with normal duties. The three Caitians are apparently now operating together, but they've shown no
tendency to perform wanton attacks on individuals, and
react violently only if approached.

"If you see any of the three crew members in question, do not attempt to restrain them yourselves. Contact the nearest security team and give details of your
sighting." Kirk thought a second, then added, "Use extreme caution when approaching the three Caitians.
They have already overpowered one security unit.

Henceforth, all security teams will operate in groups of not less than eight per team."

Kirk switched back to the Sick Bay frequency. "Sorry, Bones, but I had to relay some information to Security right away. Go on."

"Jim, there's something else peculiar about this. None of the three Caitians are especially large or strong. The contrary, if anything. Yet they put a whole security team out of commission, a team of personnel whose business is restraining the unruly. The three are all marked up: bruises, scratches, cuts, the works. Ensign Trancas is one of them."

Kirk knew Trancas, a big, burly wrestler type from a slightly high-gravity world. Hardly the sort one would imagine a trio of sylphlike Caitians could overpower, much less beat up.

"They encountered only the three Caitians?" he asked in disbelief, "and they were unable to subdue them?"

"Subdue them! Jim, you ought to see these three. Trancas was in charge of their group. He told me they never had a chance. They thought they had the three fugitives spotted, and approached them with phasers ready. Trancas says they should have beamed them on sight. Instead, when the Caitians showed no sign of aggressiveness, they tried to move them physically. That's when they were jumped, too fast to use their weapons. We know the Caitians are fast, but this other thing has me confused. Trancas says he tried to wrestle M'ress to the deck and she threw him into a clump of bushes."

"M'ress?" The communications officer had never displayed any unusual strength. "Bones, do the Caitians have some special reserves of energy they can call on at will? Perhaps something we don't know about?"

"I wouldn't think so, Jim. At least, I never heard of any such phenomenon, and the Caitians are a fairly well documented race. They've been members of the Federation long enough for any peculiar abilities to have manifested themselves. I think we're still stuck with our original hypothesis: that something they've eaten has affected their body chemistry. The unusual strength is undoubtedly a byproduct of whatever's affecting them. Whatever they ingested isn't sitting well with them."

"It's not sitting well with me either, Bones. Keep hunting, and let me know the instant you think you might've found the chemical that's causing all the trouble."

"If that's what it is, Jim. Sick Bay out."

"Captain?" Talliflores glanced over from communications. "A new report coming in. From a yeoman Loo. He's certain he spotted Lieutenant M'ress and at least one other Caitian on Deck Six."

"Already? They must have slipped away before we sealed off Deck Eight."

"If anyone could avoid patrols it would be the Caitians, sir." Vedama sounded half apologetic. "With their speed and agility, coupled to a natural talent for self-concealment, they will prove difficult to corner."

"I'm fully aware of the capabilities of Caitian physiology, Mr. Vedama." Kirk's frustration made his reply sound more biting than he intended it to be. "More than I want to be, at the moment." He sighed.

"Mr. Talliflores, redirect security personnel to cover all decks, with particular emphasis on Deck Six."

"Yes, sir." He paused, listening at his headset. "Another report coming in. They didn't slip through unnoticed. They confronted another security patrol under the command of yeoman O'Hyr. They're on their way to Sick Bay now."

Events were becoming more complicated instead of less so, Kirk mused. "All eight of them?"

"All but three, Captain," Talliflores reported. "Yeoman O'Hyr is among them. But Ensigns Suarez, Hilambo, and Chevalier were not injured and are presently in pursuit of the fugitives, having delayed only long enough to report in and check the severity of their companions' injuries."

"So three of them weren't hurt, and the Caitians backed off. Whatever's affecting them hasn't made them omnipotent, then. They haven't suddenly become invincible." He hesitated. "Still, five out of eight put out of commission without so much as capturing one fugitive isn't very encouraging either. But at least no one's been seriously hurt or killed yet."

"True, sir," Arex commented from his position at the navigation-helm. "But they will have phasers now, taken from the assaulted security team."

"Mr. Arex, I'm sure they took phasers from the first trio of security personnel they confronted, and yet they haven't so much as fired to stun anyone. That doesn't make any sense either. If nothing else, the Caitians are acting consistent in their inconsistentness." Kirk stared at the vacant viewscreen, which all too soon would be displaying a picture of Starbase 25.

Probably the base had several Caitians in its complement, which meant that M'ress and her companions had to be captured and treated before anyone from the *Enterprise* could leave the ship. A human might not be affected by whatever had possessed the Caitians, but that didn't rule out the possibility of Kirk or anyone else of another species serving as a carrier. If it *was* some kind of racial malady the Caitians were suffering from, he couldn't risk infecting the Caitians at the starbase. Besides which, the Caitians had to be caught so they could be kept from harming themselves, not to mention other personnel.

"Whatever's affected them hasn't driven them completely crazy, Mr. Arex, or they wouldn't have a thought about employing weapons, not to mention severely injuring anyone else. They've been very careful about that." A new thought occurred to him.

"In fact, their recent movements are a testament to their continued sanity. Have you noticed, Mr. Arex, Mr. Vedama, that the Caitians aren't just traveling in a random pattern to avoid the security teams? They're moving upward through the ship. Why, I can't imagine. But if they persist in their movements, and there's no reason why they shouldn't—at least, none I can hypothesize—then maybe we can make it work to our advantage. The bridge is the one level on the ship where we can isolate them and eliminate any possible chance of escape."

"True but risky, Captain," Vedama pointed out.

Kirk replied tensely. "I have three valuable members of my crew running amok, Lieutenant, and if we can stop them before they severely injure any of their fellows or irrevocably incriminate themselves, I'm going to take a chance or two."

"Captain," Lieutenant Arex noted, "if we permit them to reach the bridge unopposed and they are, as you state, not insane, then surely they will suspect something."

"Not if we're careful not to give them reason to, Lieutenant. All bridge personnel will continue to perform their usual duties, as if nothing is amiss. Mr. Vedama, signal Starbase Twenty-Five and find out what they know about periodic maladies among the Caitians. Give them a detailed breakdown of their aberrant behavior lately, plus personal résumés. See if the medical computer there has any information we might use that's not in our banks. And if there's a Caitian or two serving at the Base, try and contact them directly and explain our problem. Maybe they'll know exactly what's wrong."

"Yes, sir. We are still a considerable distance from the base and there is no deep-space relay between. There will be time between questions and reply," Vedama declared.

"Sick Bay calling bridge," the speaker at Kirk's elbow announced. "McCoy here. The injuries to the five members of the last security team are—"

"Not now, Bones," Kirk interrupted him. "The Caitians are moving upward through the ship. I have a hunch they're going to try and reach the bridge."

"Why would they do that? Surely they have no illusions about taking over the ship!"

"We don't know what they might want, Bones."

"Well if you're fairly sure they're coming there, then I'm coming also. They've already demonstrated they can exercise much more than their usual strength. Several of the injured ensigns are positive they hit at least two of the Caitians with phaser bursts when it seemed they were going to be overpowered. They're convinced that's what drove their attackers off, but they don't understand why the bursts didn't stun them into immobility. All I can guess is that their increased strength may also be coupled to an ability to at least partially withstand a phaser set to stun."

"I'll believe that, Bones, when I fire point-blank at M'ress and don't see her fall on the deck."

"Maybe so, Jim, but I'm going to bring something of my own along. It's more powerful than a phaser stun burst, but no more lethal. Ke'eloveen. It's a general tranquilizer that can be adjusted specifically for several different kinds of mammalian metabolism. It won't take long to concoct a batch gauged specifically for Caitian physiology."

"Sounds promising, Bones. Be glad to have you."

McCoy arrived on the bridge shortly thereafter. He carried a small plastic pistol with a multiple barrel. Walking over to the command chair, he showed it to Kirk, reached into a waist pouch and brought out a handful of tiny transparent darts filled with a thick golden liquid.

"Each dart holds enough ke'eloveen to put out several Caitians, Jim. The pistol can fire four darts together or individually. I hope I have enough time to fire one dart at a time. I can fire a quadruple spread in an emergency, but three darts or more striking the same person would create the danger of overdose reactions."

"I'm hoping—unreasonably—that you won't have to use them, Bones." Kirk found the prospect of facing an attack by three of his crew sobering, where others might have found it ludicrous.

McCoy placed the pistol in a ready position at his waist. "Any indication of where the three are now?"

"No. We haven't had any reports on their whereabouts for some time, Bones. Hopefully a patrol will capture them before they can reach the bridge. If not, we have one advantage: They don't know that we're expecting them here."

"How can you be so sure, Jim? They probably know that you've been receiving reports on their movements. They might assume that you *do* know they're heading here and change their direction accordingly."

"I don't think so, Bones." Kirk leaned forward earnestly. "Everything they've done so far has been with a singlemindedness of purpose."

"So you think there's a method in their madness? That they have some definite goal in mind?" McCoy seemed skeptical. "That doesn't sound like any kind of disease function I ever heard of."

"Bones, they've got to be working toward some end. I admit I don't have much grounds for believing that, but their actions almost hint that they're being controlled by something they're unable to resist, some compulsion they can't fight. I don't think they'll consider that we might be waiting for them, because I don't think that whatever's driving them leaves them much room for that kind of abstract speculation. I just wish I knew what they wanted, and why."

"We'll find out soon enough, Jim." And he added, so softly no one else could hear, "Provided we don't have to kill all three of them." McCoy moved away, leaving Kirk to his own thoughts. He took up a stance near the communications console, checking to make certain the tranquilizer pistol was still in place, ready to be pressed into hurried service.

"Remember," Kirk informed the rest of the bridge personnel, "no one is to make a hostile move or indicate that anything out of the ordinary is taking place unless the Caitians provoke us. If that happens, use your phasers on stun."

A chorus of "ayes" sounded in varying degrees of assurance from around the bridge.

"Anything from Starbase Twenty-Five, Lieutenant Vedama?"

"No, sir. They should have received our communication by now. No doubt they are trying to find something to report to us."

Kirk turned to communications once more. "Talliflores, any new word on the present location of the Caitians?"

"No, sir, nothing. None of the patrolling security teams reports a sighting since the last one identifying them from Deck Six—and no word from any other personnel, although everyone on the ship must be looking out for them."

"They're probably not even halfway to the bridge yet," McCoy commented. "Maybe they changed their minds or their imaginary unknown purpose, and are heading in a different direction."

"Maybe, Bones," Kirk conceded, "but I still—"

The turbolift doors opened abruptly. Everyone on the bridge tensed, then relaxed. It was only a couple of ensigns wearing science department insignia. And also wearing, Kirk noted curiously after starting to turn away, oddly matched blank expressions.

"Bridge—!" he started to shout.

Both technicians fell forward, unconscious. Two Caitians emerged from the lift behind them, moving low and incredibly fast and firing phasers of their own.

"—alert!" Kirk finished, even as he was ducking down in the command chair and reaching for his own sidearm.

The order was hardly necessary, since everyone had heard or seen the two bodies of the technicians falling to the deck in front of the lift. Moving forms and flashing beams of phaser power set for stun filled the bridge. That included the phasers of the Caitians, who still displayed a caution entirely out of keeping with their actions. Several members of the bridge complement were quickly immobilized by the Caitians' surprise attack.

Shielded by the command chair's bulk, Kirk was able to aim a touch better than some of his crew. One blast from his phaser struck Ensign R'leez square in the left side, under her arm. She stumbled—but didn't go down. They had been correct in assuming that whatever was affecting the Caitians had also given their bodies the ability to withstand a low-power phaser burst.

But Kirk couldn't consider increasing the power of any weapons to killing intensity. No one had been killed or seriously hurt by the rampaging Caitians. Of course, if it appeared that it was going to be a choice between hurting one of the Caitians and letting them take over the bridge . . .

Arex was crouched behind the navigation-helm console firing regularly. Holding a paralyzed left forearm tight against his side, Lieutenant Vedama provided a crossfire from the region of the science station.

One of the Caitians, R'leez again, made a rush for the command chair and Kirk. The Captain fired at the charging ensign, then rolled out of the feline's path. But it was immediately clear she wasn't after him or the command chair. She rushed past Kirk, ignoring him as she headed for the helm controls.

Arex caught her with another phaser burst. She staggered but again somehow managed to keep her feet. She was almost on top of the console and its protective, tripedal operator when she unexpectedly collapsed and fell across the helmsman's seat.

Kirk had rolled back behind the command chair, panting. Now he noticed the tiny glint of plastic reflected off the syringe-dart sticking out of the Caitian's back. McCoy had shot her with one of his tranquilizer darts.

Then something knocked him aside, moving at incredible speed. It was Ensign M'viore, the other Caitian who had arrived in the lift.

"Bones! Fire, Bones!"

Why didn't he fire?

M'viore leaped for the controls, and Arex emerged to meet her. The Edoan threw three arms around her, wrestled her off. His additional arm prevented her from dealing with him as easily as she and her companions had dealt with the members of the various security teams. Spitting and clawing while a silent Arex held on desperately, she tumbled to the deck on top of him.

"Bones!" Kirk looked around frantically for the doctor. Then he saw why McCoy hadn't fired at M'viore and why he didn't answer now. McCoy was lying sprawled on the deck, stunned by a burst from one of the Caitians' phasers.

Half crawling, half stumbling, Kirk ran to his side, picked up the half-loaded tranquilizer gun. Arex and M'viore rolled over twice before the Caitian came up on top and raised her claws for a swing at the exhaust-

ed navigator's face. Vedama and Talliflores hunted for
a clear shot at her.

Kirk turned, aimed the unfamiliar but simple device,
and fired. The syringe-dart snicked into M'viore just
beneath her upraised right arm. She sat perfectly still
for a moment, then rose and glanced at her side
uncomprehendingly. For a brief instant the expression
on her face was almost normal. Then she crumpled to
the deck.

A shaken Arex climbed slowly to his feet. Kirk
moved to stand beside him, still holding the dartgun.

"Her reserves of strength were startling, sir," Arex
told him, "much in addition to what the reports
claimed. It was one thing to listen to them, quite another to experience what they were referring to. I
found myself being rapidly overpowered." Long, high
whistling sounds—Edoan wheezing—issued from the
navigator's mouth.

"I thought she was coming for me," a puzzled Kirk
murmured. "She was looking straight at me, and
then—something more important seemed to take control of her. She forgot me completely in her rush to get
at the helm. R'leez was heading for the helm also."

"That's funny, sir," a puzzled technician replied,
from across the bridge, "I thought she was coming after *me*."

"I wonder why the helm as a final destination.
Where could they want to go so frantically?"

"We'll find out when they wake up." Arex regarded
both limp feline forms thoughtfully.

"I hope so." Kirk glanced around quickly, but the
bridge and turbolift were devoid of the one figure he
sought. "I wonder where M'ress is?"

The Caitian communications officer was closer than
Kirk knew. She was in a dark, dark place. It didn't
bother her. She was not subject to claustrophobia, and
the faint glow from the pocket light she carried in one
hand provided more than enough illumination for her
cat eyes to make out her surroundings. It was blissfully
quiet where she was working, but she wasn't calm and
relaxed. The pounding of her heart and the raging

emotions controlling her kept both her hands and mind moving desperately.

Nurse Chapel arrived with other Sick Bay technicians. The two Caitians and the members of the bridge crew who had been paralyzed by their phasers were carried from the room.

One particular casualty concerned Kirk, not because he was more severely injured than any of the others, but because his invaluable advice would be sorely missed. "How soon before Bones will recover?" he inquired as McCoy was carried off the bridge.

"It doesn't look as if he received the full force of a beam, Captain." Chapel considered the question briefly. "Not very long. In fact, he may be the first one to recover since he only absorbed a glancing blow. He'll recover faster if I give him a countering neurodrug, but he'll feel the effects twenty-four hours later."

"I need him most in the next twenty-four hours," Kirk told her. "What would Bones say if he was able?"

"To give him the drug," Chapel replied without hesitation.

"Right. Do so. What about the Caitians? I've got to know what's affected them and what M'ress is likely to do on her own, now that her two companions have been caught."

"I understand, sir. I've been working with Dr. McCoy trying to find out, and we've several members of the ship's organic fabrication staff working with us. If anything unusual got into their food, they'll find it. It's slow going, though, backchecking everything that's been processed in, say, the past several weeks. They've found nothing in the way of a foreign substance so far that might be responsible for the trouble."

"Keep them at it, Chapel. Do the best you can. And contact me the moment Bones is conscious."

She smiled. "He'll do that himself, sir."

When the last motionless crew member had been removed and the medical team was on its way down to Sick Bay, Kirk resumed his station at the command chair. Talliflores, Vedama, and himself were the only ones who had escaped the Caitians' assault.

But that wouldn't do, especially not with M'ress still unconfined.

"Lieutenant Talliflores, contact appropriate sections and have them designate on-duty qualified personnel to replace the technicians who were stunned. We need a maximum complement here, in case of any new surprises. Have backups report immediately."

He turned to Vedama. "I wonder why M'ress didn't join her friends in their attack. A third charge might have successfully reached the helm."

"It is possible, Captain," the science officer theorized, "that M'ress might have disagreed with her companions in their approach. Or she might feel different compulsions, have differing motives, and therefore didn't accompany them. Or," and he looked around with concern, "their seemingly well-planned assault on the bridge might only have been a diversion so M'ress could reach some other part of the ship."

"Possible, Lieutenant. Talliflores, give me shipwide channel again."

The communications officer complied and Kirk once more addressed the command chair pickup. "All personnel, this is the Captain speaking.

"Two of the three renegade Caitians have now been tranquilized and are on their way to Sick Bay to receive treatment. Lieutenant M'ress has not been located and presumably is still moving freely about the ship. It is possible that the recent, nonfatal attack on the bridge which you will shortly be hearing rumors of was an attempt to divert our attention from some other deck. Security teams will continue searching on their own levels and all personnel will continue to remain alert for the lieutenant's presence. Thank you."

"If M'ress has any sense left," Vedama commented, "she'll realize that she can't hope to accomplish whatever bizarre intention she and her companions had."

"Relief personnel are on their way up, Captain," Talliflores announced smoothly.

"Good. Hopefully this will all be over soon." Kirk regarded the command chair chronometer. They still had plenty of time to——

The lights went out.

Everyone spent a nerve-wracking couple of seconds in near-total darkness until the self-contained emergency lights cut in, filling the bridge with an eerie, dim glow that was punctuated only by the brilliant but localized illumination of the instrumentation faces and dials.

"I believe, Captain," said Vedama slowly, "that we now know the whereabouts of Lieutenant M'ress."

"Mr. Talliflores," Kirk said crisply, his eyes darting from dark corner to half-hidden bulkhead, "any communications from elsewhere on the ship as to her possible presence?"

"Checking, sir." Talliflores turned to his console. A peculiar expression came over his deeply tanned face. He rapidly adjusted several controls, but these actions served only to deepen his uncertainty.

Eventually he turned back to the command chair. His tone was grim. "Sir, all on-board communications are dead. I can't reach any part of the ship, and if there are incoming calls I'm not picking them up."

"Lieutenant Vedama, try through the science section. See if you can raise anyone," Kirk ordered.

Vedama likewise operated one switch after another before turning sorrowfully to face Kirk. "Sir, not only can't I contact any *one*, I can't contact any *thing*. All links with the main computer have been blocked off."

"So now we know exactly where M'ress is." Kirk found himself slowly inspecting the surrounding walls and the ceiling. "She's got to be in the service crawlway encircling the bridge." He couldn't, despite the seriousness of the situation, keep a touch of admiration from his voice.

"While M'viore and R'leez were attacking the bridge, she was busy cutting controls and connections. We were intentionally kept too busy to use any of the bridge instrumentation, or even to consider that the attack might be diversionary."

His most important remaining question was directed to the only other officer in the room. "Mr. Arex, we've lost communications and computer access. I hope that's all we've lost."

"I follow your meaning, Captain," the Edoan navigator acknowledged. "I am glad to report that we are still on course and maintaining speed. The engineering conduits, which are the most heavily sealed of all bridge–ship linkages, are too strong for her to break."

"Or maybe she doesn't want to break into them," Kirk commented thoughtfully. "If the Caitians' purpose is to take over the ship, they'll want it in operating condition." He leaned forward in the chair, added sharply, "None of this means we can't get reinforcements in here. Lieutenant Vedama, try the turbolift."

The science officer nodded, left his station, and moved to the lift. He touched the controls. The doors did not swing aside.

"Nothing, sir. Not even an acknowledgment light on the panel."

"I retract my statement on reinforcements. Apparently Lieutenant M'ress isn't dazed enough not to think things through." He smiled ruefully. "It's always pleasing to see an officer demonstrate such competence. I only wish it were under different circumstances."

"There's still the way she got here, Captain," Vedama pointed out as he moved back to his station. "Up through the service passageways."

Kirk shook his head. "You can bet that when she entered the serviceway around the bridge, Lieutenant, she took care to block off the approach behind her. The Caitians have demonstrated too much thoroughness so far, to forget something so obvious.

"However, the moment someone tries to contact the bridge—if they haven't already—and finds out that its sealed off, they'll guess what's happened and act accordingly. Even if M'ress has used a phaser to melt and seal the door to the serviceway, it won't take long for someone else to get a torch from engineering and cut through.

"And that means," he finished, hefting the tranquilizer gun tightly in one hand, "that if she still expects to accomplish whatever crazy end she has in mind, she'll have to act very soon."

But they waited in silence. There was no sound nor

sign of movement from any of the several serviceway hatches lining the interior wall of the bridge.

"Biding her time," Kirk muttered softly, "waiting for some special moment. I wish I knew what was driving her and the other Caitians to do this."

A nervous Talliflores suddenly voiced an unspoken concern. "Sir, what about our life-support systems? Couldn't she take over by interrupting our air supply?"

Kirk replied just a smidgen more confidently than he felt. "I've already thought of that, Lieutenant. She could cut our atmosphere, but I don't know if she could restore it for her own use. But M'ress is no engineer. I don't think she could modulate the air supply just enough to knock us out, and I don't believe she'd chance killing us. That would be counter to all their actions thus far. No, I think she'll try and take the bridge without doing anything so drastic."

"I admit they haven't killed anyone so far, sir," Talliflores conceded, "but if M'ress is pressed for time and feels someone breaking in behind her, into the serviceway— I just wish I knew why they're doing this!"

"Easy, Lieutenant," Kirk urged, trying to relax the officer. "If we knew that, I think we'd have the answers to all our questions."

"If you're right, sir," Talliflores mused, "why wait here for her to attack us? She's had the element of surprise with her ever since this business began."

"How do you propose to take it away from her?" Kirk could see along the lieutenant's intended path and didn't like the option it presented. At the same time, Talliflores was quite correct. Kirk didn't see how he could object to it.

The communications officer indicated a nearby service hatch. "She could be anywhere around or above us, sir. There are several entrances onto the bridge from the serviceway. She could be right here next to communications, or waiting by that one." He pointed to the hatch beneath the main viewscreen. "But she can't be behind all of them at once.

"If one of us could get through a hatch, armed with a phaser and in close quarters, he could probably hold her off despite her speed and added strength. Even an agile Caitian needs room to maneuver. One of us could keep her busy while another cut through the sealed downway to go for help. We might even surprise her enough to overpower her before she could react."

"You saw what little effect phasers had on ensigns M'viore and R'leez, Lieutenant. Each of them took two or three bursts and still didn't go down."

"I know that, sir," Talliflores argued, "but it did slow them down. If one of us used a phaser and another was ready nearby with the tranquilizers—"

Kirk was emphatic. "Absolutely not, Lieutenant. Your idea has merit, but . . . no. Keeping the tranquilizers ready right here is one of our two remaining methods to insure that the bridge is protected."

"The other?" inquired the lieutenant.

Kirk hesitated, finally voiced the one thing he'd been fighting to avoid. "In that case, we'll have to set phasers to kill."

VIII

All the Kzinti save one were engaged in setting up the stasis-field nullifier or in supervising its construction. The single exception sat in the far corner of the ready room looking miserable and unhappy as always. But that didn't prevent it from regularly scrutinizing the Federation prisoners. Sulu knew that it was concentrating only indifferently with its rheumy, sensitive eyes. The dangerous attention it was lavishing on them sprang from another organ. The telepath ignored the excitement in the room. It spoke not to its fellows, simply sat and watched and listened with its mind, hoping for unconscious betrayal of useful information from one of the captives.

One of the largest Kzinti spoke a few harsh final words to one of the others, then turned to walk over and study the prisoners. Spock had already singled him out as a leader among the collection of yowling aliens, as much for his bearing and manner as for anything he had said. The gaze the Kzin lavished on the immobile captives was more baleful than that of the other Kzinti. His entire manner hinted at impatience and a natural belligerence he did not even try to suppress.

That was fine with Spock. He preferred a direct confrontation to the subtle spying of the telepathic weakling hunched in the background.

Eyes darting rapidly from one to the next, the big Kzin examined them each in turn. Directing his words to Sulu, he spoke. His standard English was comprehensible enough, though pushed out in a rough, raspy voice, as if the Kzin were speaking with a mouthful of pebbles. The implied threat and harshness of his tone needed no clarification.

"I am Chuft-Captain. You will identify yourselves."

So much for diplomatic courtesy, Spock mused. Well, realistically they could expect nothing better.

Taking his cue from what the first officer had said before, Sulu spoke up as if it were natural for him to be in command. "Lieutenant Sulu of the Federation starship *Enterprise*." He gestured with his head toward his companions. "This is officer Spock."

Chuft-Captain appeared to find nothing unusual in Sulu's failure to identify Uhura. He regarded her once, only long enough to assure himself that she was female, and then dismissed her presence as if she did not exist.

Spock, however, was evidently deserving of somewhat more attention. "You are a Vulcan," declared the Kzin, contempt dripping from every word. "I feel no pressing need to converse with an eater of roots and leaves."

One eyebrow rose slightly, but Spock didn't reply to the taunt. If Chuft-Captain was trying to assure himself of Spock's placidity, the first officer wasn't going to do anything to counter that impression.

Apparently satisfied, the Kzin commander turned back to Sulu. "Humans are at least omnivorous," he growled with the air of one making a major concession. "You are prisoners aboard the privateer *Traitor's Claw*, a stolen police vessel."

Sulu had a questioning response ready, but having

delivered himself of this information, Chuft-Captain showed no inclination to pursue the conversation. Instead, he turned away from the captives.

His subordinates had almost finished the basic assembly of the nullifier and were beginning to place ancillary instrumentation into the complex framework. As the odd-shaped device took shape, the various members of the Kzin crew displayed increasing excitement.

One Kzin took no part in the construction of the stasis-field nullifier. His attention was reserved solely for the stasis box itself. It rested on the far end of the huge central table. Even with the former owners of the box secured within the police-web field, the guard showed no sign of relaxing his vigilance.

If the Kzin commander was reluctant to converse, then it was up to Sulu to persuade him. "Stealing must be a habit with you. The police vessel . . . *two* stasis boxes . . ." The helmsman managed to sound impressively contemptuous himself.

Chuft-Captain spun to face him. Since contempt and insult was a normal component of Kzinti communication, Sulu's manner had no effect on him at all.

"Both boxes are the rightful property of Kzin. One we found was empty. We will soon see about the one your trespassing archeologists found. Yes, we knew of those on Gruyakin—and of the box. We intercepted one of their broadcasts, you see." He looked proud. "We did not know of the box until they contacted your ship.

"Rather than assault the entire installation—an attack which would no doubt have been successful but difficult to conceal—we waited for the box to be transported off the planet. Little could we hope that only one man and two others would be sent to recover it. With that known, we hastily arranged this trap. Your disappearance," he added matter-of-factly, "will be much simpler to disguise. As for the second box," and he gestured at the glowing cube on the table, "it is rightfully the property of Kzin."

"What's all this garbage about trespassing and Kzin property?" Sulu sounded outraged. "Gruyakin is an open system."

"A system long claimed by Kzin," snapped an imperious Chuft-Captain.

"The Kzinti make it a habit to claim half the planets in the galaxy," sniffed Sulu. "It's one thing to stake a claim, another to prove rightful ownership. Saying Gruyakin belongs to Kzin is not the same thing as owning it."

"Both boxes are the property of Kzin!" Chuft-Captain's idea of rational debate apparently consisted of stating that which he believed over and over again, as if his claim would gain validity through force of repetition.

"The stasis box we found some time ago was empty," he explained, "but it served well as bait to draw you here. Now we await the inheritance rightfully ours." He gestured at the box, evidently enjoying himself. "The Slavers possessed weapons that could devastate a civilization. If the gods are with us, there will be one such weapon in that box."

Automatically Sulu's eyes traveled to the glowing container they had recovered with so much difficulty. The box itself was harmless as long as one took care—unlike the unfortunate Jaiao Beguin, back on Gruyakin—not to try to open it incorrectly. Sulu fervently wished that the Kzinti stasis nullifier wouldn't work properly. It would be a pleasure to watch the box's defensive system promptly envelop every member of the Kzinti crew in a silvery stasis field of their own.

Across the room, the Kzinti telepath frowned. Let him. Sulu grinned viciously. They had nothing else to threaten him with.

However, judging from the expertise with which the Kzinti technicians were assembling their own nullifier, Sulu's hope was wishful thinking at best. Again he could only glance at the box and pray that its contents proved as innocuous as its exterior.

Sulu had already assumed an aggressive, angry pose. Might as well maintain it. He continued to lace his comments with contempt. "The Kzinti fought four wars with humankind and lost them all," he declared. "The last one was two hundred years ago. It seems that you haven't learned a thing since."

That touched a nerve. A violent howl rattled the interior of the ship. It was as brief as it was extreme. Aware that he had been provoked beyond control, Chuft-Captain quickly bit off the roar, though it took him several moments longer to regain his composure.

When he finally, dangerously responded, his comments were phrased almost carelessly. "Guard your speech, man. None of my crew has ever tasted human meat as did our ancestors. We would welcome the opportunity."

Belligerence had its place. So did common sense. Realizing he had pushed Chuft-Captain too far, Sulu refrained from responding. The Kzin's threat was not made idly. There was nothing to be gained by advancing the time of their death. While they lived there was always the chance, however faint it seemed at the moment, of recovering or at least destroying the stasis box and its unknown contents. While their present status mitigated against that, they could do even less from inside someone's stewpot.

"Always," Chuft-Captain was saying, "you and your Federation have had superior equipment and technology. We've sought a weapon for a long time which would enable us to defeat you at last."

Sulu jumped on that. "So much for your story about being a privateer. You've just declared that you're really working for the government of Kzin."

One of the other Kzinti, possibly an intermediate officer, looked up from the work proceeding at the table to snarl at Chuft-Captain, who growled back.

"You are presumptuous," he rumbled at Sulu. "All records will show that the *Traitor's Claw* is a stolen police ship. If we are captured, the Highest of Kzin will repudiate us." He smiled, showing sharp white teeth. "No matter what happens, no one except you could possibly prove that this is anything but an illegal privateer crew. And you will not be alive to offer any evidence against us."

A low growling interrupted him. The Kzinti were stepping back from the now-completed nullifier.

Chuft-Captain snarled a reply, started toward the table. He glanced back with a final word for Sulu. "If we succeed and are not captured or intercepted, you will be meat for our tables."

There was an exchange of grumbles and gestures. A couple of the Kzin technicians made some last-minute adjustments to the nullifier. When everyone had stepped clear, the engineer in charge pulled a single switch.

The mood in the room, among captives as well as Kzinti, was one of anticipation mixed with caution. While the stasis nullifier looked efficient and the Kzinti had clearly taken every precaution with its construction and design to insure that it would operate exactly as intended, no one could predict with one hundred percent certainty exactly what a stasis box might do in any situation. For example, it might turn out to be a very intricate Slaver booby trap designed to look like a stasis box.

These fears were overcome by fascination as the nullifier acted on the box. As the nullifying field strengthened, so did the blue aura surrounding the mirror-surfaced cube. Abruptly, the box flared with a light so bright that the Kzinti had to shield their eyes and the prisoners shut theirs tightly.

The powerful flash lasted only an instant, faded as quickly as it had appeared. In its place rested an unremarkable-looking metal box devoid of its original blue halo. Chuft-Captain gestured curtly.

In response, one of the low-ranking Kzinti approached the table. He eyed the box warily. This was a duty he would have preferred to avoid, but under direct order from Chuft-Captain such a thing was unthinkable.

Very carefully, very slowly, he pushed the metal lid up and back. Nothing erupted from the box to shatter its opener or anyone else. No stasis field appeared to freeze the Kzin in time for the next billion years. For all the reaction its opening produced, the box might as well have been made of plastic in the *Enterprise*'s nonorganic fabrication section.

As soon as it was evident that nothing dangerous was going to happen, Chuft-Captain shouldered his crew out of the way in his eagerness to peer into the box. He reached the table, looked into the box . . . and stood, staring quietly.

Sulu, Spock, and Uhura all watched closely—the two humans with apprehension, Spock with an intense curiosity.

Chuft-Captain reached into the box and withdrew an object. It was small and pulsed with an inner light of its own. Sulu stared at the form, which was vaguely reptilian in outline and somehow conveyed the impression of considerable size. He blinked. The "size" was a mental suggestion, built into the shape. The glowing object was as small as ever.

A certain amount of awe came into Sulu's voice. "Could that be a solid simuhologram of a Slaver?"

"If so," Spock whispered back to him without taking his eyes off the object as Chuft-Captain set it on the table, "it is the first representation of a Slaver ever discovered. An important historical find."

Again Chuft-Captain reached into the stasis box. This time he drew out a small square of what was unmistakably raw meat. It was wrapped in a peculiar, nonplastic transparent substance. Chuft-Captain examined it, turning it over in his fingers, and spoke to several other Kzinti. They appeared to agree with him as to its identification.

"It looks like fresh meat," Uhura murmured wonderingly. "Over a billion years in that box, and it looks *fresh*. I wonder what it's doing in there."

"It may have been left inside accidentally," theorized Spock. "Or perhaps whoever placed it inside intended to come back shortly and reopen the box, and left itself a fresh snack."

Uhura glanced sharply—as sharply as she could, restrained as she was by the police web—at the *Enterprise*'s first officer, but there was no hint of humor in his expression and had been none in his words.

Chuft-Captain set the little cube of meat down next to the solid simuhologram, which might or might not be a portrait of a Slaver. Sulu thought he put the meat aside a little reluctantly. He could understand that the possibility of tasting billion-year-old meat was very tempting to a carnivore. But Chuft-Captain was not so foolish as to consume an alien substance without ample pretesting. That was a pity. If they were lucky, it might have poisoned him.

Across the room, the telepath frowned again.

Anyway, more important revelations were at hand. Suddenly Chuft-Captain bore a look of great excitement. This time his hands fairly swooped down into the box. They emerged like a hawk with a kill in its claws.

What the Kzin commander withdrew resembled nothing organic, however. It consisted of a silver-surfaced bubble some seventeen centimeters in diameter. Attached to it was a heavy pistol grip. In form it was awkwardly made, and though not designed for human or Kzinti hands, it was unmistakable as to purpose and function.

A slot ran down one side of the hand—or claw, or tentacle, or who knew what—grip. Sulu could make out six settings notched along the slot. Beside each setting were markings in an unfamiliar script. A small toggle ran the length of the slot. At present it was at the slot's topmost setting.

Wordlessly, an enthused Chuft-Captain turned the device over and over in his hands. Anticipation spread rapidly among the other Kzinti as they realized what Chuft-Captain might be holding. They growled and snarled with animation, acting like a bunch of schoolchildren at vacation time, sounding like a section of a Federation zoo.

It was a deceptive demonstration. Their unrestrained enthusiasm masked their natural viciousness. Chuft-Captain turned, using the object to threaten the prisoners.

"Nothing like this has ever been found before in a stasis box. It can only be a weapon. It *must* be a weapon. A Slaver weapon! And we of Kzin are the only ones who have it. Look close at it, human!" He walked up to the police web, shook the device almost under Sulu's nose. "This may mean the end of your flatulent Federation of pacifists and root-eaters!" He turned, walked back to display the device to the rest of the curious group.

"Is he right, Mr. Spock? Could he possibly be right?" Sulu's voice had fallen to a worried whisper.

"I fear it is very possible, Lieutenant," the first officer replied. Then he added a note of caution. "However, I do not as yet see any solid reason to share Chuft-Captain's assurance. Certainly the device *looks* like a weapon. Yet we know so little of Slaver physiology and technology. It may not be a weapon but something else entirely.

"I find little comfort in that, however," he added. "Given the design of the device, even allowing for alien vagaries of technology I must—" He slipped sideways a little, then righted himself.

Sulu and Uhura moved, half stumbling, before recovering their balance. They found they could now move from the waist up. Their arms moved slowly, as long-frozen muscles struggled to obey mental orders.

"They have relaxed the police web," Spock noted aloud. "Preparatory to doing something unpleasant with us, no doubt. Switch on your translators."

The three officers, their hands now free, activated the tiny devices at their waists. Now they could understand the Kzinti without having to rely on the obsidian-edged English of Chuft-Captain.

The Kzin commander was still speaking to several members of his crew. "Have the humans moved to the surface. Be sure they are secured there in the police web. We will utilize them to test the weapon."

"Yes, Chuft-Captain." That response from one of the other Kzinti, another subofficer. He executed an odd sort of salute, then departed. Probably, Sulu thought, to locate a suitable place above for the . . . demonstration.

Several other Kzinti prepared to leave with Chuft-Captain. That worthy paused. For the first time since Sulu had regained consciousness, he saw Chuft-Captain talking to the forgotten member of the crew. Scratching at the scraggly, drooping whiskers on his face, the Kzin telepath gazed up at his commander sadly.

"You have had time to observe the aliens," Chuft-Captain said to him. "Can you read their minds?"

The telepath's voice matched his pitiable appear-

ance. It had none of the power or strength of his
brother Kzinti. Its most distinguishing characteristic
was a distinct whine.

"I can read the one called Sulu with difficulty,
Chuft-Captain. The other human is only a female. Consequently I have not wasted my efforts on her." Chuft-
Captain made a grunting sound to indicate he
understood. "The third is a pacifistic herbivore." The
whine was augmented by pleading. "Surely you would
not force me to delve into such a brain!"

"If it is necessary," was the Kzin commander's bru-
tal reply. "I do realize that you need time to recover
from each effort at probing." That was as far as
Chuft-Captain could go toward expressing concern for
a fellow creature. The telepath did not seem very
grateful for it.

"Prepare to move them to the surface." At this order from Chuft-Captain, the remaining Kzinti spread
out and drew phasers. One Kzin moved to a nearby
wall panel and touched a control. The remainder of the
police web deactivated.

Several moments passed while the prisoners were
permitted to exercise their cramped leg muscles. Under
Chuft-Captain's direction they were surrounded by the
armed Kzinti and marched back out the way they had
entered. Other Kzinti rolled up the police web and carried it behind, along with a portable power unit and set
of remote controls.

There was a wait at the lock while the Kzinti donned
their suit armor and the prisoners were permitted to
reactivate their life-support belts. Then in small groups
they passed via the lock to the icy ground outside.

Once more Spock studied the terrain, only now it
was with different thoughts than the ones which had
run through his mind when they had first arrived on
this world of Beta Lyrae. Pressure ridging and earth
movements had broken and buckled the ice plain. If
they had an opportunity to break free of their captors,
they had ample cover to run to.

After setting up the police web, most of the Kzinti
returned to the ship. That left only Chuft-Captain,
Telepath, and two others. Apparently the Kzinti felt

confident of their ability to control their prisoners. And why shouldn't they? There was really only the human Sulu to watch. The root-eater and the female animal could be ignored.

Chuft-Captain responded to a buzz in his helmet. "Yes?"

A raspy voice sounded over the suit intercom from inside the *Traitor's Claw*. "Chuft-Captain, chemistry has finished analyzing the meat that was in the stasis box. The wrapping is composed of an unknown polymer of metal-ceramic. The meat itself is fully protoplasmic and is poisonous to Kzinkind."

That last was disappointing. Chuft-Captain glanced down at the hoped-for Slaver weapon, inspected the silvery bubble shape thoughtfully. "What of the simulacrum?"

The response came this time not from the ship but from one of the suited figures standing next to the commander. "The human Sulu," the telepath said, "believes it to be a three-dimensional representation of an actual Slaver."

Sulu was startled. He had almost forgotten the presence of the telepath. It was the first time the ragged-looking Kzin had actually given proof that it could read their thoughts. The helmsman found it gave him an uncomfortable, dirty feeling, as if someone was rummaging with impunity through his private possessions. All he could do was glare menacingly at the telepath.

"I agree with the human's assessment." Chuft-Captain was recalling the shape of the simuhologram, the impression of size and strength that radiated from it. "It would have made a worthy foe. Secure the prisoners."

Helplessly Sulu, Uhura, and Spock watched as the police web was unrolled, charged, and activated. The test completed, the web was turned off until the three captives were standing on it. Then it was switched on again and all three officers found themselves immobilized once more.

Meanwhile, Chuft-Captain had walked to a nearby rise of ice and rock. He raised the silvery device. It took him several clumsy tries to pull the trigger, since the grip wasn't designed to fit his hand.

Nothing happened.

"Perhaps the small toggle," one of the watching Kzinti suggested.

Chuft-Captain nodded brusquely, moved the toggle in the handle slot down toward the first notch and its untranslatable hieroglyphs. The toggle slid easily and freely, slipped into place as though just lubricated. But as soon as the toggle slipped home, the device started to twist in his hand as if it were something alive. Chuft-Captain made a startled sound halfway between a hiss and a snarl. The other Kzinti and the three captives were equally surprised.

To his credit, Chuft-Captain did not drop the device. The distorting writhing soon stopped. The silvery sphere had vanished. In its place, attached to the same unchanged hand grip, was a small parabolic mirror with a silvery knob located at its focal point. A series of markings with little toggle switches of their own ran across the back of the mirror's surface.

After a brief examination of the device's unexpected new configuration, Chuft-Captain aimed it at the horizon and pulled the trigger set in the hand grip. Again nothing happened. He lowered his aim until he was pointing the mirror at the ground in front of him and held the trigger down. There was no hint of radiation or any sign that the device was doing anything at all.

Snarling in frustration, the Kzinti commander raised the device until the mirror was centered directly on Sulu. Uhura made a shocked sound. Spock didn't say a word.

The helmsman stood quietly, assumed a resigned, outwardly unaffected expression. Chuft-Captain held the trigger down again. There was still no indication that the device was performing any kind of function. Perhaps, Chuft-Captain thought, the device was acting in some fashion not readily visible.

"Telepath," he asked, still holding the trigger down and centering it on Sulu, "am I not affecting him at all? Is the life-support belt interfering?"

Concentrating hysterically, Telepath looked more

than normally miserable. Uhura almost managed to feel sympathy for the poor creature. He had not wished his talent on himself.

"No, Chuft-Captain," Telepath reported, a bit too loudly, a touch too fast. "He hears a faint whine but feels no ill effect. There is a vibration in the material of his metal accoutrements but—"

Telepath winced suddenly as if struck by a solid blow, and reeled backward several steps. When he recovered, he stared wild-eyed and pleadingly at his commander. "Chuft-Captain, he is too alien. He makes me taste yellow root munched between flat teeth. I am made sick, Chuft-Captain. Please!"

"You may stop—for now," the Kzin commander informed him. Grateful beyond words, the telepath turned away and was ill inside his suit. "Be glad you need not read the Vulcan's mind."

Looking closely at the parabolic mirror and the settings on its obverse, Chuft-Captain rumbled musingly to himself and his subordinates, "It may be a communications device of some kind. Or perhaps the vibrations it produces are designed to adversely affect members of a race now extinct. Another setting, perhaps."

With a thick furry finger he shifted the hand grip toggle down to the next setting. This time he didn't jump as the device blurred and curled like a ghost python in his hand. The parabolic mirror metamorphosed into a backward-facing screen arrangement with a small lens facing forward. Several knobs were set around the entire assemblage.

Again Chuft-Captain pointed the front of the device at Sulu and pressed the trigger. Again the helmsman displayed no reaction. But the device did. The screen lit softly to show Sulu standing on the police web.

Chuft-Captain experimented with the knobs on the back of the screen and below it. One touch brought a good, sharp-edged closeup of the stiff-legged human into view. Raising his arm, Chuft-Captain produced a magnified view of the sky above. He lowered the device, stared at it admiringly.

"A good, versatile, portable telescope. They built very well, these Slavers."

"Yet it is of no importance to us," one of the on-looking Kzin crewmen pointed out. "We already have several types of good small telescopes."

Chuft-Captain made a curt gesture of agreement, touched the toggle control once more. Again the device convulsed. When the Kzin commander saw the third configuration, he permitted himself a slight, toothy smile. This one looked much more promising. Set into the handle and trigger grip was a long metallic tube. Several moldings and protrusions blistered the sides of the tube, which ended in a small, thick lens.

Following his previous pattern, Chuft-Captain aimed the end of the tube at Sulu. At the last moment he shifted it slightly to one side before pulling the trigger.

A dense red beam of coherent light emerged from the lens. It contacted the ground just to the right of Sulu's feet and the police web. Ice fragments exploded into the thin air and steam boiled upward where the beam struck. Chuft-Captain released the trigger and the beam disappeared. A modest, still-steaming hole showed in the ice where it had struck.

Sulu had not flinched, despite the proximity of the small explosion. Chuft-Captain fired again, the beam moving closer but still avoiding both the helmsman's boots and the police web. Again Sulu didn't move.

The Kzin commander was moved to admit grudgingly, "I give you credit, human. You are not afraid to die."

"I'm never afraid of the familiar," Sulu replied calmly, nodding at the Slaver device. "That's simply a laser, and not much of one at that. The Federation has had more effective weapons for over a hundred years."

Chuft-Captain permitted himself to look annoyed. Rather angrily he adjusted the toggle to a new setting. Once more the device contorted, as solid in its change as a dream before awakening.

It solidified into a short cylinder. A flared aperture of fair size appeared at its far end. Two flat metal projections extended well downward from the near end of the cylinder. They resembled stirrups so closely that

Uhura couldn't repress a start of recognition. If the downward-pointed surfaces had been attached to a small saddle, the device would have closely resembled the ostrich saddles she had used as a child.

Chuft-Captain found the device's latest manifestation far less intriguing—or familiar. He bemoaned the lack of a gunsight or anything resembling one while realizing that nothing so lethal had adorned any of the device's previous forms. Nothing for it but to try this new setting and get on with the next.

He pulled the trigger.

Instantly he was shooting backward across the ice in a seated, undoubtedly uncomfortable position. Traveling at a respectable velocity he had to exert all his strength simply to hold on to the device.

The other three Kzinti scrambled to clear a path for the errant Chuft-Captain. One bit of flame from the gushing Slaver whatever-it-had-become washed across the slower-moving telepath. He screamed in pain. Completely out of control, Chuft-Captain shot across the police web, straight at the three imprisoned officers. His force was more than adequate to carry him through the comparatively mild restraint field the web generated.

Unable to dodge, Uhura was struck on her side. The impact was sufficient to overcome the withholding force field. It knocked her off the web. Clear of the web, she rolled over, scrambled to her feet, and sprinted for the nearby *Copernicus*.

Meanwhile, one of the two remaining Kzinti noticed the injured telepath. The scorching exhaust of the Slaver device had ruptured the smaller Kzinti's suit. Scooping up the lighter telepath, the Kzin turned and raced frantically for the lighted tunnel leading to the buried ship. Telepath was howling over his suit mike, trailing a fog of freezing atmosphere behind him.

"Telepath's suit has been cut," the remaining Kzin called out to Chuft-Captain.

"Never mind that!" The Kzin commander lay just past the police web. Having finally succeeded in shutting off the runaway device, he was climbing slowly and painfully to his feet. He gestured toward the Federation shuttlecraft. "The female is escaping, fool!"

Puzzled, the remaining Kzin's gaze traveled to the sprinting communications officer. "What of it?"

"Idiot!" Chuft-Captain was trying to find his own phaser. "Human females are intelligent!"

The remaining Kzin fought to assess this piece of incredible information. Though he knew it to be true, it was no less difficult for him to cope with. But he was a Kzin warrior. Time enough to muse later. Act *now*.

Drawing his phaser, he aimed it carefully. Uhura had almost reached the shuttlecraft when the stun burst caught her neatly in the small of the back. Her body arced spasmodically; she took another couple of steps and slumped to the ground.

Replacing the phaser at his waist, the Kzin trudged off to pick up Uhura's recumbent form. Meanwhile the Kzin who had thoughtfully carried the injured telepath into the ship was returning, moving at a fast jog.

"What report, Flyer?" asked Chuft-Captain, showing more concern for the neurotic mind reader in the latter's absence than he had previously.

The Kzin called Flyer responded worriedly. "His suit lost considerable pressure before I could get him into the ship, Chuft-Captain. But he will live."

"Good. We will need him later." Chuft-Captain proffered the new configuration of the Slaver device, handling it gingerly. Flyer examined the complex arrangement of struts and tubes.

"Doubtless a personal rocket motor, some form of one-being transportation device. One could place one's feet on the pedal shapes, there, and balance carefully. With practice, one could obtain great individual mobility."

"In any case, it is certainly not a weapon," concluded Chuft-Captain.

The two argued over the precise function of the new setting as the other Kzin returned with Uhura. They broke off their discussion long enough to guard Spock and Sulu while the other warrior placed the still-unconscious communications officer on the police web. He retreated quickly and the web field was restored. Uhura slumped slightly before the field caught her, held her upright.

"Uhura!" Sulu called as best he could with his head pinned. He turned slowly to look at her. "Lieutenant Uhura!" Her eyelids fluttered, finally opened. She stared across at him, recognition that she had failed dawning rapidly.

"Nice fry," Sulu attempted to reassure her.

It did not. "I'm slowing down." She sounded bitter. "I used to run the hundred in record time. How long have I been out? Did I miss anything?"

"Not much," Sulu told her. Unexpectedly, he chuckled. "A lot of good they'll get out of that propulsion setting. I wonder how much fur Chuft-Captain lost off his backside, suit armor or no suit armor!"

"We have been fortunate," Spock said more somberly, "that none of the settings thus far employed have revealed anything superior to known Federation technology."

"Thus far. Look." Uhura tried to point, but found that she couldn't, of course. Her arm was once more held tightly motionless by the police web. Sulu and Spock turned to watch the Kzinti again. It appeared that Chuft-Captain had moved the toggle control, because the Slaver device was writhing in his hands for a fifth time.

The new shape was a total surprise. Not only didn't it resemble a weapon, or something familiar like the parabolic mirror or the laser tube, it didn't resemble anything at all. Spock had to blink to assure himself the device had indeed finished changing, because it looked as if it had frozen in the middle of its new transformation, neither complete nor incomplete but some non-Euclidian nebulosity in between.

The shape should not have been. As he watched, it seemed to alter regularly without moving, to twist and curl in and about itself in a bizarre, topologically impossible fashion. And yet, it possessed the appearance of a solid shape.

"No gun sight," Chuft-Captain murmured softly, revealing a fixation on a single thought. "No evident way to aim it. Still, it must do something." Lifting the device, he pulled the trigger.

Both subordinate Kzinti were staring fixedly at the clump of ice-covered rock Chuft-Captain was aiming at. So none of the three warriors noticed that as soon as their commander pulled the trigger, the yellow glow from the tunnel behind them winked out like a drowned candle.

Uhura nearly fell, then caught herself and stayed motionless. "Mr. Spock, I can move."

"So can I," an excited Sulu whispered, experimentally edging one foot back and forth. "The police web is off."

Spock flexed the fingers of his left hand just enough to make certain he too was no longer trapped. "The fifth setting seems to be some sort of energy absorber. Fascinating. We've had no indication the Slavers possessed anything along such lines."

"Mr. Spock, shouldn't we—?"

Spock cut the helmsman off. "Yes, but in concert. When I give the word, run for the shuttle. Remember to present as irregular a target as possible. You traveled in a straight line, Lieutenant Uhura, and while you cannot outrun a phaser burst there is a chance to avoid one."

"Don't worry," Uhura assured him grimly. She had no intention of being stopped so easily again.

"Ready?" warned Spock. "*Go!*"

Adrenaline substituted for starting blocks as Sulu and Uhura fairly exploded toward the shuttle, twisting, dodging, zigzagging across an imaginary obstacle course. Tired from her previous sprint and still suffering lingering aftereffects of the recent phaser burst she had taken, Uhura fell behind.

Spock wasn't even close. He had chosen a different path toward the shuttle, one involving a slight but critical detour. Before the startled Kzinti could react, the first officer was racing toward them.

By the time their attention shifted from the nonexistent destructive effects of the Slaver device's fifth setting, Spock was on top of Chuft-Captain. The Kzin commander turned a second too late to defend himself.

Spock wasn't fooling with anything as subtle as a Vulcan nerve-pinch. Both legs came up as Spock leaped. His full weight was behind them, multiplied by his velocity, as he slammed both feet into the Kzin commander, high up on the feline's rib cage.

Chuft-Captain doubled over as he began falling backward, let out a loud moan, and dropped the device. Landing on one hand and both feet, Spock grabbed the Slaver artifact before it could bounce twice, and was off and racing for the shuttle.

Sulu looked behind him. Three Kzinti were now firing their phasers, one aiming at Spock, the other two at the more distant humans. A rise of broken rock and ice loomed nearby, just to the helmsman's left. Seeing that he wouldn't be able to make the shuttle, he swerved sideways and took shelter behind the hillock.

Uhura tried to follow him but she was too far behind. A burst from one of the phasers caught her again. She stumbled toward the ground, her last conscious thoughts filled with anger more than disappointment.

Clutching the Slaver device tightly in one hand, Spock continued his erratic, weaving course across the icy surface. Phaser beams repeatedly struck the ground where he had been heading only seconds before. But the first officer was still running hard and fast, and the Kzinti were unable to guess which way he would head next.

Deciding that the Vulcan was too far out of range, Flyer moved to aid Chuft-Captain. The commander was still lying on the ice, doubled-up and clutching at his side.

"Chuft-Captain, what happened?"

"I would rather not discuss it," came the sharp but pain-ridden reply. "Help me into the ship."

Flyer helped his commander to his feet. Chuft-Captain winced, nearly fell as he straightened. Flyer said nothing. It was unthinkable to show sympathy.

They started toward the tunnel leading to their ship. As they walked, it became clear to Flyer that Chuft-Captain had been badly hurt, for he couldn't have walked without help. As the airlock cycled around their suits and Chuft-Captain's painful wheezing sounded in his suit helmet, Flyer was still trying to visualize the unthinkable.

IX

It had been quiet on the bridge for long moments. The emergency lighting remained on, bathing instruments and the four wait-officers in its eerie, subdued glow. Communications with the rest of the ship remained dead, as did computer control. The *Enterprise* was still on course toward Starbase 25, but she was flying blind.

Kirk idly regarded the stun setting on his phaser, resting ominously at his waist. He hefted the tranquilizer pistol firmly. Their phasers would remain set on stun. Lieutenant M'ress and the other captured Caitians were as much a part of his crew, as much personal friends, as anyone else he worked with.

But . . . the ship had to come first. It seemed impossible that the four of them, alerted and expectant, would be unable to overcome a single slim Caitian female. However, everything else that had happened so far had seemed impossible also. With their communications and computer controls out, he couldn't even switch control of the ship to the secondary bridge.

The phaser controls seemed to grow larger in his eyes, the extreme end of the setting beckoning to him hypnotically. But before he would change that, he'd try any alternative. "Lieutenant Talliflores, Lieutenant Arex, if you two would like to try Talliflores's plan, keeping your phasers set on stun and without utilizing the tranquilizer pistol, you have my permission."

"I'd rather have the tranquilizers, sir," responded a doubtful communications officer.

Kirk shook his head emphatically. "Absolutely not."

"We'll try anyway, sir."

"Good luck." Kirk turned to the science station. "Mr. Vedama, if this fails, and Mr. Talliflores and Mr.

Arex fail to return . . . set your phaser to kill." He had trouble finishing the sentence.

"Yes, sir," his science officer said solemnly.

Talliflores palmed his phaser, then left the useless communications console to stand next to a ready Arex. "Since we have no idea where she is, sir, we'll try the hatch closest to the accessway leading to the deck below us."

Moving as quietly as possible, Talliflores and the Edoan navigator edged over the service hatch. Kirk kept the tranquilizer gun trained on the hatch as Arex set about undoing the catches. The resultant opening would be large enough for a good-sized human to fit through. The tripedal Arex would find it a tighter squeeze, but Kirk estimated his navigator should also be able to squeeze through into the serviceway beyond.

"Lieutenant Talliflores," he called abruptly, as the two officers were preparing to release the last catch.

"Sir?" Talliflores was lying flat on the deck, working at the hatch cover.

"You'll move to cut through the sealed doorway to the lower decks, if it is sealed. If not, you'll go for help. Lieutenant Arex will cover you."

"But sir, I'd hoped to . . ." Talliflores began.

Kirk cut him off firmly. "Sorry, Lieutenant. Mr. Arex has already tangled with one of the Caitians and come off considerably better than anyone else." He suppressed a smile. "Mr. Arex has the advantage of being half again as dextrous as a human."

"Very well, sir," Talliflores reluctantly replied.

The last catch was released. Carefully the two officers removed the hatch plate. When neither phaser bolt nor squalling Caitian emerged from the opening, Talliflores leaned forward and peered into the dim crawlway beyond. He glanced once back at Kirk, who nodded—there could be no talk on the bridge now, not with the hatch opened. Talliflores crawled through, vanished into the darkness. After a last glance back at Kirk, Arex followed.

It was as silent as a Klingon consulate on Federation Day. Suddenly someone, probably Talliflores, shouted. Muffled yelling and sounds of a struggle followed.

Vedama took a step toward the hatchway. Kirk ordered him back to the science console.

If Arex and Talliflores couldn't overpower or outmaneuver M'ress in the cramped serviceway, sending in the diminutive Vedama would only result in the loss of another officer. Nor could he enter the fray himself and risk losing the tranquilizer pistol, their only proven means of stopping a berserk Caitian.

The hidden battle continued more quietly. Only an occasional curse, grunt, or peculiar low-pitched feminine yowl punctuated the quiet. Once, Kirk thought he heard Talliflores cry out, but he couldn't be sure it wasn't M'ress.

Then it was silent on the bridge again.

Hesitantly, hopefully, Kirk called out. "Mr. Talliflores, Mr. Arex?"

No response.

Sadly, Kirk turned to face Vedama, gestured significantly at the officer's waist. Vedama drew his phaser, made the agonizingly painful adjustment of the setting ... and sat back to wait.

"Let me take the first shot, Mr. Vedama," Kirk instructed him. "If I miss . . ." He didn't have to finish the directive, and had no desire to.

"Lieutenant M'ress?" He directed his voice to the square black eye of the hatchway. Again, no response. "Lieutenant M'ress, this is the captain. I don't know what you think you're doing, Lieutenant, but whatever you have in mind can't be allowed. Your two companions, M'viore and R'leez, have already been captured and can't help you. You haven't got a chance, Lieutenant."

The black orifice stared back at him mockingly.

He tried a different approach. "Listen, M'ress, I know you're not doing this of your own free will. You've got to realize that yourself. Whatever's compelling you to act this way, I understand. I'm not holding you and the others responsible for your actions. But this has to stop, *now*. You've got to fight whatever's gripping you, M'ress! You've got to break this madness before . . . we have to stop you."

"I . . ."

It was a faint, barely audible sound, and for a second Kirk felt he had imagined it. But a quick glance showed that Vedama had heard, too. It was more a cry than a challenge, and sounded as if it had been forced out against terrific odds.

"What is it, M'ress?" Kirk called eagerly. "I'm listening. Talk to me, talk and fight it."

"I'm angrrry . . . confused. I . . ." and she mumbled something in broken Caitian which Kirk didn't understand. The Caitian had been mixed with English.

". . . can't . . . stop . . . myself," she moaned, as if fighting with her own voice. "Must . . ."

"Must what, M'ress?" Kirk had to keep her talking. "Tell me what you need and maybe something can be worked out."

"Must . . . go home. Go to Cait."

"Your homeworld? But why?" Kirk had felt sure that when the Caitian's purpose had been revealed, it would clear up the rationale for their bizarre behavior. He was wrong. The knowledge only added one more confusing aspect to the whole incident.

"Can't . . . Must go to Cait-rrrr—." Her voice changed, overtones of anger replacing the desperate striving for understanding. "Must go to Cait now, fast. Give me contrrol of the ship, Captain. Orr . . . change courrse forr Cait."

Kirk threw Vedama a querulous look, saw that the science officer was equally bemused at the imperious request. "M'ress, we can't possibly go to Cait now. Have you forgotten the Briamos conference? We have to be there on time, to represent the Federation, or the Briamosites will probably align themselves with Klingon. You don't want that to happen, do you, Lieutenant? I know you're not a traitor."

"Must . . . go now to Cait!" It came out a half-order, half-sob. Conflicting desires were tearing M'ress apart.

"You're not being sensible, M'ress," Kirk countered, aware that none of the Caitians had been acting sensibly recently. "It's impossible and you know it. We can't miss the conference. Listen, give yourself up peaceably, right now, and after the conference I give you my word we'll go directly to Cait. You don't even have to give me a reason."

"Captain," Vedama began, "other Starfleet orders—"

"Lieutenant, I have the authority to overrule any subsequent Fleet orders in order to respond to any emergency threatening my ship—barring a Federation-wide danger." He turned back to the open hatchway.

"Did you hear that, Lieutenant?" he asked, raising his voice slightly. "I have the authority to order the *Enterprise* to Cait immediately following the conference's conclusion. I'll put it in the official log, if you want." No response. "Are you willing to bargain, M'ress? Will that satisfy you?"

"Can't . . . help," came the threatening yet pitiable response from somewhere beyond the hatch. "If you will . . . not orrderr us to Cait now, give . . . conntrol to me. Orr . . . I will . . . I *must* . . . take overr yourr brridge."

"You can't do it, M'ress." Kirk sounded more positive than he felt. "I know that you're partially immune, somehow, to phasers set for stun. Lieutenant Vedama's phaser is set to kill. He won't shoot except as a last resort. I'm holding a tranquilizer pistol, M'ress. Dr. McCoy prepared a serum keyed to the Caitian metabolism. That's how we knocked out M'viore and R'leez. The serum will do that to you, too.

"You can't possibly overwhelm two of us from the serviceway and take over the bridge before a security detail finally gets here. They're probably on their way right now, running the turbolift on bypass controls and power, or coming up through the serviceway access below us. They won't have my orders to restrain them, M'ress," he said desperately. "They won't have their phasers set for stun, or wait for me to fire first. Don't you see? You can't possibly win. There's no way you can take over the bridge."

"Tell . . . that to . . . Arrex and . . . Talliflorres," came the half-taunting, half-sorrowful reply.

"Captain?"

"Just a minute, Mr. Vedama. Lieutenant M'ress, let me think about your demand. Give me just a minute."

STAR TREK LOG TEN

"Don't want to . . . hurrt anyone," M'ress insisted, sounding as if she meant it. "But *must* go to . . . Cait . . . *now!*"

"What is it, Vedama?" Kirk whispered.

"I've bypassed normal communications and computer network, sir," he murmured tightly. "We have intership communications again. Several sections are calling steadily, trying to contact us. Several sound frantic."

"That's not surprising. If we can just stall her a little longer . . . Give me Security."

"Try your chair pickup, sir."

Kirk directed his voice toward the command chair pickup, his gaze never leaving the gaping hatchway. "Security, this is the bridge."

"Yeoman Dickerson here, Captain. It's good to hear from you. What's going on up there?"

"Lieutenant Talliflores and Lieutenant Arex have been stunned. Mr. Vedama and I are holding off Lieutenant M'ress. She's in the serviceway encircling the bridge. You must try to break through the serviceway door or come up the turbolift. She's cut all bridge power. Under no condition, except as a last resort to preserve the integrity of the ship, is anyone to use a phaser set higher than stun. Is that understood?"

"Yes, sir, but—"

"Is that understood, mister?"

"Yes, sir." The voice sounded disappointed, but the acknowledgment sent a wave of relief over Kirk.

"Then get moving, Yeoman. Bridge out." He glanced quickly back at Vedama. "Who else is calling, Lieutenant?"

"Sick Bay has priority, sir."

"Put them through."

A pause, then an anxious familiar voice sounded over the chair speaker. "Jim, are you all right? Jim?"

"I'm okay, Bones. So far. M'ress has us pinned down here, but I think we have her trapped as well. What's been happening at your end?"

"Jim, we've been doing frantic research on Caitian disorders. That's been part of the problem."

Kirk frowned. "I don't think I understand, Bones."

"We've been looking for a disease, a physical malady, something rare and unusual. It took a while for me to realize that while the Caitians' behavior might be extreme, it might have a perfectly normal cause."

"That sounds contradictory, Bones."

"Jim, I think I know what's causing them to act the way they have. Has it occurred to you that all the seriously injured personnel—security and otherwise—have been men? Or rather, male? And that the women who were part of the eight-person security team that was assaulted were incapacitated but not harmed? Listen to this, Jim."

There came a pause, and then a horrible screeching and yowling sounded over the speaker. It was a frantic, uncontrolled din, and yet somehow it seemed sorrowful rather than ferocious.

"Bones, what the—?"

"That's M'viore and R'leez, Jim," came McCoy's reply. They're both conscious again. I've got them both strapped down so they won't hurt themselves—or anyone else. Needed extra straps to keep them from breaking free. Jim, the level of Caitian-equivalent adrenaline in their blood is unbelievable! But what's most important is their Caitrogen hormone level. Absolutely crazy. Sent my diagnostic indicators right off the graphs.

"I've given them the moderating dosage necessary to bring their hormone levels back to normal . . . the dosage they should have received normally. They should both be sensible in a couple of hours."

"Dosage they should have received?" Kirk thought he saw motion at the hatchway, but decided he was imagining things. The tension had grown worse with the passing minutes. "What are you talking about, Bones?"

"When we couldn't find anything physically wrong with them, I tried to imagine what could induce a Caitian to go insane like they did. Caitians usually control their emotions fairly well. I thought about drugs, the presence of certain stimulants in their food, maybe even accidental self-hypnotism. But the chemists couldn't find anything foreign in their recent menus.

"That's when it occurred to me that maybe they weren't ingesting something they regularly took, instead of having eaten something they shouldn't have. The chemists were put off because their blood tested normal, except for the excessive hormone level. I tied that in with the suddenly realized fact that all the badly injured security personnel had been male, Jim. Couple that with the fact that our three Caitians all happen to be female—"

A definite shadow appeared at the hatchway. Kirk fired reflexively. The syringe-dart struck metal somewhere beyond the blackness and the shadow vanished.

"Neither of the ensigns is coherent enough to give me any help, but their behavior fits what I discovered in the limited Caitian biology references in the medical records. They take biannual doses of a drug called pheraligen, which moderates their body's production of Caitrogen. And that in turn suppresses the otherwise extreme reactions Caitian females used to have at this time of the year."

"This time of year . . ." Kirk finally had the answer to the mystery.

"Apparently," McCoy continued, "the pheraligen is programmed into their diets in innocuous-tasting supplements, Jim. They're so used to receiving it without having to think about it, they didn't realize what was happening to them. Since the regimen is in no way a treatment for a disorder, I didn't know about it. Programming it becomes the responsibility of the science life-support section, not medical."

Vedama had turned pale. "My department, Captain, my department. But I've never had to—"

"And Spock isn't here to check on it. Probably the facts are resting right in his daily work-log: *Caitian female personnel, semiannual pheraligen dose due.* So that's why they've been acting the way they have."

"Right, Jim. All it takes is a standard dose of pheraligen to counter the excessive hormone production and they'll return to normal."

"That's all very well and good for M'viore and

R'leez, Bones, but what am I going to do with M'ress?"

A phaser bolt erupted from the upper right-hand corner of the hatch opening. Aimed with difficulty, it struck several centimeters from Kirk's right foot. Nerves tingling from the nearness of the beam, he abandoned the command chair and limped around behind it. Vedama crouched lower but didn't abandon the science console.

"Bones, M'ress isn't sensible enough to understand what you've been saying, though I think she's trying to. She can't control herself, and I think maybe desperation's making her frustrated enough to kill. She wants to take over the bridge and change course for Cait."

"Not surprising, Jim," came McCoy's voice over the open bridge speakers. "She's only reacting the way primitive Caitian physiology's instructing her to, and there are no Caitian males on board. If there were, none of this trouble would have happened. That's why our security personnel were attacked, and then not killed. Even with their hormone level driving them insensible, they still retained enough knowledge of who they were to stop before committing murder. The injuries to our security teams were inflicted out of frustration, not malice. You've got to get one of those tranquilizer darts in her."

A second phaser burst poured from the hatchway. This time Kirk couldn't be sure the beam was still set to stun.

"She's becoming hysterical, Bones!" Kirk tried to spot the elusive lieutenant, saw only black in the hatchway opening. "She doesn't dare use too powerful a setting, though. If she damages the controls, she won't be able to try turning us toward Cait."

"Captain, if you've no objection . . ."

"What's that? Who's speaking? Scotty, is that you?"

"Aye, Captain. I've got an idea I've been working on since Dr. McCoy found out what was wrong with the two ensigns. With your permission, I'd like to give it a try. I know this business isn't my department, but—"

Kirk ducked as a phaser beam scored the top of the

command chair. "Anything nonlethal, you've got my permission, Scotty. Go ahead with it."

Kirk didn't know how long they could continue to stall M'ress. In between useless exchanges of phaser fire he conjured up every argument he could think of. None of them would have done any good, save for the fact that M'ress retained just enough sanity and sense to respond to them. So she listened and reacted, even if her comments were not particularly sensible.

Of course, Kirk knew he might be deluding himself in thinking that he was keeping her mind busy. She might be waiting for him to grow so involved in his chatter that he would drop his guard and allow her a reasonable charge at the command chair. Eventually, he knew, she would have to come to the inevitable decision that he wasn't going to voluntarily relinquish control of the ship, and that her time was running out.

That moment came sooner than she expected or Kirk had hoped.

A hissing noise reached the bridge. It came from somewhere beyond the open hatchway.

"Captain," M'ress yowled, "call . . . them off. Tell them to . . . stop trrying to cut . . . in."

"I can't," he lied. "They're operating independently of my orders, M'ress."

Her voice rose unsteadily. "I'll use my . . . phaserr on the firrst one who comes thrrough the opening!"

"Lieutenant, you haven't killed anyone yet! Fight what's controlling your mind. We know what your trouble is now!"

Not surprisingly, M'ress refused to listen.

There sounded a sharp *spang* of stressed metal giving way. Any second Kirk expected to hear the slight, deadly hum of M'ress's phaser as she made good her threat on whoever was coming through the opened serviceway.

Instead, he heard a strange yowling from the Caitian unlike anything heard thus far. It was followed by a distinct *phut*, then silence.

A figure started to emerge from the hatchway opening. Kirk raised the tranquilizer pistol, then hesitated.

So did Vedama. The figure that stepped into the dim light of the bridge would have caused them to fire instantly, except for the fact that it was carrying its head beneath one arm!

"Scotty! It worked."

"Aye, Captain." The *Enterprise*'s chief engineer looked relieved. He gestured back toward the hatchway. Sounds of moving feet came from behind it. "Dr. McCoy's inside now. And a whole crew of techs. If the damage M'ress caused isn't too serious, and I dinna think it could be, bridge functions should be"—the regular lights abruptly came back on and Kirk blinked at the bright, familiar illumination—"restored quickly." Scott permitted himself a slight smile of professional pride.

"What about Lieutenant M'ress?"

"Dr. McCoy says she'll be fine, Captain," Scott replied, "as soon as the pheraligen takes effect on her system and she's had a couple of hours' rest." Walking forward, he deposited an object in his right hand on the navigation-helm console. It was a twin to the dart-pistol Kirk still held.

As he approached, Kirk grew conscious of a peculiar, powerful odor emanating from the chief engineer. His nose twitched. Scott noticed it and grinned.

"Strong stuff, Captain. That smell's the only thing that made it work. Dr. McCoy synthesized the appropriate male Caitian pheromones to complement this costume." He indicated the furry, catlike suit he was wearing. I'm not so sure the costume alone would have let me get within shooting range, but the pheromones fooled her—or overpowered her. We only had to distract her for a couple of seconds, long enough for me to get a syringe into her." He gestured at the dart-pistol resting near the helm controls.

Kirk was putting his own weapon down. The crisis was all over, but the tenseness drained slowly from him. "What ever made you think of such a crazy idea, Scotty?"

The engineer looked embarrassed. "From a costume ball I went to, Captain, several years ago. I went dressed as a Fiorellian and a real female Fiorellian mistook me for a male of her species. To complicate matters, *she* was costumed as a human female. So it was doubly disconcertin'."

"I can imagine," agreed Kirk, slowly resuming his position in the command chair.

"Captain?"

Kirk looked over at the science station. "What is it, Mr. Vedama?" When he saw the lieutenant's position, he swiveled fully to face him, frowning. "What's wrong?"

Vedama was standing stiffly before his console, unsmiling. "I hereby present myself for arrest, sir."

"At ease, Lieutenant." Vedama relaxed, but only slightly. "It wasn't your fault. It wasn't anybody's fault, except maybe the Slavers'. They had the poor timing to present us with one of their stasis boxes at a time when Mr. Spock had to be two places at once. I'm sure that by tomorrow or the next day, in routinely checking over his schedule, you would have spotted the instructions to program the pheraligen into the Caitians' diet. It was bad luck and timing that their metabolism chose this particular time to shift into high gear.

"In fact, it's surprising you haven't overlooked more than one thing. You're doing your best, Lieutenant, and so far that's been quite satisfactory. Resume your post."

"Yes, sir." Vedama's salute was crisp.

Scott had slipped out of the suit. "Bloody hot, Captain. I don't understand how the Caitians can stand their own fur."

"They probably wonder, like all naturally furred creatures in the Federation, how we humans can run around almost naked, by their standards."

Kirk stood as several figures emerged from the hatchway. A limp form was passed to one tall medical technician. He handled the comatose M'ress easily. Her eyes were closed tight, arms and legs dangling like pale vines.

"Sick Bay immediately, Ensign," ordered a muffled voice from somewhere behind the hatchway.

"Yes, Doctor," acknowledged the tech, moving toward the turbolift doors.

Kirk was about to tell the ensign that the lift didn't work, when the doors slid aside obediently at the man's request and shut behind him. At the rate they were going, it wouldn't take Scotty's crew long to have the bridge functioning at full efficiency again.

"They'll all be all right, Bones?" he asked the figure emerging from the hatchway.

"I think so, Jim. Except for the mental inconvenience they might suffer for a while."

"How do you mean, Bones?"

McCoy walked over to retrieve first Scott's discarded tranquilizer pistol, then Kirk's. "Consider what they've done, Jim. They've tried to take over the ship. In the process they put a respectable number of their fellow crew members in Sick Bay with assorted scratches and other wounds. Generally they've behaved in a very immature as well as aggressive fashion.

"Of course, they had no control over their actions. Matter of fact, when they come around in a few hours I doubt that any of them, M'ress included, will remember much of what they did. The difficulties will come," he continued after a brief pause, "when their companions tell them what they've been up to.

"That will upset them enough, but it's the reason behind their actions which will trouble them the most. M'ress will stand it better than M'viore and R'leez because she's an officer, but I don't doubt that the two ensigns will take a good deal of kidding about what happened. I think we're going to have to cope with three very embarrassed Caitians."

"But everyone will know," Kirk said, "that they weren't responsible for their actions, that they had no control over the way they were acting."

"Easy to say, Jim, but then *we're* not the ones who have to handle the fact that we lost all composure and intelligence and spent a day acting like, well, like animals."

Kirk turned to the blank viewscreen, thought hard. "I think the Caitians will handle any joking competently, Bones. After all, they can always use the argument that we humans act like animals all the time."

X

Sulu found himself running deeper and deeper into the jumbled landscape, dodging nervously around towering blades of ice, scrambling atop slick-surface boulders to whom the proximity of organic matter was a radical if nonperceived event.

The terrain grew steadily more grotesque in outline, the horizon increasingly tortured. One would have thought two rivers of ice had rushed headlong into one another here, jammed together like massive white wrestlers. Ice and stone pressed and piled over and atop each other to create a chalcedony desert flavored by Bosch. At least the chaotic topography favored Sulu's retreat. No phaser beam stabbed at him from behind. Let the Kzinti follow him if they could—he'd have them ambushing each other.

Sulu turned another ice block half the size of the shuttlecraft, only to see a figure rushing at him. Startled, he tried to back away. Then he recognized the familiar shape and began moving toward it.

"Mr. Spock!" Sulu let out an exhausted but relieved sigh as the first officer neared. "I thought you were one of the Kzinti."

Spock replied simply by holding up the object he carried. "I have the device, Lieutenant."

"Yes, but they've got Uhura. At least, I expect they do. I'm sure I saw her fall before I got out of the open. They've also got subspace radio and have us cut off from the *Copernicus*. If they want to, they can wait for us to starve while they call for help from the nearest Kzinti base."

"No, they cannot," Spock informed him with remarkable self-assurance, "or rather, they will not."

Sulu re-examined the options open to the Kzinti that he had just voiced, and bewilderedly could find no reason why they could not do exactly what he'd claimed. "Why can't they?"

"Because I kicked Chuft-Captain." When Sulu showed no sign of comprehending, the first officer elaborated. "Consider, Mr. Sulu. Chuft-Captain has been attacked by an herbivorous pacifist, an eater of roots and leaves, one who according to Kzinti tradition not only does not fight, but does not resist. Furthermore, I gave the ultimate insult subsequent to my successful attack, by leaving Chuft-Captain alive." Spock moved to the far corner of the monolith, peered cautiously around it.

"Chuft-Captain's honor is at stake, Lieutenant. Before he can seek outside help he must have personal revenge in order to absolve himself."

"Now I understand, sir. That gives us some time, then." Sulu hesitated, eyeing the first officer intently and with admiration. "You did plan it that way?"

"Of course." Spock seemed surprised that Sulu should think of any other possibility.

"Then as long as you stay free, the Kzinti can't or won't do anything until Chuft-Captain's had his chance to regain his reputation." He looked suddenly concerned. "But they could use Lieutenant Uhura as bait to trade for the Slaver device."

The first officer examined the enigmatic construction he held. "That is so, Lieutenant. However, to this point we have not seen it display anything more powerful than devices and instruments Starfleet already has. I would actually go so far as to say that in several cases present Starfleet equipment is superior to some of the device's manifested forms."

"Maybe so." Sulu looked thoughtful. "But I have a feeling, Mr. Spock, that that won't hold true. It doesn't make sense for it to hold true. All those different settings," and he pointed to the toggle gauge, "those different functions. Why so many varied ones and why conceal them behind the initial, inert, bubble shape?" He was studying the device and thinking hard.

"What do *you* think, Mr. Sulu? What could be behind such careful concealment of functions and their multiplicity?"

"I'm not sure, but I can imagine one possibility. Suppose this thing belonged to a spy or espionage agent of some sort? He could carry the bubble shape around openly. Maybe the bubble shape corresponds to some billion-year-old personal ornament or decoration, like a bracelet, for instance. And a spy would be just the one who could make good use of something that looked harmless but could be made to serve as an energy absorber, a telescope, perhaps a communicator of some kind, a personal transport."

"I acknowledge your expertise in the field of weaponry, Mr. Sulu," said Spock readily, "but I do not see how you can determine a possible ownership classification."

"Just look at it, Mr. Spock." Sulu was convinced of his own supposition now. He took the device and held it up to the faint light. Lime-yellow gleamed on its metal surface, reflecting the life-support aura of both officers. "All these settings. I admit we don't know that a common Slaver soldier or even an ordinary citizen couldn't handle them all, but to what end? For a soldier, only the laser is an effective weapon. The other functions aren't necessary for an ordinary warrior's single objective: to kill the enemy. An ordinary Slaver citizen, if there were such a creature, wouldn't require that a multitude of functions be so cleverly disguised. But they *are* disguised.

"For that matter, it wouldn't be necessary for a warrior to have such an elaborately concealed set of functions. If the device produced a shield, well, that would be useful. Possibly the telescope, and certainly the energy absorber. But a communicator, a telescope, and the rocket transport? A soldier might have need of them all, but why put them all into a single device of tremendous technological complexity? No, the thing is too intricate—unless intended for someone who *has* to hide all those functions in a single place."

"Assuming it is a dangerous device intended for use by someone who doesn't wish it to look like that," Spock finally replied, with equal thoughtfulness, "the Slavers would have wanted to keep its secrets a secret. They would never have wanted a potential enemy to know that the device was anything other than a silvery bubble attached to a handle. If so, and if we follow your reasoning through to its logical conclusion, it seems reasonable to assume that the device possesses a self-destruct setting also."

Sulu indicated the toggle switch, which rested at the bottom of its slot. "But we've seen all the phases, all five manifestations of the device."

"Perhaps not." Spock took the device back, turned it over in his hand. "There is the null setting."

"Null setting, sir?"

"The first one, where the toggle was originally set. It is marked with a hieroglyph." One finger traced the strange writing while Sulu looked puzzled. "The device appears to be without function, at this setting. But then why should that setting be present in the first place?" Spock had the look of a mathematics professor on the trail of an errant ingredient in a catastrophe-theory problem. "Why not simply leave the device set at the telescope setting? There is no reason an ordinary person, Slaver or Vulcan or human, could not carry a small telescope about with him. Nor does the first setting correspond to a safety lock of any sort, since Chuft-Captain was able to move the toggle easily to the other five settings."

Sulu shrugged, took the device back, and indifferently nudged the toggle up to the top of its slot. Immediately the device dissolved in his hands, the fifth mode returning once more to the featureless silvery bubble shape.

It certainly looked harmless enough.

"Maybe," Sulu began thoughtfully, "it's the key to some kind of hidden setting, Mr. Spock. Maybe this manifestation is intentionally innocent. If we—" He stopped as a rumble like a distant earthquake sounded.

Beneath them the ground trembled. They turned in the direction of the sound.

Just over the rim of the highest ice block, a shallow cone shape with a flat base was rising steadily space-ward. Boulders and huge chunks of ice fell in a spar-kling rain from its flanks. It was the *Traitor's Claw*, the Kzin ship, hatched from its place of concealment.

Narrow projections protruded from the edge of the cone. They looked suspiciously like weapons, weapons which a mere police vessel shouldn't be quipped with. Sulu and Spock hugged the protective overhang of the massive boulder next to them, trying to slip their revealing life-support auras wholly beneath the shielding mass.

Within the observation room of the ship, Chuft-Captain glanced back once to assure himself that the human female remained frozen on the police web. She glared back at him with sufficient animation to tell him that she was alert and fully cognizant of what was taking place around her.

In one massive paw he held a communicator, standard Starfleet issue. He addressed himself to it while staring out the main port, which provided a moving view of the jumbled ice plain beneath the slowly moving ship. Neither of the two escaped prisoners, either the Vulcan or the human Sulu, were visible. That was hardly surprising. They were not fools and must have heard the *Traitor's Claw* lift. By now they should sensibly be well concealed in the crazy-quilt rocks below.

It would do them no good. Being familiar with human and Vulcan psychological orientation, Chuft-Captain knew that the possession of the human female was sufficient to bring the Slaver device once more into his hands.

"This is the *Traitor's Claw* calling Lieutenant Sulu," he said into the communicator. "Chuft-Captain speaks to you. We have the female prisoner. She is in good health, a condition dependent solely on your next actions. Will you bargain with us for the Slaver device or must we take harsh action to convince you?"

There followed a respectable pause during which no response was forthcoming. That did not bother Chuft-Captain. Any warrior would first consider every possible alternative before surrendering. He expected no less of the human.

"If you do not reply," he said into the communicator when a reasonable amount of time had passed without an answer from below, "it will not be pleasant for her."

Uhura might have given Chuft-Captain a reply, but it wouldn't have done her any good. She stood paralyzed on the police web, kept silent, and considered her predicament. It was probably fortunate for her, despite Chuft-Captain's patience, that Telepath was not present to inform him of her hostile thoughts.

The *Traitor's Claw* cruised back and forth over the icefields in a regular spiral pattern, searching the ragged formations below for traces of the escaped prisoners.

"Still no sign of them, Chuft-Captain," Flyer reported from his position at the controls.

Chuft-Captain snarled his acknowledgment, tried to repress a stab of pain and keep it out of his voice as he spoke into the communicator again. "I repeat, Lieutenant Sulu, we have the female human as hostage. You have something that *we* want. We will trade her life for the Slaver device."

Spock and Sulu remained well hidden beneath the overhanging lip of weathered rock. Together they had listened intently to Chuft-Captain's demands. Now Spock stared meaningfully across at his companion.

"Chuft-Captain's offer neglects certain important details, Lieutenant Sulu. Answer him."

Sulu palmed his own communicator, flipped it open, briefly considered his reply before speaking. "This is Sulu. You've taken care of Lieutenant Uhura. What about Mr. Spock and myself? If we're not included we can't consider your offer."

"You must surrender anyway," the Kzin commander's raspy voice said over the tiny speaker grid. "You cannot reach your shuttlecraft. There is no escape for you. But I will give a chance. I offer Mr. Spock single combat."

"Not interested," Sulu said immediately.

Spock only nodded. "Chuft-Captain must fight me. They could beam this entire region on low power, probably kill us without damaging the Slaver device. But he cannot risk letting me die without regaining his personal honor."

Back on board the *Traitor's Claw*, Chuft-Captain's claws contracted reflexively as he clutched tightly at the arm of his seat. Leaning to his left partially concealed the ends of the pale bandages and his uniform hid the the rest. His tail switched lightly above the deck, projecting backward through the slot provided by the Kzin chair.

"Why do you refuse? I am as the Vulcan left me," he informed the communicator, "with two ribs broken. I have not had them set. He may conceivably kill me."

Sulu hesitated, shut off the communicator while he watched his superior. Spock's attention was still on the sky, searching for the patrolling ship, but the helmsman knew that Spock had heard Chuft-Captain's words as clearly as he had. "What about what he says, Mr. Spock? Could you?"

"I kicked him over one heart, but Kzinti ribs have vertical bracing in addition to the horizontal bracing found in humans and Vulcans. His injury would still be severe, but far from crippling." He thought a moment, then added, "I compute the odds of my defeating Chuft-Captain in hand-to-hand combat at sixteen to one against, and that is assuming his injuries are as he claims."

Sulu flipped the communicator on again. "Sorry, offer refused," he said tersely. Putting the deactivated communicator away, he resumed his examination of the Slaver device, puzzling over Spock's suspicion of the innocent silver bubble shape.

Chuft-Captain stared out the fore port, at the endless fields of ice and ragged stone. Eventually, he turned his attention to the figure standing silent and frozen behind him. Uhura glared back at him.

"They think very little of you."

"Wrong." She wished she could scratch her right thigh. "They don't think much of *you*."

That provoked a vicious growl from the Kzin commander. Uhura wasn't impressed. Let them continue to consider her a dumb female like those of their own species. She would never give them an excuse to call her a coward. When Chuft-Captain turned his baleful gaze away from her and back to the fore port without saying anything else, she felt as if she had won a small but significant victory.

Sulu leaned back against their concave shelter, his

life-support aura compressing to a thin lime-yellow line against his back. Again he examined the Slaver device in great detail. Again he found nothing faintly resembling another toggle switch, hidden button, or any other kind of control that could conceivably activate some unknown setting.

Turning the device once more, in the vague hope he might still somehow have overlooked something, Sulu became conscious of something he had not noticed before. He had had the hand grip in his right hand and the silver sphere in the other. When he'd turned the device this last time, he was certain the sphere had moved slightly. He used his right hand again on the argent globe. Yes, it definitely moved!

Excited, he stood clear of the rock wall. Gripping the sphere firmly this time, he twisted sharply to one side. Nothing. He twisted in the opposite direction. This time the globe not only moved, it turned halfway around on its axis.

The familiar blurring distorted the device. This time, when it coalesced, the sphere was gone. In its place was a cone with its apex facing outward. The cone had a rounded base that blended smoothly into the hand grip. The configuration was so simple that Sulu almost shrugged it off as merely another disguise form and twisted the sphere back. But maybe the thing did something, despite its innocuous appearance.

One small, added shape gave credence to that thought. A tiny, round transparency was emplaced between the cone and the hand grip. A peculiarly arranged series of tiny lines were etched into it. They resembled an asterisk more than anything else.

Spock leaned forward as soon as the sphere shape had given way to the cone. Now he ran a finger over the strangely engraved little lens.

Chuft-Captain, he knew, would also have interpreted that tiny but significant transparency at first glance. "A self-destruct mechanism would not have a gun sight."

"No, it wouldn't," agreed Sulu readily. "Let's see what this setting does." Widening his stance, he raised the device as if it were an old-fashioned pistol. Aiming at a point on the distant horizon, he pulled the trigger.

An intensely blue beam sprang from the point of the cone, crossed into space. Slowly the helmsman lowered his arm until the blue line, which remained constant as long as he held the trigger down, touched the lowest ridge of rock and ice. There was a brilliant flare of pure white light. Sulu shut his eyes, blocking out the powerful radiance, then took his finger off the trigger. The glare vanished slowly, like a dying ember. In its place appeared a thick, rising cloud of dense gas and smoke mixed with vaporized ice and stone.

Sulu opened his eyes, stared in horror at the still growing pillar of boiling gases.

"We can't let them have *that!*"

"Fascinating," was all Spock said immediately. His attention was held by the tower of carbonized solids. "No laboratory in the Federation has ever produced a hand weapon of such power." He squinted into the distance. The cloud was finally beginning to dissipate, and he could see through it a little.

"The entire crest of the ice monolith you fired at appears to have vanished. Total conversion of matter to energy at this distance, and by a simple hand weapon."

"An army of Kzin warriors armed with these would be invincible," Sulu observed in awe, gazing at the simple cone shape he held. "One man could fight off a small ship. The whole galaxy would be their dinner table."

"And it was, Mr. Sulu, it was. I do not imagine they were called Slavers because of their benign dispositions."

"If we . . ." Sulu started to add, but something he saw caused him to pause. A rising wave of ice particles and small gravel was racing toward them like a dark cloud from the region of the destruction, carried on a disturbed wind front by the shock of the vaporization.

"Hit the dirt!" he yelled.

Both men curled up beneath their overhanging boulder, tried to press themselves into the solid stone. But like the power of the Slaver weapon, the shock wave when it arrived was far stronger than either had imagined. Both men were lifted from their places and slung through the atmosphere. Sulu did something to the

Slaver device just before he hit the ground hard. Spock landed nearby, no more gently. A faint reverse shock whistled over them a moment later, stirring both immobile bodies like sawdust on a plate. They did not move.

A few minutes later a slim, flattened shape *thrummed* overhead. In its observation chamber, one seated Kzin let out a snarl of triumph at something just glimpsed below.

"There they are, Chuft-Captain!"

The injured commander leaned forward, recognized the two motionless bipedal shapes. "Peculiar. There must have been a ground-level aftershock. They were too exposed to cope with it." He grinned. "How fortunate for us. Set down as close to them as you can manage, Pilot."

"Yes, honored one." The pilot operated controls and the *Traitor's Claw* began a slow, smooth descent. The "stolen" police vessel touched down only a few meters from where the bodies of Spock and Sulu rested unmoving on the icy surface.

Chuft-Captain glanced over at Flyer. "Bring them in. Carefully."

"Yes, Chuft-Captain." Flyer saluted, turned, and headed for the airlock.

While he was gone the rest of the Kzinti waited anxiously in the observation chamber. Uhura regarded the aliens with interest. She had hopes that Sulu and Spock were feigning unconsciousness, perhaps in a bold attempt to get themselves taken on board the Kzinti ship, where with the aid of the Slaver weapon they might have a chance to overpower her captors. So she received a rude shock when the party of suited Kzinti returned, carrying two limp forms that showed no hint of consciousness.

"They are alive, Chuft-Captain," Flyer reported to his commander as the other Kzinti stood the two former prisoners back on the police web, which had been turned off to allow them to be placed, but which was then quickly switched back on to keep them upright.

"They have sustained some bruising, mostly internal, from what our physician told me," Flyer said. "Their life-support belts cushioned them enough to keep them alive. Without those belts, I am sure they would have been scattered in pieces across the ice."

"Some bruising, yes." Chuft-Captain's right hand rubbed at his cracked ribs, touched gingerly at the bandages wrapped around his chest. Flyer handed him an object and the commander gazed down at it speculatively. "Meanwhile we have the problem of this."

His uncertainty was understandable. Before being knocked unconscious, Sulu had managed to twist the cone shape. It had once more reverted to the maddeningly familiar silver sphere.

Both officers regained their senses together. Sulu saw that the Kzinti had no interest in them for the moment. The whole crew were offering suggestions dealing with the Slaver weapon. Much yelling and growling was evident. Everyone held a different opinion, it seemed. But eventually, simply by fiddling incessantly with the device, one of them discovered the sphere twist. Or rather, *a* sphere twist. Somehow it seemed to Sulu that the globe had been turned in a manner different from the way he had done it.

Expectedly, the silver ball vanished. But the cone shape did not appear. Instead, the sphere was replaced by a smaller, rose-hued globe. A small grid was set into the top of the ball.

None of the formerly talkative Kzinti volunteered an opinion as to the possible function of this new manifestation. The device had proven too many wrong already, and none of them wished to be embarrassed in front of Chuft-Captain with an inaccurate appraisal of the device's capability.

So it was Chuft-Captain who finally had to ask for theories. "What would this be?" He pointed a thick finger at the small, reddish ball.

"I have no idea," Flyer said quickly. He glanced thoughtfully at a gauge set into the side of his armored suit. "Whatever it does, it generates power."

That revelation produced more confused yowling and growls from the assembled Kzinti.

Nor were they the only ones speculating on the device's newest, and most surprising, manifestation.

"There's a grid set into it," Spock said to Uhura and Sulu. "It may be another communications setting. Possibly related in some way to the first communicator shape keyed by the first notch in the toggle slot, but," and he almost frowned slightly, "that would seem redundant, and out of keeping with the Slaver's oft-demonstrated efficiency. Not to mention the economical, many-functions-in-one nature of the device itself. If we—"

A new—startlingly new—voice spoke in the observation chamber. It spoke in Kzinti, or at least something very close to Kzinti. It had the distortions common to an out-of-town rural visiting a large, cosmopolitan metropolis and trying to converse in the local dialect. That meant it was comprehensible, but spiced with a notable yet not quite definable difference.

It was immediately clear that the voice did not emanate from the mouth of any of the assembled warriors; this was confirmed by the manner in which they abruptly ceased all conversation among themselves. The voice sounded again. It had a faint crackle in it, like carbonation in liquid. All at once it became evident to everyone that the voice came from the little grid on top of the Slaver device's newest configuration.

"Whatever it is, it sure has the Kzinti frightened," Sulu observed with satisfaction.

"That's not surprising." Spock's placid expression showed that it wasn't. "The Kzinti, if I recall correctly, have many legends of weapons haunted by their original owners."

Uhura stared, fascinated, at the device. "Could it be a voice-response control, requiring verbal direction?"

The Kzinti had clustered closely around Chuft-Captain and the device, and the muffled sounds of conversation were all the frustrated officers could make out.

"I think not," said Spock. "Somehow it actually appears to be conversing with them." He paused, listening. "Yes. It gives replies to direct questions, and reasons abstractly where appropriate. A reasoning computer so small, capable of independent analysis and reply? Even with the subminiaturization that modern Federation technology has achieved, that is hard to believe. A computer, yes, of any tiny size you want. But one capable of reasoning and decision-making? An incredible accomplishment."

"Are you sure, Mr. Spock?" Sulu asked.

Spock listened for a while longer, then nodded affirmatively. "It is much more than a computer. Its logic circuitry must be infinitely more sophisticated than anything we have yet developed, save for huge reasoning computers such as the main one on board the *Enterprise*. This one appears capable of similar activity, and it is unbelievably smaller."

The crowd of Kzinti, their initial excitement beginning to fade, spread out from one another. So when the voice spoke again, it became loud enough and clear enough for the translators hanging from each of the prisoners' waists to interpret.

"How long," Chuft-Captain was asking the tiny rose sphere, "since you were last turned off?"

"I do not know," the stilted voice of the Slaver device promptly replied. "When I am off I have no sense of passing time."

"Very well." The Kzinti commander opted for another tack. "What is the last thing you remember?"

"We were on a mission." Spock couldn't tell from the awkward inflection in the machine's voice whether it was referring to several Slavers, or the device and a single owner, when it said "We." "I may not tell you of the mission unless you know certain coded terminology."

Flyer spoke up. "If you could describe to us the positions of the stars above the last ship or world you were on, we would be able to guess how much time has passed since then."

"Without certain code words," the computer voice informed them evenly, "I may not describe the location."

Patience was not one of the Kzinti's finer qualities. Chuft-Captain couldn't keep the irritation out of his voice when he next addressed the device. "One of the settings on you was a matter-conversion beam of tremendous power. We know that, having observed it in operation." He glanced back, smiling victoriously at

the frozen prisoners. "We all saw what it can do." He
turned back to the device. "Tell us how to find that
setting on you."

There was a pause, then, "Move the toggle until you
reach the original null position."

This affirmative response, without a single reference
to code words, produced an excited, anticipatory chattering among the assembled Kzinti, so much so that
their yowling drowned out everything else the computer was saying.

"That's the end, then," said the despondent Sulu.
"They've succeeded in communicating with the device."

"There must be *something* we can do." Uhura
fought against the invisible bonds restraining her,
found the police-web field strong as ever. Then she noticed Spock. The first officer was never demonstrative,
no matter how serious the situation; but considering
the gravity of their present predicament, he appeared
even more phlegmatic than usual.

"Mr. Spock, you know what's happened," she called
to him. "Don't you have any suggestions?"

Spock apparently did not. He was staring blankly at
the excited cluster of milling Kzinti. "Most peculiar,"
he murmured, and that seemed to constitute his final
words on the matter.

Uhura stared back at the Kzinti, but saw nothing to
inspire such a comment from her superior.

Chuft-Captain raised the Slaver weapon, brandished
it aloft triumphantly. If Uhura had no inkling of why
Spock was so fascinated, Sulu did, the moment he set
eyes on the weapon again.

It had changed, obviously in response to Chuft-Captain's request. But it had not changed into the matter-
conversion configuration. At least, not into the
weapons mode Spock and Sulu had used piror to their
recent recapture. Not one cone but a pair projected
from the hand grip now. Neither apex faced outward.
Instead, the two points faced each other. They came
close to touching, forming a distorted dumbbell shape.

Still chattering enthusiastically among themselves,
the knot of Kzinti trooped from the chamber, moving
toward the ship's airlock.

"That was not," Spock said decisively, "the total conversion beam. We must assume the weapon gave them directions for employing still another new setting."

"But if it wasn't the conversion beam . . . ?" Sulu hesitated, glanced anxiously around at the exit taken by the departing Kzinti.

Uhura, meanwhile, was shifting her attention from one officer to the other, their statements only serving to confuse her further instead of providing enlightenment.

Followed by Flyer and the rest of the Kzinti, Chuft-Captain marched outside. The Kzinti commander still walked in pain, leaning to his left and occasionally clutching at his cracked ribs. The party of armor-suited aliens moved a respectable distance from the *Traitor's Claw*. Having already observed the power of the Slaver weapon, Chuft-Captain wanted to be well clear of his ship before activating it again.

Once they had ascended a jumble of shattered ice blocks, he inspected the re-formed weapon. The double-cone arrangement looked little more like a weapon than many of the device's previous manifestations.

"Like the other configurations," he informed his subordinates, who stood below and slightly behind him, "this new one appears to be devoid of a gun sight."

"It may be a broad-beam weapon," Flyer suggested, "for use on distant or rapidly moving or multiple targets. We saw its power. There may be only a need to aim it very generally in a target's direction. It is definitely a weapon. I suggest you fire at a very distant subject."

Chuft-Captain concurred. "Very well." He assumed as formal a marksman's stance as he could manage with his damaged ribs.

"We can't let them have that weapon." Uhura fought the police web frantically. Though she exerted all the energy in her body, shoving in every direction including straight up, she was unable to move a centimeter and remained frozen in place.

Spock's reassuring comment was delivered with an

eerie calm. "They're not about to get it, Lieutenant. I think you are worrying needlessly." She stared at him uncomprehendingly. Sulu did likewise, but the helmsman had a glimmering of what the first officer meant.

"Why aren't they?" she asked.

"Assume you are a Slaver war computer, Lieutenant Uhura. A small one, to be sure, but a war computer nonetheless. You have been deactivated, you do not know for how long, but when you were deactivated there was a war in progress. Assume furthermore that it is likely, as Mr. Sulu has suggested, that you are a secret weapon in the truest sense of the term, on a secret mission of some sort." He paused a moment, continued when Uhura had had time to digest this.

"Now you are abruptly awakened by aliens you have never seen before and retain no memory of. They do not know any of the military passwords. They are certainly not recognizable as belonging to the hierarchy of possible Slaver allies. They ask you so many questions it's obvious they know little about you and are trying to find out a great deal more, particularly anything involving weapons settings. Your true owner is nowhere about." He turned to eye her expectantly.

"What would *you* think?"

Uhura didn't have to consider long before replying. "I'd think that I'd been captured by the enemy. Or at least by a non-ally."

"And when they asked you," Sulu prompted eagerly, "how to find your most powerfully destructive setting, what would you give them?"

Uhura and the helmsman exchanged meaningful glances while Spock merely stood staring thoughtfully out the main port, wishing the Kzinti were in view and yet very glad they weren't.

Chuft-Captain aimed the double-cone arrangement as best he could. Focusing on a distant hilltop, he pulled the trigger on the Slaver weapon.

Chuft-Captain vanished. So did Flyer and the rest of the Kzinti standing with him. So did several tons of ice and stone beneath them, and so did part of the hull of the *Traitor's Claw*.

In fact, everything within a radius of twenty meters of the former Chuft-Captain simply disappeared—including, naturally, the Slaver weapon. As Spock had surmised, the war computer built into the device had reasoned that the Kzinti were not entitled to operate it. Instead of the weapons setting discovered by Spock and Sulu, it had provided Chuft-Captain with its self-destruct setting.

Portions of three rooms on board the Kzinti vessel had been opened to space. The control room, a storage chamber, and the crew common room now looked out onto a near vacuum. Walls, equipment, and the ground they had rested on had completely vanished. The conversion had extended to within half a meter of Spock's left leg.

There were no aftereffects. The self-destruct setting operated much in the manner of normal atmospheric lightning: a million-volt bolt could strike a tree and a man a few meters away might not be harmed. Similarly, though the imprisoned officers had been standing frozen on the very edge of the disruption field, they had not been touched. Within the disruption field, however, everything for a radius of twenty meters from Chuft-Captain had been converted. A violent *whoosh* of air escaping from the *Traitor's Claw* was the only sound produced by the disappearance.

Spock barely had time enough to say clearly, "Activate life-support belts!" Having cut into the control room, the self-destruct field had sliced through the police web and its power supply. The three prisoners found they were able to move. Hands touched controls at their waists. Three lime-yellow auras sprang instantly into existence in the dim light of the powerless observation room.

Uhura was studying the smooth-sided, round-bottomed crater in front of them with interest. "Total-disruptor field." She wasn't worried about an attack from any remaining Kzinti. If any remained aboard, they would be too busy trying to lock themselves into airtight compartments and find alternate sources of atmosphere to bother offering hinderance to escaping prisoners.

"Yes," commented Spock. "Another conventional weapon. It would seem that the total-conversion beam Lieutenant Sulu and I discovered was the only thing the Slavers had that we do not also possess, in one form or another."

Sulu walked to the edge of the sliced-open room. It had been cut, he noted, as neatly as with any industrial phaser. The sides and bottom of the crater were smooth as glass, marred only by a few unbalanced boulders and chunks of ice that had fallen into the pit and gathered at the bottom.

"No sign of the weapon, of course." He stood straight, sighed in disappointment. "It would have looked nice in some museum."

"It would never have remained in a museum long, Lieutenant," Spock observed quietly. "There was too much power in that single unique setting. If not the Kzinti, then the Klingons or some other warlike species would have tried to possess it, to copy it, and to duplicate its destructive potential." His gaze lifted and he stared across the open pit. On the far side of the pit and intervening icefield the shuttlecraft *Copernicus* waited. Only the gaping glassy depression in the ground indicated that anything out of the ordinary had occurred on the barren planet of Beta Lyrae. The depression . . . and a small police vessel sliced as neatly as an apple by the knife of some titan.

"Strange," the first officer of the *Enterprise* mused aloud, "how the past sometimes breaks through into the present. A war a billion years old could have sparked a new conflict between the Federation and the Kzinti." He turned to face his companions.

"I think it's time for us to leave. The weapon is now history, along with the Slaver Empire. We have a conference to attend. But while we don't have the weapon, Lieutenant Sulu, at least we have something that might grace your imagined museum."

He gestured nearby. The stasis box that had contained the Slaver weapon rested near one half of a tilted table in the room. The other half of the table and the Kzinti's own empty stasis box had lain within the self-destruct disruptor field and had vanished.

"The box isn't much," Spock observed, "but even though empty it will excite those who see it. They can fill it with their imaginations."

Uhura nodded, leaned over the table's remains and tucked the box which had caused them so much time and trouble loosely under one arm. Devoid of its contents, it was only an ordinary metal container. An ordinary metal container over a billion years old.

Moving carefully downward, they made their way out of the hulk of the *Traitor's Claw*. They skirted the slick rim of the pit, a technological rabbit hole down which had vanished the belligerent dreams of Kzin. Once more on solid ground, they made their way steadily toward the *Copernicus* and a distant rendezvous with their ship, their friends, and a new race to whom the Slaver Empire was more tall tale than truth . . .

XI

The commander of Starbase 25 greeted them personally when the *Enterprise* had finished docking procedure. "Jarrod Shulda, Captain Kirk," the deceptively ordinary-looking man introduced himself. The two shook hands, turned and stared down the extended docking tube leading into the body of the station.

"We know what your mission is, Captain," Shulda said volubly, "and we've been preparing for your arrival." He checked a wrist chronometer and smiled. "Glad you made it on time."

"Was there any reason to assume we wouldn't?" Kirk wondered aloud as they turned down a corridor.

Scott and M'ress accompanied him. The Caitian communications officer appeared unaffected by her recent unfortunate experience. Soon after the pheraligen had taken effect, she and M'viore and R'leez had resumed their normal duties and shifts. Their mental readjustment was helped by Dr. McCoy's instructions to all personnel to extend sympathy and understanding to their three temporarily deranged shipmates, while mentioning any actual incidents or encounters as little as possible. The order was complied with, even by the security personnel whom the three berserk Caitians had put in Sick Bay.

"No offense, Captain. I wasn't impugning your vessel's efficiency. I'm glad you arrived on time because it will take some of the pressure off us, here at the base." Shulda tried to add some humor to a vitally important, serious situation. "Starfleet Command's mighty nervous about this whole Briamos business. They've been talking our ears off here, asking for confirmation of your arrival. I'm happy I can finally send that. Frankly, Captain, you could have arrived here the day after you received your orders and I suspect we still would have had half a dozen worried inquiries from anxious bureaucrats concerned over your slow pace."

"Well, we're here now," Kirk said easily. They were entering a small conference room and the captain added softly, "Most of us, anyhow."

Now who was worrying needlessly? He was no better than those back at Command, continually thinking about the unknown progress of the three officers on board the shuttlecraft *Copernicus*. Resolutely, he shut all thoughts of Spock, Sulu, and Uhura from his mind.

It was an effort.

A florid, plump little woman with oriental features and the air of a society matron was standing next to a small podium going over a handful of notes when they entered. She turned, saw them, and scurried crablike across the floor to greet them. All her movements were quick, her gestures expansive as a courting blue jay, voice brisk and prying.

"Captain Kirk." She extended a smooth palm, thimble-thick fingers extended. "I'm Chu Leiski, sociologist by trade, diplomatic adviser by necessity."

"So you're the resident expert on our friends-to-be, the Briamosites?" Scott was eyeing the woman uncertainly.

"Lieutenant Commander Montgomery Scott," supplied Kirk, "my acting second-in-command, and Lieutenant M'ress, acting communications chief."

"My, my, Captain, but to a stranger you'd seem to be running a thespianic enterprise. But as they say, all the universe is a stage. Please take some seats, any you like, and we'll get started. I'm please to meet you all. We've a great deal to brief you on."

A little breathless with trying to keep up, Kirk slid slowly into one of the chairs in the conference room. Sociologist Leiski moved to stand behind the podium. She put down her notes and activated the electronic readout set into the podium top.

"None of the information I'm going to impart to you is critical by and of itself, but I've included everything we know on the Briamosites. No telling, no telling when during the conference some obscure chunk of information will become crucial. The Briamosites are a very thorough people, and they admire that thoroughness in others. So that's how these briefings will run— thorough in execution and thorough in content. You have to explore a whole pool in order to find the school of minnows, sometimes."

Shutting out the homilies, Kirk asked, "Just how big is that pool? How much have we been able to learn about the Briamosites, Chu Leiski?"

"Not a great deal, Captain. Certainly not as much as we'd like to before you have to go off to this conference. That's why," and she smiled at Scott, "despite your chief engineer's compliment, I can't pass myself off as the resident expert on the Briamosites. There *are* no experts on Briamos and its people."

She leaned both elbows on the podium. "In fact, we're hoping that you and those of your crew who attend or participate in the conference will learn all they can, so they can come back here and lecture me—and all the other so-called experts." Quite suddenly, she dropped her chatty, informal manner and exchanged it for that of the dignified instructor.

Moving to a large screen, she touched a control. The screen lit up, but no pictures or words appeared on it yet. "My connection with the Briamosites comes from the fact that I was an assistant to Ambassador Laiguer. I was half observer, half adviser to him on personal Briamosite interactions. That was my specialty."

"Since you served as the ambassador's assistant and have spent more time among them than any of us, why aren't you coming with us to the conference?" Scott wanted to know.

She smiled again, briefly. "I'm not an official diplomat, nor a member of Starfleet. Just a civilian technician. I have no diplomatic credentials to present to Briamos. As I said, the Briamosites are a very thorough folk. They're as thorough about protocol as anything else. My presence in the official negotiating party would be considered insulting."

"You don't have to be part of the actual negotiating group." Scott could be persistent. "Why dinna ye just come along to give us on-the-spot information?"

"I have to stay here, much as I'd like to go," Leiski told him. "I've been assigned to relay all information on the progress of the conference from here, as it arrives from Briamos and the *Enterprise* back here to Starbase Twenty-Five. I'm to provide my own comments and analysis to accompany your reports, and in turn I'm to convey back to you any suggestions or orders they might come up with." She ruffled her notes.

"I told them I could comment, albeit a little slower, from Briamos via deep-space beam, but it apparently was considered vital in certain circles to have a knowledgeable intermediary between Starfleet Command and Briamos while the conference was taking place. That's me. Besides," she added convincingly, "in a few days you'll all know as much about the Briamosites as I do."

The lectures proceeded smoothly. Despite her pose of self-deprecation when it came to her professional accomplishments, Chu Leiski proved an adept and efficient teacher. Occasionally Kirk brought other personnel along, from Sciences, or Communications, or other departments, as Leiski's subject matter shifted to bear particularly on one section's specialty. But as the days passed with no communication from the *Copernicus*, Kirk found his attention wandering when it should have been fixed on this or that aspect of Briamosite culture.

Finally, after the last lecture, questions were put to

Chu Leiski by Kirk and other officers. She replied with answers and questions of her own.

As the room was emptying, Leiski drew Kirk aside. "I know you'll do the Federation proud, Captain. I wish I were going with you."

"Obviously Starfleet thinks you're more important to them here," Kirk told her. "I know you'd like to be part of the conference, and you will be, an integral part. You just won't be there in body."

"Oh, it's not that, Captain." Leiski was cleaning the nails of her left hand with a nail on the right and she didn't look up at him. "I hope the conference is a success, naturally, but I don't especially care if I'm a part of it. I just like Briamos and its people, that's all, and I want to make sure I have the chance to go back." She looked up now, smiled fitfully. "Do well, Captain Kirk, so I can go back?" She turned and left.

Alone in the room, Kirk felt confident for the first time. No matter how temperamental and difficult professional diplomats such as Ambassador Laiguer found the Briamosites, they had to be a people worth knowing if they could inspire such affection and interest in a woman like Chu Leiski . . .

Kirk was resting in the command chair, brooding silently. He and McCoy had been discussing items of no particular importance—a rare luxury for them both —when Kirk suddenly said, "You realize, Bones, that if they're not here by fourteen hundred tomorrow we'll have to leave without them. We can't delay departure."

"I know, Jim. I'm sure Spock, Sulu, and Uhura know it too, wherever they are."

Kirk turned, stared at the blank viewscreen. His hand tightened slightly on the arm of the command chair, but only McCoy noticed.

They should have reported in by now!

M'ress was already at her post when Kirk entered the bridge the following morning. He glanced over at her, framed a wordless question. She shook her head slowly. The message he had hoped for had not arrived.

Almost, he asked for something she could not give.

Then his lips tightened and he took his seat half angrily. "Mr. Arex, Mr. Vedama, prepare for Briamos departure."

"But, Captain," Vedama began, "can't we——?"

"The one thing we can't do, Lieutenant, is be late for that conference. We depart at fourteen hundred. I won't risk traveling at maximum velocity and the chance of an engine malfunction delaying our scheduled arrival, in order to wait any longer. You know the Briamosites' fanatic attitude toward punctuality. You attended many of the lectures yourself."

"Yes, sir. I did." Discouraged, Vedama turned away.

Arex commenced programming their course, frowned his odd Edoan frown, and called back over a shoulder, "Captain Kirk?"

"Yes, what is it?"

"Captain, our detectors show an unidentified shuttlecraft coming in."

"Check with starbase communications, M'ress," Kirk ordered quickly, hardly daring to believe.

"Yes, sirr." A pause, then she said excitedly, "They arre not expecting any shuttles, sirr. And none of theirr own arre out."

"We're too far from any well-populated worlds for easy shuttle transportation," Kirk mused.

"Call coming in, sirr," the Caitian communications officer announced. She added without waiting for an order, "Acknowledging incoming signal."

This one time, Kirk did not reprimand her.

"Shuttlecraft *Copernicus* to *Enterprise*." Spock's lean, relaxed tones gave no hint of anything amiss on board the overdue shuttle. "Request docking."

"M'ress, put me through." He waited while she nudged the necessary controls and then he spoke into the chair pickup. "Spock, this is Kirk here."

"Hello, Captain."

Kirk waited, until it was evident his first officer didn't intend to expand on his greeting. " 'Hello, Captain'? Is that all you have to say, Mr. Spock? You're three days overdue." He tried to sound accusing, but came out appearing worried. "What happened to you in Gruyakin?"

"We had to cope with the fact that the stasis box had been stolen prior to our arrival, Captain."

"Stolen?" Kirk twitched violently.

"Yes, Captain," came Spock's confirmation, calm as ever. "We recovered it only after the stasis box had placed the would-be thief in a stasis field of his own."

"Stasis field of his own?"

"That's correct, Captain. However, that was a minor problem, compared to the trouble the Kzinti caused us."

"Kzinti? Kzinti!"

"It is not like you to respond to every statement with a questioning echo, Captain." The first officer sounded mildly reproving without being outright insubordinate.

"It's not like anyone, Mr. Spock, to go after a stasis box, and then have it stolen, and then run into—" He stopped, took a deep breath. "Mr. Spock, I will expect to see you in my cabin as soon as you've docked and gotten yourselves squared away—and bring that stasis box." A sudden thought moved him to ask quickly, "Lieutenants Sulu and Uhura are all right?"

"Yes, sir," "Yes, Captain," came the almost simultaneous replies from both officers.

"Good. You can both report to me along with Mr. Spock. Maybe the three of you together can come up with one sensible explanation for your delay."

"I'm sure you'll find both the stasis box and our explanation equally intriguing, Captain," Spock assured him.

As usual, Spock understated Kirk's reaction. All four sat in his cabin. Spock was concluding their story. He had related it all, without pausing. Kirk simply sat at his desk, shaking his head in response to one part of the tale, nodding at another, staring in disbelief at still a third. The first officer did most of the talking, while Sulu and Uhura occasionally broke in to provide emotional coloration of their own. The stasis box rested on a table between them.

"And that is how the box has come to be here empty, Captain," Spock finished.

Kirk stared at the metal cube for a long moment.

"My congratulations to all of you. Merely being here is proof of how well you carried out your assignment."

"I beg to differ with you, Captain," said Spock. "We lost the contents of the box, the Slaver weapon."

"That was unavoidable, Mr. Spock. While we don't have it, more importantly neither do the Kzinti. Furthermore, the Federation still has the three of you." He studied the box. Its silvery surface shone metallically in the cabin light. "There ought to be *something* we can—" He broke off, and a slightly mischievous, slightly satanic grin appeared on his face.

"We'll take it to the conference," he announced. "Mr. Spock, you and Chief Engineer Scott can rig a small device to place inside for generating an imitation Slaver field. The box itself," he went on, leaning forward, "is every bit as impressive as any discovered. With an aura surrounding it, no one would know it's been opened. No need to tell the Briamosites, or the Klingons, and I don't think any of them will rush to open it manually, in front of all the others."

"That would be deceitful, Captain," Spock observed disapprovingly.

"Diplomatic, Mr. Spock, simply diplomatic. Remember, the Briamosites will choose between the Klingons and the Federation. I am not going to stick to Marquis of Queensberry rules when something as vital as an interstellar alliance with a race as important as the Briamosites is at stake. And especially not when the matter also involves Klingons."

"Pardon, Captain . . . Marquis of Queensberry rules?" Spock asked.

"They have to do with boxing, Mr. Spock," Sulu informed him.

"Oh yes, boxing. One of the ancient barbarous human martial arts." Sulu bridled and Spock hastened to add, "No offense, Mr. Sulu. I was referring only to the primitive, unrefined techniques of human warfare, not to fencing or the more sophisticated forms of self-defense."

Sulu looked uncertain, but relaxed.

" 'Barbarous' is the right word when negotiating with Klingons, Spock." Kirk had turned grim. "You know the Klingon watch phrase when it comes to diplomacy: 'That which is expedient rather than that which is truthful.' So we'll bend the truth a little bit ourselves. We may not actually have to lie. If no one asks us whether the stasis box has been opened, I see no reason to volunteer the information that it has."

"You are rationalizing, Captain." Spock refused to be argued out of his stance. "But considering the importance of the conference, I find, reluctantly, that I must concur with your methodology. We must show ourselves as adaptable as the Klingons."

The *Enterprise* was well on its way to Briamos from Starbase 25 and approaching the limits of Federation territory, when an unexpected buffeting struck the ship. One moment they were cruising along easily—the next, the ship was shuddering as if afflicted with metallic pneumonia. As suddenly as the disturbance began, it stopped.

"Now what could have caused that?" Kirk wondered, then added more loudly, "Lieutenant Uhura, damage report."

"All stations all decks report no damage and secure, Captain," she reported in a few minutes. "Several sections want to know what happened."

"So do I. Mr. Spock?"

The first officer was bent over his readouts, then looked up. "I am not certain, Captain. It could have been caused by any of several phenomena, external or internal." He touched a control. "Engineering, Mr. Spock here."

"Aye, Mr. Spock," replied Chief Engineer Scott. "What the devil was that?"

"You do not know, Commander?" Spock asked.

"No sir. I was hopin' you'd be able to tell me."

"I am attempting to find out by eliminating possibilities, Commander. Bridge out." Spock made several more fast checks, looked back at Kirk.

"It would appear to be an external problem, Captain." Spock appeared to hesitate. "As far as outside causes—"

Further buffeting, not a repeat of the last but stronger this time, rocked the *Enterprise* again. It had enough force to jolt small objects loose from their places at desk and console. It also lasted slightly longer than the previous shaking, and stopped just as mysteriously.

Uhura relayed the gratifying no-damage reports from each deck and section while Spock worked feverishly now at the science computer.

"I think I have it, Captain." He glanced up finally from his instrumentation. "If the information compiled by our long-range sensors is accurate, we would do well to immediately—"

He never finished the suggestion. A giant hand slapped the *Enterprise* sideways, flung Kirk from the command chair. He barely caught himself in midair to keep from being thrown against the navigation-helm console.

All across the bridge, other crew members were slung from their positions. Only Spock, who was half prepared for the shock because of what the sensors had told him, clung tightly to his seat and absorbed the buffeting. But this time the shaking didn't stop. It fluctuated from dangerous to irritating, but never ceased entirely.

Kirk crawled carefully back into the command chair. "Mr. Sulu, all ahead warp factor eight! Emergency power!"

"I'm trying, Captain," Sulu shouted after a frustrating struggle with the controls. "She's not responding properly. We're caught in something."

"Energy storm," Spock announced loudly, over the noise of the shaking. "Captain, sensors report a variable pulsar in the immediate spatial vicinity. That's what's causing the uneven buffeting. It's rotating at a high rate of speed, throwing out intermittent, unpredictable bursts of tremendous energy. I should have recognized the cause sooner but—" He broke off, concentrated on keeping his seat as a violent *spang* sounded through the fabric of the ship's hull.

Kirk thought of a hammer pounding on a metal pail—and they were inside the pail.

"Captain!"

Kirk instantly recognized the urgent voice shouting over the chair intercom.

"Hang on back there, Scotty."

"What's going on, sir? The strain on the engines tryin' to hold us to a course through this is makin' my stress gauges look drunk. And the hull's showin' strain, too."

"Variable pulsar, Scotty."

"What? But how did we get so close? Shouldn't . . . ?"

"I know, Scotty. Let's wonder about that later. Bridge out." He rolled to his right, remembered the sensation so well described in books of sea captains of old. "Mr. Sulu, change course. We can't fight through this. Compute to—" He held on, gritting his teeth, forearm straining as another violent jolt battered the ship. "Compute position of pulsar, utilizing sensor readings, Mr. Sulu. Engage course directly opposite to plotted wavicle flow!"

"Aye, Captain!" A brief pause was long enough for the *Enterprise*'s superfast navigation computer, operated by Lieutenant Arex's skilled three hands. Then Sulu fed it to the helm. Abruptly the *Enterprise* came about, although there was no sensation of turning on the bridge: The curve the ship was making was far too gradual for it to affect the artificial gravity field.

The buffeting gentled, the galactic storm falling to a electromagnetic zephyr, but didn't cease completely.

"How are our shields holding, Mr. Spock?"

The first officer checked his instruments. "Still holding, Captain. I would be surprised if we have not suffered some external damage, though. We were caught utterly unprepared, and our shields are not designed to absorb that kind of intense radiation bombardment anywhere but at different spots at a time, as in a phaser attack. The storm enveloped us completely."

He checked his readouts again. "We absorbed saturation-level bombardment for nearly two minutes." Someone on the bridge whistled in awe. "We are fortunate to still have power."

"I know we've been lucky, Mr. Spock. But if we'd struck that storm at a sharper angle, plunged deeper into it before we realized what was happening, we'd have less than power." Everyone knew what Kirk was implying. A variable pulsar, at close range, could put out more than enough energy to fry the best-shielded vessel in space. The *Enterprise* had barely escaped being turned into a vast, metal coffin.

It was a nervous moment as another tsunami of energetic particles rocked the ship. This was the last one of any kind, powerful or gentle. Seconds later the warp drive had outpaced the wave front assaulting them.

"All right, Mr. Sulu." Kirk discovered half the muscles in his body were still contracted, forced them to relax. "Compute a new course and bring us back toward Briamos . . . and keep a slight curve out on the new heading." That ought to keep them clear of the receding pulsar's most powerful outbursts.

"Damage reports coming in, sir." Uhura listened a moment, then added more quietly, "They're not negative this time."

"I don't doubt it." Kirk readied himself. "Anything of real significance?"

"Several sections on Decks Seven and Eight report external structural damage in their area, sir. Estimate is that a portion of hull plating will have to be replaced."

"Contact Engineering and inform Chief Scott— though he may know about it already. Tell him to put a couple of crews to work on the damage. They'll have to rig something temporary as best they can. We can't afford the time to go back to Starbase Twenty-Five for formal repairs."

"Our appearance when we arrive in orbit around Briamos will not be the best, Captain," Spock pointed out.

"I know, Spock, but I'd rather show up looking a little bruised than not show up on time. According to what I heard during our briefings, if we're late we might as well not show up at all."

"I have already examined a part of the briefing material in detail, Captain, and I concur." The science officer turned his attention to the fore viewscreen, which showed only steadily burning normal stars forward. "A near thing. We should take time to report the hazard."

"That's right." Kirk turned, glanced over his shoulder. "Lieutenant Uhura, give me Starbase Twenty-Five contact."

Uhura worked busily at her console. Kirk waited
. . . and waited. "Lieutenant, what's the delay?"

"I'm sorry, sir. Apparently some of our external
communications facilities were damaged by the energy
storm. I've finally gotten through to the base, but I can
only receive audio at the moment."

"That'll do, Lieutenant. Inform Engineering and
have Scotty get on that damage also."

"Starbase Twenty-Five," came a pleasant, mildly
concerned voice over the bridge speakers. "Lieutenant
Jorgenson speaking. Go ahead, *Enterprise*."

"Mr. Spock, you have the coordinates?" The first officer nodded. "Tell them, then."

Spock switched on his own pickup. "Lieutenant Jorgenson, are you recording this transmission?"

"Yes, sir."

"Very well. We have just ridden out a violent energy
storm, radiation put out in ship-crippling bursts by a
variable pulsar of," and he read off several figures, giving galactic position and the pulsar's estimated frequency of critical-intensity outbursts.

There was an unexpected silence at the other end.
Kirk and Spock exchanged puzzled glances. "Do you
copy, Starbase Twenty-Five?" Uhura finally asked.

"We copy," came the lieutenant's voice, "but . . .
would you mind giving those figures again please, sir?
Especially making certain of the coordinates?"

"The coordinates were correct the first time," replied
Spock evenly, "however," and he repeated the entire
sequence of identifying numbers.

"But that's impossible," Jorgenson insisted. "Those
figures can't be right!"

"I assure you that it is not impossible and that our
figures are correct." Spock sounded just the faintest bit
peeved. "Are you denying that we just experienced the
situation described?"

"No, no . . . it's not that, sir. I've counterplotted
your figures against the base charts and we have that
pulsar clearly marked. There are four beacons of
deep-space broadcast capability set well clear and
equally spaced around that pulsar to warn approaching
ships of the danger well in advance."

Kirk's thoughts tumbled over one another. "This is Captain Kirk speaking, Lieutenant. We certainly weren't warned. We picked up no beacon transmissions." He glanced sharply to his left. "Lieutenant Uhura?"

"No, sir!" She looked shocked. "You can't miss an emergency deep-space beacon. Not even if I wanted to. I didn't pick up as much as a cautionary beep."

Kirk hesitated, but Spock spoke into his chair pickup. "Are you sure about those four beacons, Lieutenant?"

"Positive, sir," came the reply, crackling with static due to the *Enterprise*'s damaged communications network. "It says here in the manual that they're fourth-degree amplitude broadcast, too, and were serviced only two years ago. You should have picked up at least two signals well in advance of any potentially damaging energy surge."

"It seems most unlikely, Captain, that two recently serviced beacons of that type should fail simultaneously." Spock sounded unusually grim.

"True, Mr. Spock." Kirk chewed his lower lip, looked thoughtful. "Still, there can't be many ships passing this way. They *could* have failed."

"Possible, Captain," Spock conceded. "I am not denying that, only saying that the odds are large against it. Deep-space warning beacons are powered and designed to remain operative without inspection for a hundred years. That two of them should fail together in so short a time . . . I find that a difficult concept to accept."

"So do I, Spock. But at that moment that's one of only two possible explanations I can think of. And I don't like thinking of the other one."

"That the beacons were intentionally tampered with?"

"Yes. Although I admit that seems little more reasonable than a simultaneous double failure." He paused, then directed his voice to the chair pickup once more. "Starbase Twenty-Five . . . Are you still there, Lieutenant?"

"Yes, sir."

"Report that at least two of the four beacons and possibly more apparently have become inoperative."

"*Inoperative,* sir? But that's impossible also."

"There's no other explanation, Lieutenant. Not unless all our external sensors and communications equipment has been rendered completely useless." Uhura shook her head violently. "And I'm assured that's not the case.

"Put in a report and have Starfleet maintainance get a repair team out here to check those beacons as soon as possible." He paused, and added even though he knew the answer, "Could those beacons have been destroyed by an energy surge from the pulsar itself, Lieutenant?"

"No, sir. According to the manual here, those four beacons are Class-AA-shielded. Nothing short of a full nova would knock them out. I just don't understand this, sir."

"Neither do we, Lieutenant, although we have a suspicion and it's not pleasant. However"—he took a deep breath—"we are still on course for Briamos and expect to arrive slightly delayed but still within the time parameters set by the Briamosites. You can report that back to Starfleet Command for us."

"Will do, sir. And, sir?"

"Yes, Lieutenant?"

"If there's negligence proven in this case, someone's going to pay for it."

"I have news for you, Lieutenant," Kirk replied. "If there's *no* negligence proven, someone's going to pay for this."

XII

Other than the unexplained incident involving the unbeaconed pulsar, the flight to Briamos was devoid of surprises. That pleased Kirk just fine. One near disaster before the conference had even been convened was quite enough.

Briamos's main system, containing two populated planets including the Briamosites' homeworld, was impressive. And Briamos itself was as beautiful a world as any in the Federation. Its twin world of Niamos, orbiting farther out, was smaller but equally attractive.

Clearly the Briamosites had not squandered the natural opportunities nature had given them. The deep-range scopes and sensors on the *Enterprise* indicated highly developed populations on both planets. With Niamos, an inhabitable world, hanging only seventy-five million kilometers off in space, the ancient Briamosites had been gifted with a natural reason for developing space travel.

While they did not possess warp-drive capability as yet, and journeys between the three close Briamosite solar systems involved—by Federation standards—unconscionably long times, the vessels that Kirk saw when they approached Briamos were superbly designed and very efficient-looking. So much so that Chief Scott was of the opinion that the Briamosite ships could be adapted to warp-drive technology, and therefore fast deep-space flight, with few modifications. No doubt that capability would be one of the first items the bargaining Briamosites would seek in deciding who to ally themselves with. But it would hardly be critical. Both the Federation and Klingon could offer Briamos high-speed FTL technology.

No, the Briamosite decision was likely to hinge on less definable reasons.

Five warships, each nearly as large as the *Enterprise*, drifted out of low orbit to greet them.

"We're being scanned and hailed, Captain," Uhura reported.

"Have a good time but check your weapons first," murmured Kirk as he admired the lines of the approaching ships. "Let's keep in mind that they're likely to be cautious at the same time they're displaying impatience. Put them through, Uhura."

The screen cleared instantly and they saw their first Briamosite. Their first live one, Kirk reminded himself. He had studied those features at lecture session after session. The actual sight, therefore, was expectedly anticlimactic. He now knew Briamosite features as well as those of M'ress, Arex, or any other nonhuman Federation race.

Since the screen proportioned everything, one couldn't tell from the portrait that the alien stood over two meters tall, this being the Briamosite average. Partly, the alien resembled a human being who had walked in front of one of those ancient amusement park fun-house mirrors (the one that made fat women happy by squeezing them to an unnatural thinness while stretching them to Watusi heights). The forehead was high, the head itself long and narrowed. But it was not a hollow-cheeked skull face. The Briamosites were thin, they were not living cadavers.

The one regarding them now did not smile. Neither did he frown. Not much could be told from that, one way or the other. Even sociologist Chu Leiski hadn't been able to learn much about Briamosite expressions during her limited sojourn on their world, and the shy people had been reticent to discuss the meanings of their occasional facial grimaces and twitches.

One thing they did know, Kirk remembered: as long as a Briamosite did not on first greeting show lower canines and groan softly, he or she was at least offering a neutral greeting.

The eyes were stretched like the rest of the gangling body. Ellipsoidal orbs peered out at Kirk, their pupils eerily small. As if to counterbalance the high, narrow skull the ears were wide pleated shapes like the wings of a bat, and roughly that size. They stuck out boldly at right angles to the nearly hairless pate. A three-centimeter-high gray fuzz ran in a straight line from the forehead down below the back collar, much in the fashion once favored by certain primitive Amerinds of Earth.

The figure spoke. Considering the small size of the mouth opening, the words that emerged sounded quite normal in inflection and pitch. Now that he was speaking, the Briamosite gestured freely with one hand or the other, hands which ended not in fingers but in four small, flexible tentacles, each tipped with a pointed claw painted a color different from that of its seven fellows. The ears moved also, in a manner which Kirk recalled from his notes as signifying friendliness. While the two arms were jointed much like human arms, the weaving boneless tentacles gave them a decidedly graceful, supple look.

As the speaker moved, the pins holding his toga to one high shoulder sparkled. Stripes which Kirk recognized as indicating rank ran across the upper folds of the garment. The skin beneath those folds was a light gray-green, hairless but definitely not reptilian in appearance.

"To you greetings, Captain Kirk of the Federation ship *Enterprise*. Am I—I am Colonel-Greeter Pliver here to welcome you to our system home and to conference." His ears swayed in agitation like those of a nervous rabbit. "Worried I was that you might not be here in time. You have arrived barely six vilvits the polite side of deadline."

"We're sorry, but we were delayed," Kirk explained quickly. Then he recalled the view that the Briamosite's portrait had replaced. "That's quite a welcome you've given us—five warships. You, Colonel-Greeter Pliver, make me feel like an honored guest. But all those weapons aimed in our direction kind of counter the effect."

"Apologies are extended," said Pliver.

At first Kirk thought the Briamosite might be struggling with an unfamiliar duty; but that impression had changed swiftly. Already Kirk was coming to regard the alien as a slickly professional diplomat the Federation Diplomatic Corps would have been proud to match wits with.

"We felt it necessary to provide an escort," Pliver continued smoothly, "for your own protection."

"Protection from what?" a new voice wondered. Kirk glanced back, saw McCoy emerge from the turbolift and stride onto the bridge.

"Hello, Bones. I was just going to ask that myself." He returned his attention to the viewscreen. "We can take care of ourselves," he said meaningfully. "Who do we need so much protection from?"

"Why, from mutual enemies yours, the representatives of Klingon. They have been here for," and Kirk thought he detected just a hint of reproach in Pliver's voice, "three days."

"Klingons . . . As I told you," Kirk went on, "we ran into some trouble on our way here. If you take a look at the damaged exterior of our ship you'll have some idea of why we were delayed."

"I have already noticed the damage, during your initial approach from deep space, on our scanners." He didn't sound particularly sympathetic, Kirk noted. "Most unfortunate. Assuming, I am, as little as we know about you of the Federation, that you are telling me a true story, Captain Kirk. I would hate to think that Federation of yours thought so little of us as to send a second-class damaged ship to represent them because it was not needed somewhere more important."

Almost, almost Kirk said the first thing that came into his mind. But he recognized it as a clever ploy, and a test. Pliver had deliberately baited him, testing his patience, his pride, his ability to maneuver mentally in a stressful situation.

Calmly, he replied, "The *Enterprise* represents the finest class of ships in current Starfleet operation, Colonel-Greeter Pliver. I assure you that our damage is as genuine as it was unwished. You may have the opportunity of inspecting it yourself, if you desire."

"Perhaps sometime during the conference," Pliver responded pleasantly, having tried Kirk and not found him wanting.

McCoy leaned close, was careful to keep his voice below pickup range. "They're a handsome people, Jim, if this one's any indication. And sharp operators." He turned, strolled casually toward the science station as Pliver, with an excuse, begged a moment's pause. No doubt to report the results thus far to his superiors.

"Five warships to protect us from the Klingons, eh? Mighty solicitous of our health, wouldn't you say, Spock?"

"I detect a familiar note of sarcasm in your tone, Doctor," the first officer replied. "The Briamosites, in preparing to ally themselves and their future with either the Federation or Klingon, are only exhibiting a cautionary xenophobia natural in such a situation. Clearly the presence of these warships is designed to insure that we do nothing unpleasant, should the conference not proceed in our favor. We would not, of course, but the Briamosites cannot be sure of that in their own minds. I am certain a similar escort surrounds the Klingon ship.

"While they do not possess warp-drive technology, from the appearance of their vessels and from Commander Scott's engineering analysis I would estimate they have ample firepower to blast any unruly visitor from their skies, be it Federation cruiser, Klingon, or both.

"Also, the presence of the warships constitutes an important show of force for Briamos. They naturally wish to impress us with their power and potential so that we will make our most generous offers of alliance and they will be able to obtain the best for their systems." Spock paused a moment, added, "I believe the presence of the five ships is best described by an ancient human saying once employed by the primitive tribes called nations. 'Showing the totem,' I think it was." There was a touch of disgust in the Vulcan's voice.

" 'Showing the flag,' " McCoy corrected him. "What's the matter, Spock? Didn't individual tribes on Vulcan ever show the flag?"

"Perhaps far in our past we did, Doctor," Spock conceded. "However, we disposed of our ritualistic slogans and totems much earlier in our racial history than humanity did."

Pliver returned to the viewscreen. "Your orbital coordinates are as follows, Captain. They have been transcribed for your own instrumentation systemology. You see, we have done our homework, too."

As always, there was no evident movement of the mouth beyond the minimum necessary to form the requisite words. But Kirk was beginning to relate certain significant hand and ear motions to what he had learned during the series of lectures at Starbase 25, and if he was interpreting them correctly now, it meant that

Pliver had, in addition to his sleek diplomatic style, a well-developed sense of humor.

"I'm sure you have," Kirk complimented him. "We've heard a great deal about your energy and abilities." That ought to earn the Federation a diplomatic point or two, he thought. "Mr. Sulu, stand by to receive coordinates."

"Standing ready for input, sir. Standing by, Colonel-Greeter."

Pliver looked pleased and a little startled at being so acknowledged. His expression didn't alter, but he read the coordinates with a definite flourish. "These will place your ship in close proximity to the Klingon vessel, Captain."

"Just a minute," Kirk said hastily. "If we may have any preference as to orbital location—"

"It is preferred," Pliver broke in smoothly but firmly, "that the vessels carrying both ambassadorial staffs remain in the same area. This will simplify," he added reassuringly with a friendly wag of batlike ears, "communications and transfer of personnel from both ships to the place-of-conference. That is located in a small resort community a modest distance from our capital city. It is on the seacoast, which is a region I am told you should find pleasant. The climate may be somewhat warm for you, but not unduly so. It was determined at high levels that it would be best to hold the conference in one of our most desirable, exclusive recreational areas as opposed to a stuffy, formal official structure in some city crowded. Landing coordinates for shuttle or transporter will be provided shortly. Until then, Captain Kirk, a pleasant forward looking-to."

Pliver switched off. Kirk couldn't be sure whether that last twist of ears indicated expectation or downright friendship, but either would be a sign that this first contact had concluded successfully.

"End transmission, Captain," Uhura said formally.

A snicker sounded from close by the science station. McCoy wore a wide, half-sardonic smile. "I like the Briamosites already, Jim. Some of their top politicians have seen a chance for a free vacation, so they're going to hold it on the Riviera instead of in the capital, where their constituents could keep an eye on them—assuming they're ultimately responsible to a constituency, of course."

"I beg your pardon, Doctor. *The* Riviera? That is a generalized human term, an adjective and not a noun."

"It wasn't always, Spock. Long time ago, it referred to one specific site on Earth. Nowadays any coast area on any world that proves especially hospitable to settlement is known as a Riviera site. Putting this conference in the local version of it," McCoy chuckled, "is a sign of the Briamosites' humanness."

"Yes," said Spock, his disappointment evident, "I'm afraid you're right, Doctor."

McCoy responded cheerfully. "Don't worry, Spock. One day soon we'll run across a race that wants to join the Federation and behaves exactly like Vulcans."

"A day I look forward to, Doctor, with great anticipation," the first officer replied. "However," he added in a more analytical tone, "it appears that the Briamosites possess many admirable qualities. I am looking forward with interest to the conference."

"On that, we both agree," finished McCoy.

Under Sulu's direction, following coordinates given by the Briamosites, the *Enterprise* was moving slowly toward the orbital station assigned to it. The five Briamosite warships shadowed the Federation cruiser every kilometer of the way.

"What the Colonel-Greeter Pliver said about placing our ship and that of the Klingons close together in order to facilitate transportation and communication is undoubtedly true, Captain," Spock ventured conversationally. "At the same time, a superficial reason masks the real one."

"Oh, there was never any question in my mind about it, Mr. Spock." Kirk thoughtfully stared at the viewscreen, which showed two Briamosite warships shining between the scanner and the green-blue world farther below. "They want both us and the Klingons together, nice and neat and accessible, so they can keep an eye on us all with a minimum amount of worry."

"Approaching designated position, Captain."

"Thank you, Mr. Sulu. Let's see what our counterparts and fellow arguers look like."

Sulu switched on the forward scanners. A small dot appeared, barely visible against the great cloud-covered bulge of the planet Briamos.

"Increasing forward magnification," Sulu declared.

The dot leaped at them. Sparkling in the viewscreen was a Klingon cruiser, analog to the Federation's *Constitution* class. It was an immaculate technological vision, hanging in space like an abstract jewel. Every centimeter of its surface shone brilliant and mirror-bright. The winged shape looked as if it had rested in a Starbase vacuum dock for months.

McCoy let out an appreciative whistle.

"She really shines, Jim. The Klingons must have polished her hull from bridge to engines."

Spock wasn't impressed. "I apparently have more confidence in the Briamosites than you do, Doctor, judging by your reaction. They seem too intelligent to me to be overawed by such superficialities as mere appearance."

"I tend to agree with you, Spock," Kirk continued grimly. "But you have to admit that with the damage we suffered from that pulsar we don't present a very impressive sight alongside that." He paused, leaned forward in the command chair, and squinted hard at the viewscreen.

"Jim, something the matter?" wondered McCoy.

"The ship." Kirk was lost in some thought of his own and spoke almost inaudibly. "I recognize that ship . . ." Then he sat back, added loudly, "The rogue planet, without a sun. The world of the illusion-masters who tested us—"

"We're being scanned, sir," Uhura interrupted, "by the Klingons this time."

"Yes. If they have a hailing signal out, acknowledge it, Lieutenant."

"They do, sir," she reported immediately. "Making contact."

A face formed on the screen; dignified, impressive, with a very un-Klingon bent toward humor. Most important of all, it was familiar. Dangerously familiar.

"Jim," McCoy whispered, "you're right. I remember the illusion-masters and our contest there. And . . . I remember *him*. Isn't that—?"

"Kumara," Kirk said sharply. "The Klingon I went to the old experimental Interspecies Academy with. Yes, that's him."

"The Klingons have clearly," added Spock, who also recognized the face, "chosen their best to represent them."

About that time the transmission must have cleared on board the Klingon ship, for the Klingon captain's eyebrows lifted in recognition. "Well, James Kirk. A surprise to see you again, Jim. Twice in the same year. A pleasure."

"One we could do without," grumbled McCoy.

Kumara glanced to his right, eyeing something off-screen. "I am just studying my other forward scanners, Jim, as you approach. It seems that these Briamosites trust you no more than they trust us. I'm glad to see their suspicion isn't one-sided. I can tell you, it took quite an effort to stay diplomatic in the face of their arrogant reception for us. There are four warships boxing my ship. Two against nine, then, if anything should go wrong."

"You make alliances as fast as you break them, Kumara," Kirk replied tightly. "It seems to me you talk awfully confidently—and dangerously as well. How do you know they aren't monitoring this frequency?"

"Their vessels and civilization are impressive for a primitive race," Kumara admitted. "But we tested this with a shuttlecraft of our own several days ago. They do not possess the equipment to break in and eavesdrop on this particular frequency." There was a pause as the Klingon captain glanced at something or someone out of view and made a disapproving sound.

"Dear me, Jim," he said when he turned his attention back to the screen pickup, "it appears that your ship has suffered a considerable amount of damage. Not very appealing to look at, I can assure you. What happened?"

"We were caught," Kirk said slowly, seeing no reason to conceal the matter, "in a wavicle barrage from a variable pulsar. A supposedly beaconed variable pulsar. The damage almost was severe enough to keep us from arriving here in time for the conference." He leaned forward again. When he spoke, his voice had assumed a low, threatening undercurrent of accusation. "I don't suppose, Kumara, that you have any idea what caused those beacons to malfunction?"

The Klingon captain looked offended. "Am I expected to know the position and disposition of every petty Federation navigational device? I sympathize with your concern, naturally."

"Of course you do," murmured McCoy sotto voce. "We can see that you're all broken up over it."

"So you had nothing to do with it, then?" Kirk persisted.

"To say that my ship was responsible for the destruction of an interstellar navigation beacon is inflammatory, besides being personally insulting, Jim."

"I could care less how you interpret it," Kirk shot back. "Did you destroy those beacons?"

"We destroyed no navigational beacons," Kumara replied with great dignity. Then he added in a slightly less formal voice, while finding something of extreme interest in the underside of his fingernails: "We were, however, patrolling routinely on our way to this conference through the fringes of the disputed territories. We did encounter a couple of malfunctioning fragments of space debris, hazards to navigation, actually, which we promptly eliminated so as to prevent the possibility of an accident to any vessel of Klingon or Federation."

"Then you *did* blow out those beacons!" Kirk slammed a fist down on one arm of the command chair, glaring furiously at the calm face on the viewscreen.

"Hazards to navigation, Jim," Kumara corrected him.

"Your pardon, Captain."

"Who's that?" Kumara looked to the right on his screen, saw Spock's outline flickering in and out of his view. "Ah, the inimitable Commander Spock."

"I might remind you, Captain," said Spock flatly, "that the destruction of Federation property, in particular something of a nonmilitary nature such as a navigational beacon, is in direct violation of the Klingon–Federation subsidiary articles of peace as appended to the Treaty of Organia."

Kumara shook his head, looked very tired. "I told you and will tell you for the last time, gentlemen, that we destroyed no navigation beacons. We torpedoed several nonfunctional pieces of free-floating metallic debris, that's all."

"The beacons," Spock continued, as if the Klingon captain had said nothing at all, "would not have been broadcasting unless there was something to broadcast about. Specifically, imminent danger from a high-intensity burst of radiation from the pulsar they were placed around. So if you destroyed them at a time when no such outburst was imminent—and there is no other way you could have approached the beacons near enough to do so, without first receiving an all-clear from them—*then* you could say they were nonfunctional.

"Furthermore," the first officer continued, "to say in the first place that an object as small and low in mass as a beacon could present a hazard of any kind in the little-frequented section of space where they were located is absurd. A starship traveling at warp-drive would barely take notice of the impact a beacon-sized object would make against its meteoric shields as it disintegrated. And the chances of such a collision occurring are small enough to border on the infinitesimal."

"Ah," countered Kumara, wagging a cautionary finger, "but they are finite, Commander."

"That may be so," Spock began, "but—"

"And no matter how slight the possibility, we of Klingon always seek ways to improve the space lanes and make them safer for travel by any ship."

"Kumara," said Kirk softly, barely holding his anger in check, "I am reporting your destruction of both beacons to Starfleet Command. An official protest will be registered with the imperial government, and—"

"Oh, come now, Jim," the Klingon captain chided him. "Why waste the power? There's no way you can prove that my ship was responsible for the so-called demise of your precious beacons. In fact, there is no way you can prove we were even in the area, which," he added quickly, "we were not, of course."

"He's right, Captain." Spock looked disappointed. "Our claim is not supported by fact, only by supposition and deduction."

"Good enough for me, Mr. Spock," Kirk snapped, a mite testily.

"True, Captain, and for myself also. However, Starfleet will not regard it so. Certainly not enough to base a protest on, one which could trigger a grave interstellar incident. There would be charges and countercharges, and without proof . . ."

"Spock's right, Jim."

Kirk didn't look around. "I know he's right, Bones. But this is one time I wish he wasn't."

"From what I can overhear of the discussion taking place around you, Jim, involving some of your officers, I would presume, you'd best heed their advice. They are quite correct. You can't do a thing." The Klingon captain sounded very pleased with himself.

"On the other hand, Kumara," Kirk mused dangerously, "I could apply inferential logic of my own regarding the destruction of the beacons and use that as grounds on which to take appropriate retributive action."

Kumara's veneer of good fellowship—never thicker than need be—abruptly vanished. So did his air of affected courtesy. No longer did he resemble some peculiar hybrid. He had turned thoroughly Klingon in expression and manner, although his reply was still more controlled than the average Klingon captain would have managed, considering the implications of the threat Kirk had just made.

"If it's a fight you're looking for, Jim, we'll be most happy to oblige you."

"No." Kirk leaned back in the command chair, satisfied at the result his warning had produced. "I was just getting tired of that oily grin of yours."

As if on cue, the expression in question reappeared. "Which oily grin, Jim? This one?" Kumara had a real sense of humor, a genuine rarity among Klingons, making him all the more dangerous.

Now that Kirk had indicated he had no intention of opening hostilities, the Klingon captain once more relaxed. "No, naturally we cannot fight, Jim. This conference is far too important to interrupt with petty squabbling among ourselves. Of course, once our friends and allies the Briamosites learn firsthand of the natural, ingrained duplicity of the Federation, then with their numerous well-armed ships about to assist us, I might reconsider."

"Don't count on their help in anything, Kumara. They're not your friends and allies yet."

"In good time, Jim. Merely a formality, as you will discover. I have preparations to make. Until the conference, then . . . ?" And without giving Kirk a chance to reply, the transmission from the Klingon cruiser terminated.

" 'In good time,' " Kirk muttered, mimicking his Klingon counterpart. "In about twenty million years, maybe, but not before."

"I don't believe the Briamosites will be around in twenty million years, Captain," Spock pointed out philosophically. "Most species are—"

Kirk sounded tired. "I don't think they will either, Mr. Spock. I wasn't being serious. I only meant to say that—never mind. Obviously Kumara destroyed those beacons. They have an excellent intelligence service. Undoubtedly they knew we were coming and which direction we were coming from: Starbase Twenty-Five.

"With that in mind, they eliminated the beacons so we wouldn't know when the pulsar was going to emit a dangerous outburst of radiation. All of which was intended to prevent us from attending the conference. They could have canceled the beacons and, traveling at maximum velocity, still have arrived here three days ago as Colonel-Greeter Pliver informed us.

"You saw Kumara's first expression, Bones. He wasn't expecting us to show up at all. Thought the pulsar would finish us." Kirk smiled grimly. "Well, we've a few more surprises we can spring on him."

"The important thing is that we're here," McCoy pointed out. "We'll outmaneuver Kumara at the conference. Klingons have a bulit-in aversion to diplomacy that will eventually undo their standing in the eyes of the Briamosites. That's for sure."

"Not entirely sure, Doctor," Spock cautioned. "One must realize that this Kumara is not a typical Klingon. He appears capable of subtlety and even courtesy. Furthermore, there is the unsightly condition of the *Enterprise*. The damage we have sustained has already given the Klingons the first few points with the Briamosites."

"I still can't buy that, Spock."

"If you have studied the recordings of the lectures given at Starbase Twenty-Five, Doctor, you will recall that the Briamosites attach a good deal of importance to personal appearance." He indicated the main screen, which once again showed a view of the gleaming Klingon cruiser. "A detail to which Captain Kumara and his crew have clearly paid much attention. The contrast between his vessel's appearance and that of our own can only be to his benefit. Remember," he added after a pause, "humans originated the ancient saying about the importance of first impressions."

"Mr. Spock, even the Briamosites will pay most attention to the last impression. That will be the critical one, and we have something very impressive to demonstrate the power of the Federation with. That." He pointed to the corner, where the empty Slaver stasis box rested unobtrusively.

"The artifact, Captain? You still intend to employ trickery to convince the Briamosites that the box is unopened and untouched?"

"I do, Mr. Spock. Toward the Briamosites *and* the Klingons. You know firsthand what a Slaver stasis field looks like. Surely you and Mr. Scott can build a small device which can fit inside the box and simulate such a field?"

"As I mentioned once before, Captain, that should not be too difficult." Spock still didn't appear enthusiastic about the idea.

"No one will test the field," Kirk pointed out, seeking to convince his first officer, "because the only sure way to do that would be to open the box, and none of the Klingon delegation is likely to be lugging a nullifier around."

"You really think the box will be that impressive to the Briamosites, Jim?" a dubious McCoy asked.

"I do. Not just the presence of the box, Bones, but the fact that we would bring it down to an alien world with us, just to demonstrate our friendship. The Briamosites are very sophisticated, remember. We can't risk thinking of them as an inferior race. In straight intelligence they're likely to be the equal of any member race in the Federation. They have everything but warp-drive technology.

"I'm sure they know about Slaver stasis boxes, if only by reputation. So I'm expecting them to react toward our box exactly as we'd react if some strange people came to negotiate with *us*, carrying an unopened stasis box like a loaf of bread, purely for us to admire.

"It'll be even more impressive," he went on enthusiastically, "because we've brought a stasis box knowing that Klingons will be present. That fact should impress the Briamosites more than the presence of the box itself. A lot more than a shiny ship!" He smiled expectantly. "Kumara will be even more impressed and surprised than the Briamosites—just as I would be if he'd brought an unopened stasis box with *him*."

"We have no formal treaty as yet with the Briamosites, Captain," Spock reminded him. "What certainty have we that they will not attempt to take the box for themselves? Revelation of our prevarication when they find the box is empty and its field a fake could drive them into the Klingon orbit permanently."

"If they steal the box, Mr. Spock, I'm not sure they're the type of people the Federation would want as fellow citizens anyway. But I don't see that happening. Too many imponderables. For one thing, I don't think they have enough familiarity with stasis fields to construct a stasis nullifier."

"Klingons do," McCoy observed. "They could simply ask the Klingons for help in opening the box."

Kirk grinned triumphantly. "And there's the catch, Bones. Just because they steal the box from us doesn't mean they'd want an alliance with Klingon. Furthermore, in order to gain Klingon aid in opening the box, the Briamosites would have to trust it to Kumara's care more or less.

"While the Briamosites have a lot of firepower ringing both the *Enterprise* and Kumara's ship, it's still possible that either of us could outrun them before they could seriously damage us. And I don't think the Briamosites are naïve enough to trust Kumara with a stasis box, either stolen or one of their own.

"Besides, theft of a stasis box from us would be tantamount to an excuse for war on the part of the Federation. As advanced as their civilization is, I don't think the Briamosites are ready militarily to take on either Klingon or the Federation, and I believe they're realistic enough to know that.

"No, their best bet is to be truthful and straightforward throughout the entire conference, to play fair with both sides and not risk their whole future on something silly like stealing an archaic alien artifact. They might envy us the stasis box, but I don't see them chancing all their hopes on a single theft."

"Kumara won't feel that way, Jim," McCoy continued.

Kirk shook his head. "Yes he will, Bones. Consider: If he tries stealing the box, he'll have to do so in front of, or at least with the knowledge of, the Briamosites. That would constitute a breach of Briamos's neutrality, not to mention an insult to every high Briamosite official attending the conference. The result would be to drive Briamos into the Federation."

"I see now." McCoy nodded slowly. "You're planning this whole incident with the box, half hoping the Klingons *will* steal it."

"That's the idea, Bones. Of course, once Kumara discovers that the box has long since been opened and emptied, he'll come running back to Briamos squealing in outrage about the treachery of the Federation and its deceitful minions—that's us. But by then it'll be too late, if I read the Briamosites correctly. If I've learned anything about them from all those lectures, it's that they're basically a decent, honorable people. Once offended by the Klingons, I sincerely believe they'd remain firmly allied to the Federation, no matter what Kumara might claim after the fact."

"Which makes it all the more important for us to convince them to join with the Federation, Captain, in the event that Kumara does not try to steal the stasis box," Spock reminded them both.

Kirk turned in the command chair. "I'm not arguing that, Mr. Spock. How long will it take for you and Scotty to concoct something to put inside the stasis box that will simulate a Slaver field?"

"In our spare time, Captain?"

"No, this is a priority assignment, Mr. Spock. You should begin immediately."

"Very well, though the entire idea still strikes me as tending too much to the childish . . ."

"So was the Trojan Horse, Spock."

The first officer didn't reply as he walked over and picked up the box of Slaver metal. After a brief examination to refamiliarize himself, he turned to Kirk and said, "I estimate three hours to plan the device and design the schematics and another three or four to build and install it in the box."

Kirk looked satisfied. "Fine, Spock. Go to it."

Spock headed for the turbolift.

As events developed, it was fortunate that the first officer's estimates about the time required were accurate. Colonel-Greeter Pliver called now to inform them that the first meeting of the conference had been scheduled to take place at 0900 ship-time the following morning.

Later, when the device had been designed and computer-tested, Spock was able to leave the details of construction to Scott and his engineering staff and head for his cabin—to sleep, and with worried thoughts about the critical conference ahead . . .

XIII

The Federation delegation consisted of four smartly dressed officers: Kirk, Spock, Sulu, and Uhura. They met in the main transporter room the following morning.

"This first meeting will probably consist mostly of introductions," Kirk was saying as the four walked toward the transporter alcove. "You know: 'Captain Kirk, meet the esteemed president of Briamos's second stellar system. Esteemed President, First Officer Spock. Captain Kumara, greet Captain Kirk,' and so on. Everyone says much, means little, and generally uses the opportunity to size up his counterparts. But just because no vital issues are likely to be discussed doesn't mean this opening meeting isn't important, Mr. Sulu." The helmsman, who had been sunk partly in his own thoughts, looked startled.

"Your collar is folded in on the left side, Mr. Sulu," Kirk said sharply. "Straighten it."

"Yes, sir." Sulu hastened to do so. "Do you think the Briamosites care enough about appearances to have researched our uniforms so they can check on our individual appearances?"

"I don't know, Mr. Sulu," Kirk said easily. "They might not know a Starfleet dress uniform proper from an engineer's work coveralls. But," he added quietly and meaningfully, "*I* do."

The helmsman double-checked his straightened collar.

All four officers looked splendid in their dress uniforms as they stepped up into the transporter. Spock carried the Slaver stasis box in both arms. The box was bathed in a delicate blue aura; in appearance it was indistinguishable from the cerulean halo the originally unopened box had been enveloped in when Spock had first seen it back on Gruyakin VI.

Second Engineer Dastagir was manning the transporter console. Kirk turned to him. "Engineer, you have the coordinates for setting down which the Briamosites provided for us?"

"Yes, sir," came the ready reply. "Already programmed into the computer, sir. Ready when you are."

Kirk nodded once. The four officers assumed a waiting stance on four separate disks in the alcove. As soon as they were properly positioned, Kirk signaled to Dastagir. The second engineer initiated transport.

Gradually the four stiff figures were replaced by four

pillars of flickering metallic iridescence. The figure-pillars began to fade . . . and coalesce . . . and fade again. And coalesce again.

Startled, Engineer Dastagir hurriedly checked dials and readouts. Everything read normal, all instrumentation reported proper functioning, yet . . . the four columns of energy had still not vanished. There was such a thing as abnormally slow transport, affected sometimes by a surge-delay in the transporter equipment, sometimes by localized planetary effects. But as the seconds slid away, Dastagir could rule out either of those possibilities.

Something sparked from the console. A nervous, crackling sound filled the room. Fragments of multihued energy broke from the four fluctuating pillars and appeared to drift between them, filling the transporter alcove with an illusion of rainbow snow. Pops and snarls filled the room as confused mechanisms growled in frustration at one another.

Within the alcove the four figure shapes were oscillating wildly now. At the strongest point of coalescence the four officers were discernible down to individual characteristics. At the weakest, when they had become amorphous cloud forms, they seemed almost to blend into a single glittering sphere.

Frantically Dastagir threw switches, overrode, backed up, compensated for. Oscillation intensified but transportation did not take place.

Faced with a disaster of frightening proportions, Dastagir did the only remaining thing he could. He threw the emergency control which would freeze energy levels within the transporter alcove in their present mode. Additional power flowed on request into the transporter mechanisms to lock the four fluttering, uncertain figures within the alcove in place, together with the indistinct swirl of energy surrounding them.

Once the control had been cut in, nothing changed. The four figures neither coalesced nor grew any dimmer. Energy levels held suspended. That gave Dastagir time to do what any intelligent engineer in his position should have done: call for help. Sweating, fumbling at the intercom control, he waited anxiously for a reply.

It came promptly, its calmness contrasting violently with his own excited, anxious self. "Bridge here. Commander Scott speaking."

"Commander, sir, this is Dastagir Engineer Second, down in the main transporter room, sir."

"Slow down, Dastagir." Scott had immediately detected something in the usually imperturbable engineer's voice. He sat a little straighter in the command chair. "Trouble?"

"Yes, sir, I've locked them on emergency hold and—"

"Calm down! *Exactly* what's the matter?" A horrible suspicion was forming in the chief's mind. "Did the captain and the others get down yet?"

"No, sir, that's just it. And I don't *know* what's the matter. I've double-checked everything and the transporter insists it's functioning properly and it's not—" Dastagir stopped, caught his breath, rambled on rapidly. "I had the Briamosite coordinates programmed in and was beaming-down Captain Kirk and the other officers when something went haywire."

"Haywire's not an acceptable engineering term, Mr. Dastagir," said Scott sharply. "Elaborate."

"As near as I can make out there's something producing a field distortion in the transporter, sir. I couldn't beam them down and I can't pull them out of it, so I threw in the emergency lock. They're field-frozen now. And there's something else happening I've never seen before, some kind of energy–matter interaction taking place on the transporter itself."

"So you threw the field lock?"

"Yes, sir." Dastagir sounded desperately unhappy. "It was all I could think of to do."

"Don't . . . do . . . anything . . . else," Scott ordered Dastagir, spacing the words out for extra impact. "I'll be right there." The chief engineer hit the off switch on the intercom, spoke toward the navigation-helm console. "Mr. Arex?"

The Edoan looked back at him. "Yes, sir?"

"Assume command. We're experiencin' a malfunction with the transporter the captain's usin'."

"How bad?" asked Arex, worried.

Scott was already racing past communications and a curious M'ress on his way to the turbolift. "It doesn't sound good. I canna tell for certain until I see for myself."

Once inside the lift car, Scott pressed the emergency override. This sent the car directly to the transporter room, bypassing all other demands on the car's service and producing puzzled stares from several waiting crew members scattered about the ship as their anticipated lift went racing past their respective call stations without stopping.

As the chief entered the transporter room his gaze went first to the alcove. He saw the flickering silhouettes of sparkling wavicles fluttering on the four transporter disks, noted the energetic abnormality coloring the air around them.

Those observations were superficial. The real definition of what lay within the alcove would be found in readouts and dials on the instrument console. He was checking them out immediately, balancing their stubborn readings against the impossibilities registering visually within the alcove.

Dastagir stood helpless to one side, watching, ready to assist if he was needed.

"Any sign of any unusual activity in the mechanisms before the trouble became apparent, Mr. Dastagir?"

"No, sir," the distraught engineer replied, hands clenched tightly at his sides. "I tried readjusting the matrix, canceling the initial input—everything I could think of. Nothing worked. They just continued to oscillate." He licked his lower lip, gazed at the alcove. "It's the blurring of the field parameters that has me really worried, sir."

"Probably nothing to get excited about," Scott lied. "Get Dr. McCoy and a medical team up here." He nodded in the direction of the alcove. "They might need some dressin' up when we bring them back."

If we bring them back, he added silently to himself. Better not even consider that.

He took a handful of tools no less intricately formed than McCoy's surgical instruments and dropped to a prone position, on his back. Once the base panel in the console was off, he slid his head inside, reached in and up with boths hands, and set to work on circuitry no less sensitive than the organic variety McCoy operated on.

At Dastagir's request, and explanation, Dr. McCoy, Nurse Chapel, and several meditechs arrived in the transporter room several minutes later. All of them stared dumbfounded at the particulate storm suspended within the alcove.

"Scotty, what happened?" asked an anguished McCoy.

"Don't know for sure, Doctor," Scott told him, his voice tinged with strain. His head did not emerge from the bottom of the console. "I'm tryin' to find out now."

"But Jim, Spock, the others—"

"They're no worse off now than they were when this started, Doctor," replied Scott. "Engineer Dastagir had the sense to throw a lock on the entire system when he couldn't figure out what was happenin'."

McCoy's thoughts were running down predictable paths. "The Klingons," he began furiously. "They've done something to—!"

"I dinna think so, Doctor," Scott's cautious voice broke in. It reverberated faintly inside the console. A couple of moments later he emerged, holding several strange-looking, gleaming tools in his right hand. Both hand and tools looked damp with a transparent fluid thicker than water and McCoy knew the engineer had been adjusting fluid-state switches.

"Damaged wavicle rectification system," Scott said tightly, wiping his wet palm on his pants. "I hope that's all it was. Those switches shouldn't ever bust, but once in a while they do. Our luck these took a bad moment to rupture." He turned to the console, put his tools down, and glanced briefly at Dastagir. "Let's bring 'em back, mister."

"Yes, sir." Dastagir moved to stand alongside the chief and assist, while McCoy, Chapel, and the rest of the medical team stood aside and looked on anxiously.

Dastagir threw a switch and Scott's hands moved simultaneously on familiar controls. The wavering, banshee whine of the transporter abruptly softened, steadied, and then strengthened. The background field of waltzing energies vanished, leaving only four cylinders of fire. Crackling and sputtering no longer issued from the console.

The four pillars in the alcove intensified, melded into four recognizable, well-dressed figures. Scott meanwhile kept his attention fixed on one particular gauge. When its luminescent pointer reached a certain number, he threw a large switch.

All four figures solidified. The envelope of energy surrounding them vanished, and the whine from the transporter dropped to nothing. The four collapsed into various, sprawling positions on the alcove disks.

McCoy and the rest of the medical team were at their sides instantly, Scott and Dastagir a few seconds after. Scott leaned over the kneeling form of McCoy. The doctor had rolled Kirk onto his back and was passing a medical tricorder over the motionless form of the captain. Scott saw no visible damage, but he knew that any serious injury the officers might have suffered would probably not be easily noticeable.

McCoy started at the top of Kirk's head, grunted in what sounded like a gratified manner when he had reached Kirk's neck, and continued passing the compact device down the unconscious captain's body until it passed over his feet. A few readjustments to the instrument and McCoy repeated the pass, moving from feet to head this time. Then he relaxed visibly.

"He's all right," he told the expectant Scott, glancing back up and smiling in relief at the engineer. "Heartbeat, brain functions, involuntary muscular activity, everything, all his vital signs read normal—adjusting for his unconscous state, of course."

"Same here, Doctor," reported Nurse Chapel. She was bending over the lanky shape of Spock.

The reports were identical from the technicians examining Sulu and Uhura. "They're okay, then?" asked Scott.

"Looks like." McCoy rose.

Kirk's eyelids were beginning to twitch and his head to move from side to side. A low, tired moan escaped his lips. McCoy knelt again on one side and Scott on the other. Together they helped the groggy captain to his feet. Scott looked briefly at his wrist chronometer.

"If you can certify them all right, Doctor, we'll take them down to the bulk transporter."

"But the Klingons—" McCoy began.

Scott shook him off. "I told you, Doctor, the Klingons had nothing to do with this. Either it was unexpected but plausible equipment failure, or else we suffered some concealed damage from that pulsar outburst we rode out. And the captain has to be down on the surface within the hour, to attend that conference. Remember the Starbase lectures. The Briamosites make a religion of punctuality."

"But surely they'll accept a reasonable explanation for a delay, Scotty?"

"I wouldn't count on it. These people strike me as bein' basically good folk, but they've got their peculiarities. And I canna blame them for bein' nervous about this conference. If the captain and Mr. Spock and the lieutenants can be there on time, they've got to try and make it."

McCoy's reply was hesitant but positive as they supported the swaying Kirk. "I don't see why they can't go . . . so far, Scotty." Looking over a shoulder, he saw that the other three officers had also been helped to stand.

Under the doctor's direction, the four stunned officers were helped stumblingly out of the transporter alcove. Kirk walked like a man drunk, as if he couldn't find his balance. But by the time they had walked-carried him as far as the console, he shrugged off their support. Putting out both hands, he braced himself on the console, then turned, leaned against it, and raised his left hand to his forehead, wincing. His eyes opened, and he seemed to see them for the first time.

"Mr. Scott, Doctor McCoy . . . What happened?" There was an odd lilt to Kirk's otherwise normal voice, as if the captain hadn't yet regained full control of all his faculties. Neither the chief nor McCoy paid much attention to it. After the disturbing experience of being frozen in a transporter field for an abnormal length of time, a few mild side effects were only to be expected.

Scott explained. "There was a malfunction in the transporter, Captain. Maybe due to damage received from that pulsar we encountered. We had put you all in limbo for a while until I could get it fixed. You gave us all a bad scare."

"Oh . . . I guess that explains it." Kirk paused, then frowned and stared at Scott. " 'Captain' . . . you called me 'Captain.' "

Scott and McCoy exchanged glances. "Naturally, sir," said Scott, as gently as possible.

"Are you feeling all right, Jim?" McCoy was watching Kirk closely.

"Jim?" Kirk's voice sounded a touch higher, more tenor, than usual. Part of that could be attributed to shock at his recent experience, but not all of it. "Why are you calling me that?" Now the captain sounded— and looked—a little scared.

"What else should I call you, Jim? What's wrong?" Privately McCoy was thinking: temporary amnesia. But no . . . Kick recognized his name and title, merely wasn't identifying with them. Something else was wrong, then.

The three officers stared at each other as if paralyzed, until a new voice broke in: "Scotty, Bones! What in the name of the seven black holes has happened?"

Both men turned together. Sulu was eyeing them in a most authoritative fashion. The helmsman released himself, started toward Scott and McCoy—and almost fell. Startled, he looked down at his feet, registered surprise and astonishment, and then came toward them again . . . walking carefully as if treading on eggshells.

"Jim? Sulu?" McCoy's dazed gaze switched back and forth between captain and helmsman.

Sulu's eyes traveled over his lower body. He extended both arms out in front of him, rotated them over and back. His hands went to his face, felt the features as would a blind man touching a friend. His eyes widened.

"Oh my god! What's happened to us? What's happened to *me?*" He gestured shakily toward the body of the captain. "If I'm Kirk, in Sulu's body, then who are you?"

"I'm Lieutenant Uhura, of course," replied Kirk's body, in that peculiarly modulated tone that was so like Kirk's normal voice yet wasn't. Then Uhura-kirk looked down at herself. She said nothing for long moments.

"*I'm* here, Scotty, Bones. In Sulu's body." Kirk-sulu eyed them both, amazed and stunned.

"It would appear," put in the voice in Lieutenant Uhura's body very calmly and rationally, "that while we were in the malfunctioning transporter field a part of each of us was switched."

"A most important part," Kirk-sulu agreed, staring over at the now-alien shape of his science chief. "That *is* you, Mr. Spock?"

The first officer spoke to them, from Uhura's body, with Uhura's voice. While the tones were unquestionably those of Lieutenant Uhura, the choice of words and flatness of speech were those of Spock. "It is, Captain." He started toward them, stumbled for one of the few times in his adult life, and moved on much more cautiously.

"It would appear, Captain," Spock-uhura said, addressing himself to Sulu's body, "that I am not quite myself." McCoy did a double-take—he was beginning to wonder who *he* really was—but Spock was serious as ever. The joke was unintentional. "That *is* you in Lieutenant Sulu's body."

"It's beginning to look so." Kirk-sulu still sounded overwhelmed by it all. Turning, he stared across at the stolid form of Mr. Spock, who was carefully inspecting himself, running hands over his body, head, and, most particularly, a pair of unfamiliar ears.

"Since everyone else has been accounted for . . ." There was no need to finish the comment. But the voice in Spock's body finished for him, and confirmed the inevitable. "Yes, it's me, sir," admitted Sulu-spock. "I feel so strange, sir. This body . . . so many subtle differences. I feel different, altered. Not ill, exactly. Just queasy."

"I would sympathize with you, Lieutenant," said

Spock-uhura, "but at least you have ended up in a body of the proper gender. If you wish to compare unnatural feelings," and at that Spock-uhura glanced down meaningfully at its curvilinear form, "I believe mine far exceed yours. Nothing could feel more awkward than this. I find myself in a body of different sex and different race. I believe I can cope sufficiently with the mind, but the rest will take careful work."

"Don't count on being unique, Mr. Spock." Uhura-kirk was experimentally walking in a small circle, testing out a different arrangement of mass and new, more powerful musculature. "I didn't exactly end up in an easy-to-compensate-for container either, you know." She almost stumbled again, caught herself, then grinned.

"No wonder I nearly fell down the first time I tried to take a step, McCoy. The captain uses a longer stride than I'm used to."

"The question remains, what can be done to put us back where we all belong?" Kirk-sulu's attention was focused on the wide-eyed face of the ship's chief engineer.

Instantly, every other eye in the transporter room turned the same way.

Scott collected himself, thought a moment, and started to reply . . . to Uhura-kirk. Correcting himself, he shifted to address the body of Lieutenant Sulu.

"Nothing right away, I'm afraid . . . Captain," he told Kirk-sulu apologetically. Turning, he bent over and reached into the still-open console panel near the floor. He withdrew a small rectangle, about twenty centimeters long, which was filled with microcircuitry. It looked like a piece of metallic turf.

As he spoke, his fingers wove an intangible web over the battered, damp panel. "Everything that's been damaged on this I've either bypassed or replaced. The key to the personality–mind switch you've all experienced is locked in place on this panel.

"To put you all back to your original bodies, I've first got to figure out exactly what went wrong. Then I have to trace the one minuscule portion of the damage that produced the personality switch and change current flows, matching energy levels and duration precisely all the way, mind you, so that when you go back into the transporter the personality changes will reswitch themselves without doing further damage to some other portion of your bodies or minds."

He let the panel dangle carefully from one palm. "It's not," he added meaningfully, "a five-minute job for a maintenance tech to perform with a hammer and chisel."

"Wait a minute," said an excited Sulu-spock. "The transporter computer bank holds memories of all our transporter patterns. Why can't we just go to another transporter, desolidify ourselves, and then have the right patterns punched into the transporter so that when we're recombined it will be in the correct pattern ... and proper bodies?"

"I dinna think it's that easy, Lieutenant," Scott began to explain. "If you'd been completely dematerialized in the transporter and then fully rematerialized elsewhere, I might be willin' to try it. But that didn't happen. Only part of your patterns were switched, and it was before full dematerialization had taken place." He shook his head. "No, I dinna think it's a good idea. It might even make things worse than they are now."

"I don't believe any of us could stand that, Mr. Scott," said Spock-uhura.

"That's for certain," agreed Kirk-sulu. "Things are going to be hard enough to cope with as they stand." He faced Scott again. "I don't expect miracles, Scotty. How long before you can localize and repair the troubled sections?"

Scott glanced down at the tiny panel, which had suddenly assumed enormous significance. "I kinna say for certain, sir. At least a couple of days. I dinna want to take a chance with you all in the transporter until I'm sure as I can be that I've fixed it."

"A couple of days?" Uhura-kirk glanced down at her massive—to her—linear shape. "I don't know if I can handle a couple of days in this body, Mr. Scott."

"I'm afraid you'll have to, Lieutenant," said Kirk-sulu meaningfully. "We'll all have to."

"But what about the conference, sir?" she wondered.

McCoy nodded. "That's right, Jim." He checked his own chronometer. "You're supposed to be down on Briamos for the conference's opening session in two-thirds of an hour."

"They're expecting Mr. Spock and myself," noted Kirk-sulu. He pointed at first Uhura's body, then Sulu's. "That means that the four of us are still going to have to attend. It's too late to change designated envoys, and I don't think the Briamosites would accept anyone below captain's rank as a designated ambassador."

"But how are we going to manage, sir?" wondered Sulu-spock. "It doesn't seem possible."

"It *has* to be possible, Mr. Sulu. We can't ask for a postponement of the conference time without offending the Briamosites, and even if we could there's no guarantee that Scotty will be able to fix the transporter and put us back in our own bodies," and he added hastily, unable to leave so grim a thought without hope, "in a reasonable amount of time."

"What precisely do you propose, Captain?" Spock-uhura looked on with interest.

"Mr. Spock, the captain and first officer of the U.S.S. *Enterprise* will be present at this conference." His gaze wandered to his own body (how strange to be staring at a self that was not a mirror image), now inhabited by the personality of Lieutenant Uhura, and to that of Mr. Spock, in which Lieutenant Sulu was currently residing. "So will Lieutenant Sulu—that's me. And Lieutenant Uhura—that's you, Mr. Spock." Uhura's head nodded once. "What you and I do is not particularly important. We're lower-ranking officers, attending our superiors. We won't be closely watched.

"Mr. Sulu, you and Lieutenant Uhura will be acting as principals in this little play. So your imitations will have to be much more convincing. Mr. Sulu, at least you're in a body of proper gender, one not unlike your own in build and musculature." He turned his attention to his own ghost shape. "The success of this pantomime, Lieutenant Uhura, and of the entire conference, rests on your shoulders—even if they happen to also be mine." His own eyes were staring back at him expectantly. To his surprise, he found he had to repress a slight shiver.

"For one thing," he went on, "you'll be operating under the constant scrutiny of the Briamosites. Now, Captain Kumara knows me, but not intimately. I don't know how much he remembers in the way of personality traits and habits from our time together at the defunct Interspecies Academy. Probably not a great deal. But you'll have hormonal and other physical responses, the normal reactions of a male human body, to cope with. Some of them may surprise you at unexpected moments. Somehow you're going to have to act natural, nonetheless."

"I don't see that I'm going to have it that much easier, sir," objected a concerned Sulu-spock. "At least Uhura's in a human body. Talking about unexpected hormonal reactions, I'm in a Vulcan body. Already I'm feeling, well, itchy."

"It should not be overly difficult, Lieutenant," Spock-uhura insisted quietly. "All you have to do is act sensibly."

"That's easy for you to say, Mr. Spock," countered Sulu-spock testily.

"And you'll have to learn to control your facial expressions," Spock-uhura warned the lieutenant. "Those grotesque distortions of lips and mouth, the unnecessary head gestures must be eliminated if you halfway expect to . . . to . . ."

Spock-uhura halted in midsentence, staring at nothing in particular. "Most peculiar," the first officer finally murmured in Uhura's bell-like voice. He looked up at Dr. McCoy. "I presume, that my near outburst just then is what might be called an emotional response."

"Possibly, Spock. If so, it was very mild." McCoy considered carefully. "You raised your voice, but that's not necessarily an indication of emotional coloring."

Spock-uhura placed both hands against his forehead, winced at something that was not pain. "I feel most unusual, Doctor. My self appears reluctant to follow directions." Abruptly, the hands dropped and

Spock-uhura looked at Kirk-sulu primly. "This is going to be more difficult than I first assumed, Captain."

"It's not going to be easy for any of us, Mr. Spock." Kirk-sulu sounded firm. "But it has to be tried. Otherwise Briamos will ally itself with Klingon. I'm willing to chance anything to prevent that from happening.

"We have a couple of things going for us, however. Briamosites know very little of human behavior. Our ambassador," he added drily, "didn't strike me as your average human being anyway. So much of our seemingly aberrant behavior can probably be explained away, if we do anything awkward. It will be more difficult to fool the Klingons, but they think all humans are a little crazy in their behavior anyhow."

"That is not entirely a Klingon assessment," noted Spock-uhura pointedly. "The present situation would only tend to reinforce that belief."

"We might stall the Briamosites for an hour or so now, Mr. Spock." Kirk-sulu looked thoughtful. "We have to. We're going to need that hour to give ourselves a crash course in each other. But for several days? No, never." He walked over to confront his own body.

"Lieutenant Uhura?"

"Yes, sir," his own voice, but an oddly higher tenor, responded promptly.

"You are going to have to become me. At least, you're going to have to well enough to fool the Briamosites and the Klingons. At least our voices weren't switched. You're speaking with my vocal cords and my lungs. You've served as acting captain several times. This is another of those times, only you're going to have to be more than just acting captain. You're going to have to be Acting Captain James T. Kirk."

"I'll do my best . . . Lieutenant," she replied. Both of them smiled.

It was good to see himself looking so confident, Kirk thought a little crazily. He still felt as if he were talking in a dream. Any minute now they would all wake up, back in their own bodies, ready for the conference— everything all right again.

Then he realized his exuberance might be due in

part to the fact that he was in a more youthful, responsive body. They would have to watch for subtle as well as blatant differences like that during the conference.

"We're all going to have to exercise some to get used to our new bodies," he went on. "Our strides, as Lieutenant Uhura has pointed out, are different now. So are our reaches. I can't have myself, meaning you, Lieutenant Uhura, reach for a stylus only to miss it and clutch empty air. Enough errors of that sort and sooner or later the Klingons would catch on that something's definitely wrong with us. Once that happened, they would find ways to take advantage of us, to our detriment regarding the Briamosites."

He turned to Spock's watching form. "As for you, Lieutenant Sulu, you're going to have to talk like a Vulcan, think like a Vulcan, act like a Vulcan."

"I'll manage somehow, sir," Sulu-spock replied calmly. "I mean," and he seemed to stand a little straighter, "I will endeavor to execute my assignment to the best of my abilities, Captain."

"There is no need to overdo it, Lieutenant," cautioned Spock-uhura mildly.

"Let's move to the main briefing room," Kirk-sulu instructed them. "We'll work on our individual acclimatizing there." He turned to regard the watching McCoy and Scott. "Scotty, you get to work on that panel." He indicated the tiny board which had caused all the trouble. "Requisition all the technical assistance you need."

"Aye, Captain. Maybe we'll get lucky." There was more enthusiasm in his voice than in his thoughts.

Kirk-sulu's gaze shifted. "Bones?"

"Yes, Jim."

"What kinds of side effects can we expect to encounter from now on?"

"Besides the obvious ones of getting used to a strange body, Jim, of walking easily and reaching normally and other physical activities, there may be mental shifts of the kind Mr. Spock just experienced." He looked helpless. "I can't predict what else might happen."

"I know that, Bones, but speculate the best you can."

The *Enterprise*'s chief physician thought a moment, aware of concerned eyes on him, eyes that were slightly haunted. "You personally shouldn't have too much trouble, Jim. You're in a human male body not greatly different from your own. You might have to concentrate on restraining yourself in certain situations."

"Restraining myself how, Bones?"

"You're operating a considerably . . . well, not considerably," he hurriedly corrected himself, "but younger body than the one you're used to. It will react faster, move more rapidly than your own—as excellently conditioned as that one is.

"You already brought up reaching for something and coming up short. It works both ways. You have to be careful not to reach for something in a hurry. Your hands are liable to get there before your mind thinks they will. You could hurt or at least embarrass yourself."

"What else?"

"Listen. I think you can all cope with the physical changes," McCoy said convincingly. "It's the other problems that worry me. Your mind, Jim. How do you feel mentally? Can you remember everything?"

"Everything I try to," Kirk-sulu informed him.

McCoy looked pleased. "Then the personality transfer extends to full memory as well. That should make things easier. You'll have it easiest of all, Jim."

"What about the others?"

McCoy walked over, confronted Spock's body. "Lieutenant Sulu?"

"Yes, sir?"

"I wish I had some practical advice to give you, but I don't. How do you feel?"

"A little funny, Doctor. But it's not overpowering me. I can handle it." He frowned, then hastily wiped the expression from his face. "I just feel generally . . . well, not depressed, exactly. But dull—as if, as if I can't get excited or sad about anything. It's not that the laughter isn't in me. It's there, in my mind. But . . . for instance, I was trying to think of something funny to say just now, when you spoke about retaining our memories. I thought of an old joke that applies, and it's one that usually breaks me up. I recognized the humor in it, recognized it's as funny as ever, but . . . I couldn't laugh."

"Vulcan control," said McCoy, without a trace of a smile. "Try, Sulu. Think of the joke again. I want to make certain your own mind isn't in danger of being submerged in something alien you can't handle. See if you can consciously override the endocrinal suppression."

Sulu struggled with himself. Then a faint smile appeared on the face of Mr. Spock. It widened slightly, and the first officer laughed. It was a little forced, but a laugh nonetheless.

"Please don't do it again, Lieutenant," Spock-uhura requested. "The unnatural sight makes me ill."

"I don't think he will, Spock," Kirk-sulu told his first officer. "Bones, does that convince you that Sulu will keep control of his thoughts?"

McCoy nodded.

"Good. From now on, Lieutenant Sulu, you're going to be a model Vulcan, aren't you?"

Sulu-spock nodded, once. "As phlegmatic and poker-faced as possible, sir."

Spock said nothing. McCoy turned, walked over to confront Uhura's form. He had to consciously lower his gaze, so used was he to staring *up* at the first officer.

"And what about you, Spock? How are you coping?"

"Adequately, Doctor," came the lilting response from Spock-uhura. "But some of the sensations I am experiencing are truly remarkable. It is an intriguing experience, one filled with ample opportunities for discovery. But I fear I may experience some physical difficulties, contrary to your primary concern over our mental reactions. My thoughts are reasonably lucid, my control over them seems firm. But this physical configuration is sufficiently, radically different from my natural self. I'm afraid I find it a bit clumsy."

"Clumsy?" Uhura-kirk looked upset. "What do you mean, 'clumsy,' Mr. Spock?"

"No offense is intended, Lieutenant. It is clumsy only to me. For example, I find that I must cope with a considerably different and to me not especially efficient distribution of mass. It's a question of leverage and muscular control. I do not think I could ever master it, but I believe I will, with practice, be able to manage it."

"Speaking of distribution of mass . . ." Uhura-kirk began accusingly.

"That's enough, Lieutenant," Kirk-sulu said sharply. "You're not reacting the way I would, are you? You're the captain now. Don't forget it."

Kirk's face assumed an expression of embarrassment. "Sorry, sir. I forgot myself, for a moment."

"If it helps," Kirk-sulu added with a grin, "consider your predicament a temporary promotion."

"If this is what I have to go through to make captain someday," Uhura-kirk replied with a shy little smile, "I think I'd just as soon stay in communications. Don't worry, sir," she finished briskly. "I'll make an efficient you."

"I'm sure you will, Lieutenant. Neither Kumara nor his staff knows us well enough to recognize personal idiosyncrasies, so your imitations won't have to be letter-perfect. The way I sometimes rest my chin on one hand when I'm thinking, for example." Uhura-kirk promptly placed her chin on her right hand and looked pensive. "Or the way Mr. Spock raises his eyebrows when something surprises or especially interests him." Sulu-spock promptly lifted both brows and assumed a distinctly supercilious look.

Kirk sounded pleased. "That's the idea, Lieutenant. Only keep Mr. Spock's comments in mind and don't overdo it. Better to act like a humanlike Vulcan as opposed to a caricature." He hesitated, then went on. "It'll be best all around for us to keep everything—our words, our movements, everything—as simple and brief as possible. That will help to minimize opportunities for error. Opportunities the Klingons can only turn to their advantage. Let's go."

He turned and headed for the turbolift, walking carefully and working to adjust his pace to Sulu's slightly different way of walking.

"Bones," he said, glancing back at McCoy, "if you

can think of anything else we ought to watch for, let us know in the briefing room. And, Scotty, no matter where we are, even if we're down on Briamos and in conference, you get in touch with me—meaning Lieutenant Sulu—the instant you've corrected the transporter and are ready to try switching us back."

"Aye, Captain, you can be sure I'll do that. Even if it means insultin' our sensitive friends the Briamosites."

Moving like a quartet of drunken ensigns on leave, the four officers entered the turbolift. When the doors had closed behind them and the telltale alongside indicated the car was moving on its way, Scott turned his attention from the wavicle rectifier to the introspective Dr. McCoy.

"Did you mean what you said, Doctor, about them being able to handle their transposition?"

"I didn't see any reason to be overly pessimistic, Scotty." He looked concerned. "But I don't know, I just don't know . . . There are several psychology tapes I've got to run through. In case any problems do arise, I want to be prepared to treat them as best I can. Let's just say," and he gestured at the little rectangle of complex circuitry Scott was holding so carefully, "that the best thing for them would be to fix the transporter and put all of them back in their own bodies." He turned, his gaze traveling to the turbolift doors behind which his fellow officers—and friends—had departed. "Dual-personality delusions are easily treatable, Mr. Scott, but when there's a physical as well as mental basis for a psychosis, then I can't help but worry . . ."

Neither officer said another word. McCoy led Chapel and the rest of the murmuring medical team into the returned turbolift. Scott turned to the second engineer standing expectantly nearby. He held the almost-dry circuit panel up to the light, turned it slowly over in his hands, tilting it this way and that. Then he lowered it, and sighed.

"Dastagir, tell Loupas and Krensky we've got a little job to do. Tell them I'll be right there to detail what's got to be done. Tell them to forget about their off-time. No one in Engineering's going off-time until this cursed piece of electronic guts is turned right-side up again."

"Yes, sir." Second Engineer Dastagir moved to the intercom to relay the chief engineer's instructions. Scott moved toward the turbolift doors.

And far below, the anxious Briamosites listened unhappily to the asked-for hour delay and wondered about the courtesy of their maybe-allies of the Federation . . .

XIV

Nearly an hour later the frenetic discussions filling the main briefing room were interrupted by an apologetic beep from the room intercom. Kirk-sulu moved to the desk, thumbed the receiver switch and acknowledged the call.

"Yes, what is it?"

"Mrr. Sulu, I— Oh, I'm sorry, Captain. We werre told and it was all explained forr us, but—"

"Never mind, Lieutenant M'ress," Kirk-sulu told her. "No need to be embarrassed. Sometimes I get confused myself as to who I am now. It's hard enough for us to cope here." He looked back into the room at the three familiar and yet not familiar forms, all discussing matters of great import among themselves. "I'm not sure any of us are easy at mind. That's our problem, not yours. We have to convince the Klingons and the Briamosites, not our fellow officers."

"That's what I'm calling about, sirr," the communications officer purred. "We just rreceived communication from below. I spoke with that Colonel-Grreeterr Pliverr, the Briamosite liaison? He was concerrned that ourr delegation had not beamed-down yet."

"Concerned or angry, Lieutenant?" Kirk-sulu asked.

"My imprression was of a perrson willing to extend concessions, sirr, but at the point of losing patience."

Kirk checked his, or rather Sulu's, wrist chronometer. "We still have a few minutes, according to the extension the Briamosites granted us, but Pliver has our interests in mind by reminding us, Lieutenant. Contact

Pliver and inform him we're on our way to the transporter room and should be greeting him in person in a very few minutes."

"Yes, sirr. Brridge out."

Kirk clicked off, called for attention. The discussion ceased and the other three looked at him expectantly. "We're out of time. Mr. Spock." Sulu-spock nodded. "Lieutenant Uhura." Spock-uhura smiled . . . weakly. "Captain Kirk?" Uhura-kirk said, "I'm ready, Lieutenant."

Kirk-sulu looked grimly satisfied. "Let's go to the masquerade, then." He led the way to the door and they left the briefing room.

Kirk-sulu and Spock-uhura stopped in the hallway. The other two officers did likewise. There was an uncomfortable pause. Then Uhura-kirk muttered, "Oh," turned down the hall, and started for the turbolift. Sulu-spock fell in alongside her, his stride natural and seemingly unaffected. The two "lieutenants," as was proper, followed.

"That's better, Lieutenant Uhura," Kirk-sulu told her. "How are you handling me?"

"All right so far, sir," Uhura-kirk replied. Kirk still felt he was listening to an echo everytime she spoke with his voice, his lips. "But it seems a little more difficult to concentrate." They entered the turbolift. "It's fighting the tendency of my body to pull me one way, when my mind tells it to behave another. The hormone differences, I think. I keep feeling emotions that I know are unnatural . . . but for this body, they're perfectly natural."

"Your mind," Spock-uhura told her, "is battling the captain's instincts. We will have to be on constant alert against doing anything without thinking first. One of us could be in full mental control over our present bodies, but while thinking of something else that body might react naturally, producing an awkward situation. This is a war with ourselves. We must take care never to let down our vigilance."

The turbolift deposited them near another of the personnel transporters, on the opposite side of the ship from the damaged one. Scott awaited them there. He had left reconstruction of the critical panel to his subordinates long enough to handle the beam-down of the captain and the others personally, this time.

Uhura-kirk marched over to the console, said firmly, "All right, Scotty, we're ready for beam-down."

"Very good, Captain. I—" Scott stopped, startled, to stare in disbelief at the captain's face. "Are you—?"

"No, Scotty, I'm still over here, where you left me." Kirk-sulu gestured with a hand. "You're speaking to Lieutenant Uhura."

"What do *you* think, Mr. Scott?" Uhura-kirk asked hopefully in the captain's familiar voice.

"I think," a dazed Scott muttered, "I'd better get that wavicle rectifier fixed in a hurry or there won't be a sane person left aboard this ship." He waved an arm weakly. "Go ahead, I'm ready."

The four officers moved away from the console and took their places in the transporter alcove.

"Is there a possibility, Mr. Scott," wondered Spock-uhura, "that we could be reintegrated into our proper forms when we emerge on Briamos?"

Scott shook his head slowly. "I seriously doubt it, Lieu—Mr. Spock. There's no question that in order to return you all to your own bodies you have to be reassembled through the altered path of the original rectifier. But if it means anythin'," he added, "I hope I'm wrong, Mr. Spock, and you're right."

"We can hope," Kirk-sulu murmured as the chief engineer energized the transporter.

"I hope you set down in a nice, quiet chamber somewhere where initial observation will be by as few Briamosites as possible, Captain," Scott said. Kirk barely had time to nod Sulu's head as the transporter took effect.

He felt the usual disorientation, the blurring of vision and thought. It was joined by an unexpected sense of fear. But it passed, and along with it Kirk's momentary worry that their experience had given them all a phobia against using transporters.

They rematerialized on the surface of Briamos. Kirk started to slump, caught himself—and stood erect more rapidly than he normally would have. Since he had been learning the past hour to compensate for a strange body, handling the slightly higher gravity of Briamos was easy. He saw the others adjust with equal swiftness.

Sadly, Spock did not get his wish. Unspoken exchanges between him and his companions indicated that they were still firmly ensconced in the wrong bodies.

Nor was the chief engineer's hope fulfilled. Instead of the nice, quiet reception room they had all hoped for, they found themselves standing on a tall reviewing stand covered with a green canopy and lined with pennants and banners, facing four tall, attenuated Briamosites, whose slimness was accentuated by their attire, making them resemble more than ever animated scarecrows.

All four aliens were elegantly clad in bright emerald uniforms. Red striping sliced across the lower third of both jacket and pants legs. They wore, male and female alike, decorative tiara crowns. Each of these was cocked at a different but rakish angle on their high skulls, and sparkled with multicolored cabochons of different stones. Whether the tiaras were a badge of office, a sign of rank, or simply an article of clothing Kirk couldn't decide.

Less attractive by far were the five figures standing on the other side of the Briamosites. Captain Kumara was flanked by four of his own officers. They wore their own dress uniforms and were a blaze of barbaric design and color. Perhaps they were more colorful, Kirk mused, but they were certainly less dignified, even a bit childish. Whether they would appear so to the Briamosites, of course, was another matter.

Kumara made a Klingon sign of greeting, smiled slightly at Uhura-kirk. "Greetings to you, Jim. We were worried that you wouldn't be able to join us."

"Hello, Kumara," Uhura-kirk said, even as Kirk caught himself. He had almost replied to the greeting. The transition from the familiar surroundings of the *Enterprise* to this vast open plain and reviewing stand had been abrupt enough to unbalance his carefully prepared Sulu-image. He had spent so much time help-

ing Uhura learn to act like himself that he'd nearly
slipped up. Fortunately, Uhura *was* prepared, and
she'd handled herself well already.

"In fact," she added, "I was worried about how
depressed you'd become if we didn't arrive. You are
sure you're feeling all right?"

Kumara responded with a tight-lipped little smile.

Kirk felt a surge of elation inside. Kumara showed
absolutely no suspicion that anything was wrong. They
just might carry the incredible impersonations off—if
their luck held.

"Greetings to you, Captain Kirk." Kirk recognized
the by-now-familiar face of Colonel-Greeter Pliver as
the tall Briamosite moved to gesture at Uhura-kirk.
"Sorry are we for whatever problem delayed you from
arriving at the appointed time, and certain am I that it
will not so trouble you again."

This was a veiled warning about punctuality, Kirk
knew, which they'd better heed. They had already
presumed on the Briamosites' version of courtesy once.
Another such request would push them into the poorly
understood realm of local insult.

"We had some trouble with one of our transporters,"
Uhura-kirk explained truthfully, without going into details. "I'm sure it won't happen again. Our delay bothered us as much as it did you, Colonel-Greeter. If
there's one thing I can't stand it is people who can't
keep their appointments."

A derisive snort sounded. It came from the knot of
Klingon officers around Kumara.

"It's not," Uhura-kirk went on, "that we had any
desire to minimize the pleasure of your company, you
understand. It was only that our transporter operator
disobeyed orders. He was reluctant to inflict the dis-
tasteful company of certain others on us. The person's
intentions were worthy, but his insubordination could
not be tolerated." She glanced toward the Klingons and
made a face. Kirk was amazed at how disgusted he
could look when he wanted to.

Her insinuations struck home. One of the Klingon
officers bridled at the hidden insult, but was restrained
by a dour Kumara. A tall Briamosite standing behind

Pliver made a small muffled sound that Kirk took to be local laughter. He forced himself to keep from smiling. Uhura's story had not only explained away their hour-long delay, it had apparently made them the first winners in the exchange of greetings. Of such tiny asides were powerful alliances forged.

"This is Sarvus, Leader of all the Briamosite systems, final arbiter of multiple-world decisions." Pliver introduced them to the elegantly appointed, two-and-one-half-meter-tall Briamosite who had stifled his laughter at Uhura-kirk's comment. "And Vice-Leader Chellea," Pliver continued, indicating the tallest member of the naturally towering alien delegation.

Leader Sarvus stepped forward, leaned like a willow to his right. His right arm curved downward to slap lightly against his slim right thigh.

"Pleasure in making your acquaintance," said Uhura-kirk. Kirk watched as his own body imitated the formal Briamosite bow-and-greeting, arm hooking down, back of the hand rapping the thigh. Uhura had gained considerable command of Kirk's musculature by now and she performed the subtly difficult movement with admirable smoothness.

Kirk started to relax just a little. Inspection showed that Kumara and his companions still suspected nothing. He found himself really believing that they just might be able to bring off the masquerade.

Uhura-kirk turned to face him and Kirk forced Sulu's body into an attitude of attention. "My executive officer, Mr. Spock." Sulu-spock stepped forward, nodded slightly in typically perfunctory Vulcan fashion, and said nothing. That was just as well, and in accordance with their plans prior to beam-down.

Uhura, occupying Kirk's body, would be forced to do a lot of talking. But there was no reason why the rest of them couldn't remain as quiet as possible. The less they said, the fewer the opportunities for making a fatal mistake.

"My helmsman, Lieutenant Sulu," Uhura-kirk went on. Kirk stepped forward, felt his strange body bow respectfully. "And communications chief, Lieutenant Uhura." Spock manipulated Uhura's body, stepping

forward to bow and in the process nearly falling over.
Clearly he still hadn't quite mastered the intricacies of
feminine musculature, particularly that of Lieutenant
Uhura, which would require more adjustment to handle
than the average female form.

He caught himself, dropping to one knee and then
rising hastily before falling flat on his face. Kirk forced
himself not to move. Instead, he watched for the expected reaction among the Klingons—and got a
pleasant surprise. None of them were looking in his
direction. They were chattering softly among themselves
and hadn't noticed Spock's slip.

But why should they be paying attention? Kirk reminded himself. Uhura and Sulu were only subordinate
officers, hardly worthy of notice. Kirk and Spock had
already been introduced. Kumara was looking over a
shoulder and conversing with one of his aides. Maybe
their present situation would have more advantages
than disadvantages, Kirk mused. He and Spock could
observe the Klingons closely, without being subjected
to similar attention. Kumara and his associates would
be watching their original bodies, now inhabited by
Sulu and Uhura.

He tried to overhear their whispered conversation,
and failed. It didn't seem important, though. One of
the officers was smiling the particularly unhumorous
Klingon smile. Certainly there was no sign they regarded Spock-uhura's slip as anything other than a
simple stumble.

Nor did the near fall appear to have bothered the
Briamosites. Perhaps they weren't quite as sensitive as
Kirk had been led to believe.

"Leader Sarvus will now speak," announced Colonel-
Greeter Pliver portentously. This was the signal for
Klingon and Federation officers alike to forgo their
own conversations and stand attentively.

The Briamosite leader withdrew a small book from
one breast pocket, opened it to the first page, and began to read. The speech was long, but the pages turned
quickly. It was a carefully worded, thoughtfully
prepared speech. It expressed feelings of friendship for
both the Federation and Klingon peoples, declared a

desire for extensive future relations of mutual benefit, and promised not so much as a grain of sand to either side in return for concessions and benefits the Briamosites were seeking for themselves.

Clearly the local precepts of diplomacy were as fully evolved as Briamosite technology. They were in no hurry to join either the Federation or Klingon, and it would take considerable persuasion to change their minds. Nor could they be fooled. But Kirk knew that the pressures both sides were bringing to bear on Briamos to join one side or the other would eventually force them to do so.

The Leader finished, closed the back of the tiny book. There was silence. The Briamosites appeared to be waiting for something. Uhura-kirk turned, glanced back helplessly at Kirk, which was a mistake, though it would probably have been worse for all of them to continue facing each other quietly, grinning like idiots.

Kirk knew what should be said. "Yes, sir, a wonderful feeling which we would greet our hosts with in kind," he murmured expressionlessly. Uhura recovered quickly, turned and repeated what the captain had just said, in somewhat different words so that it wouldn't smack of an echo.

But the damage had been done. As Uhura-kirk spoke, Kirk saw Kumara eyeing the "captain" uncertainly. Kirk began to sweat, though it did not show.

"And so we thank you for your magnificent welcome, Sarvus of Briamos," Uhura-kirk was saying. Kirk felt the words sounded a little stilted, but he doubted the Briamosites would notice. "We extend to all of Briamos and its sister worlds the best wishes and hopes of the United Federation of Planets. I, too, hope that our future dealings may always be this pleasant, enjoyable, and relaxed, and that together we may continue as equals to extend civilization a bit farther into the galaxy."

Kirk let out an internal sigh. Uhura had remembered all the speech, once he, as Sulu, had jogged her memory. He'd kept the formal reply purposefully short, eliminating many flowery phrases the psychodiplomats at Starfleet Command had thought would appeal to their hosts. The couple of sentences were enough—and Uhura had still almost forgotten them entirely.

The Briamosite officials appeared satisfied, though, despite the brevity of Uhura-kirk's response. As she had recited the speech, Kirk had seen the initially suspicious Kumara relax and lose his puzzled expression. But . . . it had been a near thing.

His worst suspicions were confirmed as soon as Uhura finished. Kumara was always more dangerous when relaxed. "It looks like you're not feeling too well, Jim," he murmured to Uhura-kirk. "A bit nervous, perhaps?"

"As a matter of fact," Uhura-kirk replied quickly, "my big problem is that I might be too relaxed, Kumara. I don't have anything to be nervous about . . . unlike some people I know."

The speed of her response was good, but the wording sounded a touch bitchy to Kirk, and was hardly the way he would have replied. But it seemed to serve where it counted most, among the Briamosites. They sensed strength instead of Kumara's implied uncertainty. Fortunately, Kumara didn't have a chance to follow up his initial accusation, or he might have succeeded in rattling Uhura.

Colonel-Greeter Pliver stepped physically and verbally between Kumara and Uhura-kirk. "We have prepared a parade somewhat. We call them something else, but 'parade' will serve. This is our way of displaying for you, Captain Kirk and Kumara Captain, part of our culture in a way we hope is entertaining to you all." He waggled his ears, and Kirk recognized the Briamosite version of a chuckle.

"If paraders seem they especially happy, is not because they are glad to see you necessarily. For purposes of parading, today was declared local metropolitan holiday so paraders could take off workings to participate. Are being compensated for not working."

Uhura-kirk nodded slightly. That was the correct response. Kirk was permitted the luxury of smiling, although it was with Lieutenant Sulu's face.

Every time the Briamosites hinted at their sense of humor, Kirk was elated. It was one area where the

Klingons couldn't hope to compete, lacking much of any kind of humor other than the sadistic. However, he cautioned himself, the grin fading, it would be better not to count on the aliens reacting in any predictable fashion until the conference got underway and he had a chance to see how their hosts reacted to serious matters.

A great fanfare of brassy but bizarre music rolled across the grassy sward in front of the reviewing stand they stood on. It sounded like violins and organs competing with damp bagpipes. At a signal from Pliver, the visitors followed the Briamosite leaders out from under the concealing canopy. Kirk took in their surroundings.

The metal-and-wood reviewing stand was nothing extraordinary, a simple construction designed to be functional rather than impressive. Across the open green-blue field Kirk saw spires, lofty and attenuated like the Briamosites themselves, rising from the distant resort town where the conference hall was located. A curving slice of deep azure, like a blue plate viewed almost edge-on, showed where the ocean of the northern hemisphere backed onto the town.

The fanfare became a rather dizzy march. Variously dressed ranks and clusters of well-organized Briamosites strode back and forth in front of the parade stand. Their long limbs swung supplely as they walked.

The four Briamosite leaders beamed approvingly as each new group appeared. Uhura, using Kirk's body, dutifully tried to mimic their appreciation. It wasn't easy. Nothing was spectacular about the parade, though the Briamosites appeared to feel otherwise.

After the parade had run for half an hour and there was still no end in sight to the flag-waving, uniformed ranks before them, the inflexible Klingons were beginning to twitch noticeably. Kirk knew that the sight of "inferior" beings passing in seemingly unending waves before them was enough to crack even Klingon self-control. One officer snapped at another who was crowding him too closely, and only a harsh, single word whispered by Kumara kept them from fighting on the stand.

The parade continued for another two hours. By

then Kirk could almost feel sympathy for Kumara, who looked about ready to scream. When the last rank of marchers had faded across the plain, the final banner receded into the distance, Leader Sarvus turned to both visiting captains. He wore a blank expression but his ears fidgeted happily, the Briamosite version of a politician who has just surveyed his constituents and seen a healthy majority of favorable votes.

"Gentlesirs, what think you? You have just seen forty-five (untranslatable noun) representing all the continents of the several worlds of the United Systems of Briamos."

"Very impressive," Kumara lied quickly, always first to flatter.

"Very much so," said Spock-uhura, "I wish only we could see it over again."

The comment produced pleased fluttering from the ears of the four Briamosite officials. It engendered the exact opposite reaction from Kumara and his cohorts. The prospect of sitting through a repeat of the just-endured parade was almost more than they could bear.

Nevertheless, it gave Kumara an opportunity to display his remarkably un-Klingonlike diplomacy. "We also would enjoy a repeat," he said with a perfectly straight face, "but too much pleasure in a single day dulls one's mind for more serious endeavors. Hopefully another day."

"No doubt you are right," an impressed Leader Sarvus admitted. "Until tomorrow, then, at the conference hall within the town, at the appointed time. You will transporter coordinates for the conference place be given."

One of the Klingons stepped forward to huddle with Colonel-Greeter Pliver. After a moment's hesitation, too brief to cause comment, Kirk-sulu moved to join them to record the coordinates.

"These will bring you down by the lakeshore, in the chamber itself within the building," Pliver told them after they had both noted the series of numbers that would tell their respective transporter computers where to set them down. "The structure itself is not an official one, but part of a large recreational complex, so your surroundings may a bit informal seem."

"We are looking forward," Leader Sarvus was saying to Kumara and Uhura-kirk, "to hearing the arguments and persuasions of both your governments." For a moment the supreme leader of the Briamosite peoples looked troubled. "Actually we do not seek an alliance so soon, but external considerations seem to be forcing us inexorably in that direction. I need hardly tell you both," he cautioned more firmly, looking at each captain in turn, "to present the strongest arguments you can muster. The Council of Greater Briamos will base its decision on the evidence you present to us in these coming few days. Once concluded, we of Briamos will abide permanently by that decision."

"All of us are looking forward to the first session," said Sulu-spock.

"Until tomorrow-time, then," murmured Uhura-kirk softly.

"Yes, until tomorrow." Kumara responded now to one of his officers, who called for him to move aside so they could be transported up to their ship. Unable to resist a last stab, Kumara half smiled at Uhura-kirk. "We are in a hurry to return to our ship so that we may supervise maintenance procedures, Jim. That is a function treated with notorious sloppiness in the Federation, a characteristic of most Federation activities—as anyone can tell by looking at the *Enterprise*."

"Our damages would not have been incurred," Uhura-kirk responded loudly, for the benefit of attentive Briamosite officials as much as for Kumara's ears, "*despite* interference with navigational beacons, if we hadn't been so involved with the recent recovery of an interesting artifact. An artifact," she said, directing her words now to the Briamosite leader Sarvus, "which we will present for your edification and inspection during the conference, sir."

Kumara looked dubious and curious all at once. "What sort of artifact?" But Uhura-kirk didn't get the opportunity to reply.

The Leader was speaking. "We not really are interested in archeological matters right now, Captain Kirk.

There are far more important matters to be dealt with."

"I believe you'll be interested in *this* artifact," Uhura-kirk insisted. "It is, in a way, part of our presentation. A means of showing you the thoroughness with which we of the United Federation explore our own worlds and those around us. The artifact will not take up much space, and will be an interesting diversion to all attending the conference." She noticed the Klingons staring at Kirk's body. "*You* should find it interesting also, Captain Kumara."

The Klingon commander looked interested in spite of his attempts to appear otherwise. What sort of trick did Kirk have up his braided sleeves this time? Why haul an old bottle or some such relic into as critically balanced a conference as this one?

Kirk-sulu noted the effect of Uhura's words on the Klingon captain, but didn't smile. They had already gotten something out of the Slaver stasis box, and without even having to display it. Kumara was worried about the mysterious artifact. Good! The more it troubled him, the less ordered his dangerously fertile mind would be, and the fewer opportunities for creating mischief of his own he would have.

"As you say, Jim," the Klingon finally finished lamely.

Kirk-sulu watched with his companions while the four Klingons dissolved, taking with them a Kumara so rattled that he had forgotten that by leaving now, Kirk would have the last word with their hosts.

True to her training, Uhura didn't waste the chance. "You must excuse our friends the Klingons," she said. "Anything new and alien to their own culture makes them uneasy."

There, that was a suitably neutral statement, but one loaded with overtones they would begin to work on the Briamosites' minds after this day was done.

They were ready to beam-up. Kirk almost pulled out his own communicator. Fortunately, Sulu-spock reacted fast and did the same a step ahead of him.

"Mr. Scott?" Sulu-spock said into his pickup.

"Yes . . . Mr. Spock." Scott's response was broken by an infinitesimal pause.

"You may beam us aboard," Sulu-spock informed the distant chief matter-of-factly. "I have new coordinates to program in for our beam-down tomorrow."

"Very good, Mr. Spock. Standing by."

"Tomorrow—with expectations of benign developments," Colonel-Greeter Pliver told them with that odd little sideways bow of the Briamosites. His words and attitude were as warm as official neutrality permitted, but Kirk felt confident that the Greeter was on their side.

However, he reminded himself, it was not Pliver's vote that counted, but those of the three distinguished aliens conversing in low tones behind him.

XV

Somewhere elseness became the norm for a moment or two. Then they were greeted by the familiar surroundings of Transporter Room 3. A smiling chief engineer rushed around toward them from behind the transporter console as soon as the four had fully coalesced.

He went straight toward Kirk's body. "Captain?" His voice was hopeful, hesitant.

"Sorry, Scotty," Kirk had to say. Scott looked over at Sulu's shape, where the words had been generated. "I'm still in Mr. Sulu's body. All four of us are still switched around."

Scott fought hard not to look disappointed. "I tried a couple of little things, sir, with the console levels. As much as I could without risk of makin' things worse." He shrugged. "It was an unreasonable hope."

They stepped down out of the alcove, walked over toward the turbolift doors. Scott stopped to gaze longingly at the transporter.

"We're still workin' on the original damaged rectifier, Captain," he informed them. "I've also been

workin' with the computer, on Mr. Sulu's suggestion
that we use your original recorded patterns to beam
you out and then back in—hopefully back in your
proper bodies." He shook his head sadly. "I still don't
think it'll work, Mr. Sulu." He directed his words to
Spock's watching form, where the helmsman's mind
was still housed. "But if the realigned rectifier should
fail for some reason, then we'll have no choice but to
try it anyway.

"Still, I'm afraid that if I send you all out and bring
you back, and you're still not correctly reintegrated,
you might never be able to get your own bodies back.
Overlapping pattern fixation on the false patterns
you're now using would prohibit ever reversin' the situation."

"We'll try it as a last resort only then, Scotty,"
Kirk-sulu agreed.

"I hope we dinna have to, Captain," the chief engineer told him. "You might all end up frozen in these
bodies for the rest of your natural lives."

Spock-uhura glanced down at himself, at the body of
the communications chief. "The prospect of remaining
forever locked in this form is indeed appalling, Mr.
Scott."

"I'm not thrilled about it either, Mr. Spock,"
Uhura-kirk told him firmly. "I'd like nothing better
than to, to repossess my own body." Her hands gestured at herself. "The chemical balance of this male
envelope initiates some of the most absurd reactions."

"We'll all be glad when"—he was careful not to say
"if"—"we're back where we belong, Lieutenant," Kirk
assured her soothingly. "Keep us posted on progress
with the rectifier, Scotty. Oh, how's the stasis box coming along? We'll probably take it down with us tomorrow."

Scott was glad of the chance to report some good
news. "All ready for you, Captain. It's on the bridge. I
couldn't put it in your cabin," he added a mite apologetically, "without forcin' the door seal, and I didn't
want to do that."

"It's just as well, Scotty. There's nothing to hide
from the crew, and I don't think I can get into my own

cabin myself now. The voice and retinal patterns that the door lock would recognize belong to that body," and he pointed at Uhura, "not to Mr. Sulu's, where I'm presently residing. If I need to get into my own cabin, Lieutenant Uhura's going to have to come along."

The four officers took the turbolift to the bridge. Although everyone on board the *Enterprise* had by now been thoroughly apprised of the quadruple body switch—mind switch, rather—it still took personnel encountering it for the first time a few minutes to get used to addressing Captain Kirk as Uhura and Sulu as Captain Kirk, and so on.

As Scott had promised, the stasis box was waiting for them. It rested on a small stand next to the left arm of the command chair. Kirk-sulu walked over to it, and was joined by Spock-uhura. "It certainly looks real enough, Captain," the first officer said.

Kirk had to admit that it did. Using Spock's descriptions of the original box, the engineering department had inserted something into the box which produced an encapsulating blue aura. The top of the box had been resealed by some exotic weldfill technique, as much art as metallurgy, so that with his face only a centimeter away Kirk couldn't see where the box had been opened.

Reaching out, he picked it up, his hands feeling a faint tingle from the false stasis field. "*I'm* convinced, Spock. But will it fool the Klingons?"

"Even sensor equipment will produce information insisting that the aura," and Spock-uhura indicated the box, "is a genuine Slaver field. The Klingons will not be given an opportunity to inspect the box closely. Furthermore, Klingon has encountered only one stasis box in its entire history of stellar exploration, and that was several hundred years ago. They are not as familiar with the artifacts as we are and so are unlikely to know enough to expose the fraud."

With that, the first officer resumed his position at the science station. The ensign he replaced couldn't help staring as he moved aside. He knew Spock was taking over, but all he could see was Uhura.

This caused Kirk to look around the bridge. The

captain was manning communications, and he, as Sulu, was seated in the command chair while Spock was serving as helmsman and Uhura was at the science station. That view of the bridge would be certain to set Kumara thinking. Instead, Kirk decided to give his Klingon counterpart something else to dwell on.

"Lieutenant Uhura."

"Yes, Captain," she replied in his own voice, from her position at communications.

"If you pick up any transmissions from Kumara's ship, or from the surface, acknowledge them but do so mechanically. Under no circumstances provide visual communication. And if the Briamosites or Kumara desire to speak to me, Lieutenant, you'll have to answer."

"I understand, sir," she replied. Kirk didn't think he could ever get used to conversing with himself.

So far everyone had performed admirably under impossible circumstances. Uhura had played Kirk reasonably well. It said something for the camaraderie that normally existed on board that they could imitate each other so efficiently. Kirk had to stay alert constantly, though, to make certain those imitations never degenerated into caricature.

They had succeeded in avoiding any serious psychological problems. Those might still lie ahead, he knew. Give the body's normal endocrine system long enough and it would begin to affect the minds housed in unfamiliar surroundings. The sooner the conference below could be concluded successfully, he knew, the better their chances would be. Meanwhile, they could only remain vigilant and hope Dr. McCoy's worries found no basis in fact.

Spock was walking back to his own cabin, musing on the intriguing but distressing events that had left him imprisoned in this cumbersome, awkward form. Thus far he'd been able to repress anything seriously upsetting. He could imitate—as long as nothing terribly drastic was required—human reactions. But he was still very much himself.

Before leaving for rest and recreation period, until

they beamed-down tomorrow, all four of the officers had gone over their personal needs with that other mind inhabiting their natural bodies. All indication of amusement absent from her voice, Lieutenant Uhura had warned Spock above all not to forget taking the several monthly capsules her system required, which he would find in the dispensers in her cabin. Spock assured her he would not.

It was difficult enough to face the possibility that he might have to live the remainder of his life in this human body. He was not about to risk getting it pregnant. Not that, he had hastened to assure her, his own mind could in its wildest moments conceive of permitting that to happen. But she made him promise to take the supplement capsules nonetheless. Spock could have quarreled with her on personal grounds. But since the communications chief regarded the subject so emotionally, he decided to humor her.

He stopped. Someone was standing in his way. Spock moved to go around him. The man, a tall ensign from organic fabrication whom Spock didn't recognize, moved to block his intended path.

"In a hurry?" the ensign said, grinning in a moronic fashion not becoming to a member of Starfleet forces. He leaned on one hand against the corridor wall.

"If you will kindly let me pass," Spock said with a touch of irritation.

"Hey, now!" The man shifted to block Spock's new attempt to walk around him. "I know you're a superior officer and all, but I didn't think you'd already forget about . . ."

It suddenly occurred to Spock that possibly all the crew, certainly not all those on long sleep cycles, had learned of the transformation of the four officers into different bodies. This ensign's familiar attitude toward a superior officer was decidedly unbecoming, but that was a matter between him and Lieutenant Uhura, a matter in which Spock had no particular desire to interfere.

Fighting the peculiar hormone reaction all at once surging through the body he inhabited—a fight which required the most vigorous application of mental discipline—he tried to explain. "I am not Lieutenant Uhura, Ensign."

The man stared at Uhura's face, heard Uhura's voice. His initial bravado turned to confusion, puzzlement. When he spoke he sounded a little hurt.

"Now, what's this all about?" the ensign broke into a wide grin. "You didn't always used to stand on rank."

Spock rushed on, hoping to spare this unfortunate individual any further embarrassment. "There was a transporter semifailure. It resulted in the transfer of the minds of your captain, your executive officer, and Lieutenants Sulu and Uhura into the wrong bodies upon reintegration. That is the present disturbing state of affairs. They will remain this way until Engineer Scott can trace and correct the trouble with the damaged transporter."

"Oh, come on, Uhura! What are you feeding me? You're Uhura . . . Lieutenant," he added, a touch accusingly. "Tell me I don't know how to recognize—"

"I happen to be Commander Spock," Uhura's voice informed the ensign frostily. "Presently I am inhabiting Lieutenant Uhura's body. Lieutenant Uhura's mind is located in the body of Captain Kirk. If you will take the time to contact the bridge, or any of your fellow shipmates who doubtless heard the announcement while you did not, you will find that what I am telling you is the truth."

The ensign's face ran through a remarkable gamut of expressions in a short time. "You're joking with me, aren't you? This is some kind of game you're playing." The man didn't sound as positive as before. "Look, if it was something I said—"

"There's an intercom." Spock-uhura indicated the grid-and-panel set into the corridor wall. "Contact whomever you wish and check what I say."

"All right. All right, I will," the ensign responded, with the air of one about to call a bluff. "We'll call this joke off fast." He thumbed the intercom.

"Excuse me, is Yeoman Anderson there?" A pause, during which the ensign smiled faintly and Spock-uhura stood quietly waiting. "Yes, Anderson? This is

Ensign Kearly. Hey, did something go wrong with one of the transporters recently? I heard this hysterical story that the captain, Mr. Spock and—"

A strong female voice at the other end spoke from the grid. "Yes. Don't you know about it, Kearly? Damnedest thing . . . I guess you must have been deep in sleep cycle. Seems that in trying to beam down to Briamos there was some kind of problem with the transporter. Rumor up from Engineering says that it was caused by that pulsar wave we ran through a while ago." The ensign's face, as he listened to this, was drawn.

"Anyway, it seems like everyone trying to beam down got all shifted around, wrong mind in the wrong body. It's hard to believe, I know, but I've personally—"

"Never mind, Yeoman." Ensign Kearly sounded a bit shaky. "I just wanted to confirm it." He clicked off, turned to stare at Uhura's form. He looked, and sounded, as if he were confronting a ghost. "Then . . . you really *are* Commander Spock?"

The first officer replied as gently as he could. Still, he was unable to keep all the irritation out of his voice. "Believe me, Ensign Kearly, this present situation is not more palatable to me than to you, or to anyone else—least of all Lieutenant Uhura."

"Yes, ma'am—I mean, sir." The ensign executed a hurried, harried salute, excused himself, and moved rapidly away. Spock was allowed to continue on uninterrupted, with ample time to consider the peculiarities of human interrelationships.

Spock's comment to the ensign about the unpalatability of the present arrangement was an understatement as far as Uhura was concerned. Presently, the communications chief was resting in her own cabin. A technician with special clearance had had to open it manually for her, since Kirk's face and hands wouldn't key the door seal any more than his tenor would substitute for her higher, more delicate voice.

Although the captain's body she was imprisoned in was in excellent condition, compared to her own she found it awkward, clumsy, and oddly unmobile. Funny, she thought, leaning back on her bed, how one could grow so accustomed to something like a body. After all, what was it but an envelope of flesh to provide mobility for the mind?

Experimenting in the privacy of her cabin, she tried to sing a favorite song, the one she had composed for her grandfather back on Earth. In place of her beautiful, throaty tones the room filled with an excruciatingly harsh, unmelodic gargling noise. It might have passed as a cry for help, but certainly not for music. She sat up in amazement that so grating a sound could issue from her throat.

There were any number of other things about her present body that made her feel uncomfortable. The best thing she could do would be to ignore them and try to relax. She lay back down again. The sooner she had her own body back, the better. The thought of spending the rest of her life in this lumbering masculine shape appalled her at least as much as did the prospect of spending the rest of his life in her body did Mr. Spock.

By the following morning, Engineer Scott could only report that the sensitive work on the damaged rectifier was proceeding as fast as he dared permit.

Kirk-sulu carried the stasis box in a large, unadorned container as the four prepared to beam down for the second day of conference, and the first real negotiating session. To hide their deception, the container had been made large enough to hold both the box and the false field it was generating, since a true Slaver stasis field would have appeared outside the walls of a smaller container.

A familiar but never comfortable instant of notbeing, and the four officers found themselves in a modest but impressive domed chamber large enough to hold a hundred people easily. The floor was composed of slabs of irregularly cut stone resembling gold-veined marble. The entire wall on their left was made of long slim panes of some transparent glassy material. Kirk noted that it appeared to lighten and darken to match the changing sunlight pouring into the chamber. There were probably occasional clouds outside today, he thought.

They walked toward the window-wall and he saw that the chamber and the building they were in were set on a hill overlooking a broad swatch of ocean and beach. Towering sandstone cliffs streaked with horizontal bands of brown, orange, and maroon lined an imposing headland in the distance. Small craft of unusual design and construction swarmed like insects within the quiet water of the bay.

Kirk recalled what Colonel-Greeter Pliver had told them about this being a very popular resort area, within reach of the capital city. Trying to imagine himself one of the happy, thin aliens cavorting in sand and water below, he wondered how many of the local honeymooners—assuming Briamosites had honeymoons—partygoers, or ordinary vacationers realized that an interstellar conference was taking place only a couple of kilometers away from them. Or if they cared.

Come to think of it, if a similar work-halting conference were being held on Earth, the average citizen would shrug and wonder if he might squeeze out another day of vacation without offending his boss. After all, the future of the universal civilization was a trifle compared to the travails and adventures of everyday life. Fortunately, Kirk knew, there were those who took the business of civilization somewhat more seriously. They became philosophers or artists.

Or they joined Starfleet.

A long *U*-shaped table was set up near the window-wall, just out of reach of the invading sunlight. The rest of the chamber was empty of furniture, giving it a spaciousness one usually felt in far larger halls. The two prongs of the *U* faced into the room while the curve backed against the window-wall.

Leader Sarvus and Vice-Leader Chellea sat at the apex of the *U*-curve. They were flanked by Colonel-Greeter Pliver, who now rose as the Federation representatives approached, and several other undoubtedly important members of the Briamosite hierarchy whose faces were new to Kirk. One of them sat particularly stiffly. His clothing and manner marked him as a military man. Empty seats, four to a side, lined the outside of both horns of the table.

"Greetings, Captain Kirk, Mr. Spock, and Lieutenants," said Pliver, walking around the table to shake hands human-fashion with each of them. He conducted them to their chairs on the near side of the *U*. The seats were a bit tight and narrow for the human pelvis, but the four officers managed—though Spock, in Uhura's body, had a difficult moment.

Pliver glanced curiously at the large box Kirk was carrying. "What does the lieutenant carry, Captain?" he asked, talking to Kirk's body. "The artifact?"

"Yes," replied Uhura-kirk. "We'll unveil it later." As Pliver seemed satisfied with that and didn't press for details, Uhura wisely kept quiet.

Kumara and his attending officers arrived a few moments later. They took the four seats on the horn of the table opposite their Federation counterparts.

The Briamosites promptly opened the conference by reasserting their humanlike characteristics. Every official present, lips firm and ears wagging like flowers in a strong breeze, delivered a substantial speech, including Sarvus and Chellea. No one intended that his part in this important occasion should fail to be entered into Briamosite history. In addition to a sense of humor, it was clear the inhabitants of Briamos were developed politically. So Kirk, Kumara, and the other guests listened while the officials of Briamos detailed variously the importance of the conference: what they hoped might be achieved by it, their desire to maintain friendly relations with both governments no matter which one they eventually entered into alliance with . . .

The self-important speeches, Kirk knew, were a characteristic common to immature races. Even the member races of the Federation hadn't entirely outgrown the juvenile aspects of government.

"I now declare open this conference," Sarvus declaimed at last. "We of Briamos look forward to hearing from each of you at length." Kirk tensed. The time had come for formal presentations, and serious business.

It was the signal for the opposing executive officers,

in this case Sulu in Spock's body, to rise in turn and deliver long prepared presentations. For Sulu-spock, the words had been constructed by the best Federation psychopoliticos at Starfleet Command and then relayed out to Starbase 25. Sulu-spock read the sentences mechanically, spelling out as clearly and persuasively as possible the advantages which would accrue to Briamos if they aligned themselves with the Federation.

Kirk knew the speech would have been more impressive and had greater impact if it had been delivered half extemporaneously by Spock himself, since Spock had the words fully memorized. But that wasn't possible. Kirk noticed that Spock, in Uhura's body, was following Sulu's recitation closely.

The Briamosites didn't appear offended by Sulu-spock's reading of the prepared statement. As Kirk had hoped, they seemed more interested in content than form. All Sulu had to do was maintain a posture of Vulcan detachment, keep his voice a monotone. That was easy enough. The only problem in rehearsing the speech back aboard ship had been to restrain Sulu during the more emotion-charged sections of the speech. After much practice he had been able to recite the words without overly emphasizing any of them. Just as he was doing now.

If anything, it was even flatter in tone than Spock would have presented it. They had decided to err on the side of reality rather than risk having Sulu reveal anything by trying to drive a particular point home.

From Leader Sarvus and Vice-Leader Chellea down to the lowest-ranking official present (a representative from one of the outlying Briamosite worlds), the assembled alien officials received the address quietly. Occasionally they would nod or jerk their heads in meaningful but indecipherable fashion, or lean over to whisper briefly to some colleague. They did not interrupt, with either applause or boos, or with questions or comments.

When Sulu-spock concluded the speech and sat down, Chellea responded with a short paragraph of thanks, then asked Kumara to present his side. The Klingons' executive officer acknowledged his captain's nod, rose, and loudly proclaimed the Klingons' hopes and intentions.

Kirk bristled at some of the claims and outright falsehoods contained in the speech, but restrained himself. First of all, it wasn't Lieutenant Sulu's place—the body he occupied—to raise objections unless his comments were specifically requested. Secondly, Kirk knew that they would have ample time later to counter the Klingon arguments and make objections of their own.

Looking smug and satisfied, Kumara's first officer concluded his speech in a burst of fiery rhetoric accusing the Federation of intending everything for Briamos from child-stealing to slavery, and resumed his seat. His smile shrank considerably when, much to the surprise of both parties, the Briamosite officials removed tiny devices from beneath their portion of the table. On touching controls, each instrument regurgitated long scroll-like strips of plastic opacity imprinted with dots and dashes and curlicues. Both Kirk and Kumara expected that their words would be somehow preserved, but they hadn't expected each official to make his or her own personal record. It displayed a thoroughness Kirk had not given the Briamosites credit for. He should have.

After thoughtful inspection of their individual scrolls, the officials looked up at their visitors. And the questions began. They favored neither side. The assembled Briamosites fired questions rapidly, almost impatiently, at the respective speechmakers.

Both Kumara's executive officer and Sulu-spock responded as best as they could. Once, another Klingon officer replied to a question from Vice-Leader Chellea when the executive officer seemed at a loss for words. That was what Kirk had been hoping for. When the Briamosites offered no objection to the new speaker, it meant that he, in Sulu's body, and Spock, in Uhura's, could now offer their own expertise during the questioning.

So as the questioning continued relentlessly, when "Spock" or "Kirk" appeared slow to respond or unsure of certain answers, Kirk felt this was more than made up for by the impressive speed with which the two subofficers, Lieutenants Sulu and Uhura, answered the queries. Indeed, even the Klingons appeared impressed by the literate, thorough responses the two Federation lieutenants provided in response to certain difficult questions posed.

Once, a particularly unsubtle inquiry was made by one of the Briamosite officials in regard to the depth and preparedness of the Federation's armed forces, in reference to something the Klingon executive officer had mentioned in his speech. Everyone was surprised when communications officer Lieutenant Uhura responded. They were more than surprised, they were astonished at the lengthy list of impressive figures, details, and placements—all unclassified—which were provided, seemingly with effortless recall.

Kumara in particular eyed Uhura curiously, wondering at the apparently unrehearsed expertise she had demonstrated in a matter not related to communications.

"Isn't it a fact, Lieutenant," Kumara said quickly, when Spock-uhura had finished reeling off the stunning array of statistics, "that the starship grouping monitoring Starbase Fourteen was removed only two months ago because that section and the races in it weren't thought worth protecting by Federation officials?"

Kirk watched Spock-uhura closely without trying to betray his concern. Kumara had concocted a tricky question. It was true, as the Klingon had claimed, that Starfleet forces had been withdrawn from that sector recently. But that had nothing to do with not wanting to extend protection to federated peoples in that area. However, it did show the extent and efficiency of Klingon intelligence.

Actually, the ships had been transferred to airdock for normal maintenance and overhauling and were scheduled to return to their positions in another two months. But it looked, if one viewed the matter as Kumara did, as if the Federation was guilty of indifference to the people of Sector 14, or at least of gross negligence. Kumara could argue that the reappearance of Starfleet vessels in that sector now would be a Federation attempt to cover their error and curry favor with the Briamosites.

Sometimes, however, when the best-laid plans of mice and men went awry, they could lead to equally efficacious new plans. Such was the case now, as Spock turned a physical disadvantage into an advantage. "I cannot answer you, Captain Kumara," Spock-uhura claimed. "A communications officer is not privy to such detailed information about military maneuvers. Since it doesn't pertain to my specialty, I can't confirm or deny your report. Ship movements are more in the province of navigation."

Kirk promptly picked up his cue. "I'll be glad to check on unclassified movements in Sector Fourteen and report back to this assembly," Kirk-sulu declared. "I do know that ships are often called from duty for standard maintenance." He looked at his own body. "Isn't that true, Captain?"

"I am not permitted to confirm information of such a sensitive military nature," Uhura-kirk replied, fast enough to earn an order of merit.

There! Those multiple responses countered Kumara's accusation while leaving the facts sufficiently ambiguous to forestall the need of a specific reply.

Kumara accepted his semantic defeat with good grace. It was only one of dozens of similar verbal battles that would be contested across the conference table before the day's session drew to an exhausted end.

The session went on into the early Briamosite evening, which was later in arriving than that of a normal twenty-four-hour human day. The setting sun of Briamos was turning the sandstone parapets across the bay to ribbons of grainy flame, and lights were winking on on the pleasure craft circling beneath them, by the time the questioning finally came to an end.

Uhura-kirk rose. "If there are no more questions from our hosts—"

Kirk-sulu broke in hurriedly, "One more item on today's agenda . . . Captain."

Uhura-kirk recovered quickly. "I was about to bring

it up, Lieutenant." She remained standing, gestured toward him. "The presentation and display."

Kirk-sulu felt relief he didn't show. Standing and picking up the crate they had brought from the ship, he moved between the table horns.

"A stand or small pedestal of some sort will be helpful, sirs," he told the Council, directing his voice toward Pliver.

The Colonel-Greeter wagged his left ear, touched a switch set into the table before him. A section of seamless wall slid aside, revealing a pair of huge, armed Briamosite soldiers. The Colonel-Greeter barked instructions at them. They vanished into the wall, reappeared moments later with a single-stemmed pedestal-table.

Kirk wasn't surprised by the presence of the armed troops. Such grim visages were present to insure that in the event the conference didn't continue in an atmosphere of sweetness and light, the Briamosite hosts would be protected from Klingon–Federation belligerence. Automatic weaponry would have been more efficient, but the presence of live troops would be effective enough, he knew.

"You can show it at any time, Lieutenant Sulu," Uhura-kirk told him.

"Yes, sir."

Picking up the container, he placed it on the pedestal and began unsnapping the side and top panels. When the last latch had been flipped, he touched a switch in the base of the container. Dramatically, the top and all four sides fell away simultaneously, revealing the glowing stasis box.

Expressions of amazement filled the chamber. They came not from the phlegmatic Briamosites, but from Kumara and his officers.

"What is this artifact you have brought to show us?" Leader Sarvus inquired, eyeing the box intently.

Kirk-sulu went on to explain about the ancient, extinct civilization of the Slavers and the isolated relics of their culture, the stasis boxes, which were occasionally discovered in scattered parts of the galaxy. As the story continued, several of the Briamosite officials wagged their ears in recognition and appeared more and more impressed. That meant that the wonders of the stasis boxes were at least known to the people of Briamos.

"As you can see," Kirk concluded, gesturing with Sulu's hand at the softly glowing cube of Slaver metal, "this stasis box has not yet been opened. It could contain an ultimate weapon, any kind of valuable device, or nothing at all. But to show you our good faith and our confidence in the people of Briamos, we've brought it here for you to see."

"Even though," Uhura-kirk added meaningfully, "we knew there would be Klingons present."

"It's a fake!" Kumara rose angrily, trying to divide his attention between Kirk-sulu, the box, and Leader Sarvus. "They wouldn't dare bring a real, unopened stasis box here to display on an unallied world. Especially," he added with a loaded grin of his own, "knowing that there would be representatives of Klingon present."

When neither Sulu-spock, Spock-uhura, or Uhura-kirk elected to respond to Kumara's accusation, Kirk decided to risk appearing a bit authoritative.

"If one of your officers has at his waist a standard-issue imperial science 'corder, you can see for yourselves."

Kumara stared curiously at Sulu's form for a moment, then shrugged, his mind too busy with more important matters to follow up the impossible suspicion that had briefly occurred to him. He eyed one of his subordinates. "Kaldin. Let him use yours." He looked at Sulu. "I assume you'd prefer to run the analysis yourself, Lieutenant, rather than let one of my men near your precious 'stasis' box?"

Kirk-sulu nodded, walked over to the Klingons, and took the compact instrument from the glaring officer who proffered it. Carefully he passed the device over the box, making certain the setting on the instrument was not set too deep, where it could pick up traces of the metal within, modern metals which Scott had used in constructing the Slaver-field falsifier. He also avoided the edges around the top of the box, where Scott had resealed it.

Then he turned and handed it back to the Klingon officer, walked back to stand next to the pedestal, and waited. There *was* a chance he might have mispassed the 'corder, that it might have detected a hint of the chief engineer's handiwork.

Apparently he hadn't. The Klingon officer read the readouts on the device, performed a few hasty calculations with a separate instrument, conferred with the other subofficer on his left, and turned a grim, solemn gaze on his captain.

"Sir, the box is Slaver metal."

"You're certain of that, Kaldin?" Kumara asked tensely.

"There can be no mistake with these readings, Captain," Kaldin insisted, gesturing with the 'corder. He extended the hand holding the device. "Slaver metal cannot be faked. Even if it could, the metal readings translate according to their nuclear bonds as being over a billion years old, and that *certainly* cannot be faked. To last until now, any metal would have to have been encased in a Slaver stasis field. Check the readouts for yourself, sir."

Kumara wrenched the small instrument away from the officer, glanced briefly at the readings and handed it back. When he looked up at Kirk-sulu again his expression was more speculative than anything else. "Very well. So you do dare. But how can I be certain that it is a real unopened stasis box? Simply because it's Slaver metal is not proof enough."

The conversation was beginning to revolve around Kumara and Kirk-sulu, a dangerous development. Uhura-kirk recognized the danger, spoke quickly to the captain. "Mr. Sulu, Captain Kumara is doubtful that we're telling the truth. Why don't we produce some facts he can't argue with. Let's open the box for all to see—right here, right now."

"Yes, sir," Kirk-sulu acknowledged. Turning, he took a small cutter from his waist and extended it into the field. Evidentally he was going to use the thumb-sized flamer on the box's upper rim.

The reaction was uncertainty among the Briamos-ites. Among the Klingons, who were familiar with stasis boxes and their properties, the reaction was much more predictable. They were on their feet, star-ing in disbelief, except for one officer who was hunting frantically for a place to hide.

All of Kumara's usual poise temporarily deserted him. He was waving both hands wildly, his gaze switching nervously from Uhura-kirk to the ready Kirk-sulu. "Wait . . . ! Jim, have you gone mad?"

Kirk-sulu activated the miniature cutter and moved the high-intensity, dark blue flame closer to the metal of the box.

Desperately Kumara whirled to face Leader Sarvus. "Sir, I beseech you, stop this! The humans have gone crazy. You can't just open a Slaver stasis box with some crude tool. It could set off a disruptor bomb or some other ingenious Slaver trap within the box. A special device is required to open the box safely." He turned disbelieving eyes back to Kirk-sulu and the threatening little flame. "We could all be killed!"

"You want proof, we're going to give it to you," said Uhura-kirk indifferently. "Existence is a game of chances. We're not afraid."

"Just the same, Captain Kirk," urged Leader Sarvus, a mite shakily, "we would prefer that if there is any truth in what Captain Kumara says, you do not demon-strate your courage so recklessly. There is no need." He indicated the box with a long, graceful arm. "*I* be-lieve you."

"As you wish, sir." Uhura-kirk looked toward the box. "Never mind, Lieutenant Sulu."

"Yes, sir." Kirk-sulu flicked off the cutter, replaced it at his waist. He fought to keep from grinning at the look of relief that appeared on Kumara's face. Well, he could hardly blame him. If their positions had been re-versed, he doubted he would have been crazy enough to try and call the box bluff.

"It is true, honored leader," Uhura-kirk was telling Sarvus, "that a Slaver stasis box must be opened care-fully. But there is no need to be concerned when the openers have confidence in their abilities. A stasis box is nothing more than a simple technological toy. Its age doesn't imbue it with any mystic properties. It's all a matter of basic physics." She glanced back at Kirk-sulu. "Isn't that right, Lieutenant?"

Kirk-sulu nodded, then reached out and gave the stasis box an impressive little shove. The box and aura fell to the hard, polished floor. This was a calculated risk, designed to demonstrate beyond argument for the benefit of the Briamosites how courageous and self-assured the representatives of the Federation were.

Of course, if Scott's aura-simulator should break loose inside the metal container, and the aura vanish without any other sign of disruption, Kumara and his colleagues could turn from frightened to threatening. But Kirk was worrying needlessly. Mindful of the captain's pre-set plans, the ship's chief engineer had secured the box's fake components tightly. The box bounced, but its blue halo continued to glow steadily.

The two Klingon subofficers yelped despairingly and dove behind their seats. Kumara's executive officer winced visibly, but held his position. Kumara did likewise, but his hands tightened on the edge of the table.

Kirk-sulu approached the box. He gave it a short kick. It went bumping and bouncing toward the Federation side of the table, while a couple of Klingon officers orchestrated each bounce and tumble with appropriate moans.

"I do wish," Kumara finally felt compelled to request, "that you wouldn't let him do that, Jim."

"All right." Uhura-kirk smiled. "I think we've amply demonstrated relative values of, well, not courage, but confidence."

"Insanity, you mean," Kumara whispered by way of reply, his eyes still fixed to the box.

"Lieutenant?"

Kirk-sulu picked up the stasis box, placed it on the table in front of his chair, and sat down.

Glowering furiously but helpless to do anything, the Klingon officers resumed their seats.

Leader Sarvus rose, placed both hands and long, limber fingers on the table before him as he regarded Kirk and Kumara. "The Council will retire for private discussion of today's session, gentlebeings. We must debate among ourselves all that has been told and . . . shown to us. Everything will be considered. If you desire them, refreshments will be brought to you. Since we may require additional information or elaboration of material already put to us, we request that you do not leave until we formally adjourn this meeting."

"That's fine with us," said Uhura-kirk pleasantly, after a rapid and unnoticed glance over at Kirk-sulu, who nodded confirmation of the Leader's request.

"And to us," rumbled Kumara, still eyeing the stasis box as if he expected it to leap across the open space between them and blow up in his face.

"We will return in," and the leader named a figure that corresponded to about two Federation hours. If Kirk's suspicions regarding Briamosite politics were even partly correct, the figure Sarvus mentioned was decidedly optimistic. He didn't expect the Briamosite council to conclude their deliberations in double the indicated time.

Not that that bothered him. He was prepared to wait. Events had proceeded well for the Federation. A glance at Spock-uhura showed that his first officer was also optimistic about the outcome of the conference.

There was a rustling of soft-legged chairs as the various Briamosite officials slid away from the conference table. A panel in the curving wall slid aside and the officials disappeared into an unsuspected chamber. That left the four Klingons and four Federation officers seated quietly facing each other.

Kumara had turned and was huddled with his subordinates. They conversed in whispers. Kirk and his companions did likewise, glad of the opportunity to drop their mimicry for even a few minutes.

"Captain, I've never been so terrified in my whole life," Uhura confessed in Kirk's own voice. "I never used to know what stage fright was. Now I do."

"You were terrific, Uhura," Kirk assured her. "And you, Mr. Sulu. You make a very convincing Vulcan."

"Thank you, sir. I had an excellent instructor."

"I must add my own congratulations, Lieutenant," said Spock in Uhura's mellifluous tones. "You've imitated me quite convincingly. I must say it is a strange sensation to attend a conference and watch while one's own self replies to arguments, answers questions, and moves about independent of one's own thoughts. It is very much like a dream."

Kirk's estimate of Briamosite decision-making ability was correct. At least four hours had passed before the assembled knot of gangly aliens filed back into the conference chamber and resumed their seats. They looked exhausted, mentally worn, but satisfied. Clearly they had reached agreement on one or more points.

Leader Sarvus alone did not sit down. Instead, he made a complex gesture with both hands, his amazingly flexible hearing organs dancing like the sails of toy boats in a spring breeze. "The Council of Briamos has decided."

Kirk leaned forward in surprise. So did Kumara. Neither captain had expected a final dispensation this quickly.

Sarvus noticed their heightened attentiveness, smiled with his ears. "We of Briamos do not do things in haste, but we like to do them without of time being wasteful. We do not feel further information is warranted or necessary. Enough has been presented, combined with what we already have learned, for a lasting decision to be handed down.

"Toward the unsuccessful side, we wish no animosity." Kirk tensed in spite of himself. "We wish to remain friends with all. But it has been determined that it is in the best interests of the United Systems of Briamos to ally itself with the United Federation of Planets."

Kirk began to smile broadly. He glanced to his right—and what he saw killed the smile instantly. Fortunately, the Klingons were so outraged and excited at the Briamosites' announcement that they didn't notice Spock was also smiling. If they had noticed that inexplicable anomaly . . .

"*Ssst!* Mr. Sulu!"

Sulu-spock looked down at the insistent whisper, the smile fading curiously. Kirk grinned back, hugely, grotesquely, and pointed casually to the "science officer's" mouth. Sulu-spock looked blank for a moment, then shocked, as he realized what had happened. The smile vanished instantly from his face and he resumed the dour expression more suited to a Vulcan executive officer.

Kirk returned his attention to the rest of the chamber. No one had seen the unnatural smile. Certainly none of the Klingons had, or they wouldn't be raving with such single-mindedness at their Briamosite hosts.

"Sorry I am," Leader Sarvus declared in a firm, no-nonsense voice. "But Council its decision has made. We have all the factors considered and balanced in objective fashion. We see no reason to change that decision. Nor can you present any additional evidence which would lead us to do so." He paused to let the Klingons absorb that. "Until tomorrow when we will an official leave-taking have for both sides, is suggested strongly we—"

"I have some suggestions of my own," a furious Kumara broke in. He was wholly Klingon now, his veneer of carefully cultivated gentility obliterated by the brusque finality of the Briamosite decision. "Since you have chosen to display the irrational obstinacy of so many of the more primitive races, you leave me no choice now but to—!"

Kirk had his communicator out and was in the process of activating it. He was too late. Kumara had come to the conference prepared to deal with any eventuality, including the Briamosites' announced decision. The Klingon did not bother with a communicator, with orders or directions, but simply touched a switch at his waist.

A vast humming filled the chamber, the heartbeat of a huge yellow glow that enveloped various sections of the room. Members of the Briamosite council scattered in confused panic. At their cries, wall panels slid aside and armed, alert Briamosite guards rushed into the chamber. But there was nothing for them to do, no one for them to arrest, no antagonists for them to subdue.

The Klingons, the four Federation representatives, and Leader Sarvus of the United Systems of Briamos had vanished with the glow.

Kirk realized what was happening before they re-materialized on board the Klingon cruiser. So incensed was he at Kumara's action that he nearly spoke out of turn—and out of character. Luckily, his companions were as furious as he was.

Sulu, carefully maintaining his Vulcan pose, spoke first as waiting Klingon guards herded the prisoners out of the transporter alcove. His angry but controlled comments reminded the others that they were still imprisoned in the bodies of their friends and shipmates. "This is a direct violation of the Federation–Klingon treaty," Sulu-spock declaimed. "Such an action is tantamount to a declaration of war."

"I would hardly go that far," countered Kumara thoughtfully. There was no humor in his words, but he seemed less apoplectic now that he was safely aboard his own ship and once more in control of events.

The prisoners were escorted down a corridor and into an elevator shaft. "The Federation–Imperial treaties have power only within Federation—Imperial space," Kumara declared pleasantly. Kirk badly wanted to respond to that statement, but forced himself not to. It wasn't his place.

Uhura-kirk had to speak for him. "The systems of Briamos lie within the areas covered by treaty."

"That's so," conceded Kumara as the elevator moved. "However, within an inhabited, intelligence-dominated, technologically advanced system such as Briamos, the treaties have no force. Briamosite independence takes precedence over outside agreements. If we were acting outside the region claimed by Briamos, then all treaties would be in effect. Within their system, Briamosite jurisdiction has precedence," he added smugly. "We're prepared to argue the point with the Briamosites, not the Federation."

"You're basing this kidnapping on a legal technicality," Spock-uhura risked adding. "Submitting your specious argument to jurisprudence will reveal holes in it large enough to drive a starship through, Captain Kumara."

Kumara eyed Uhura's form curiously. "You dabble

in interstellar law in addition to handling communications, Lieutenant?"

"A hobby only," replied Spock-uhura, promptly shutting up. It was exceedingly painful, but Spock was going to have to force himself not to reply to the Klingon commander's continued perversions of logic. Lieutenant Uhura wasn't supposed to know about interstellar law.

"Don't talk to me of technicalities," Kumara countered.

"Technicalities!" Uhura-kirk exclaimed in disbelief. "You call the abduction by force from a treaty conference of your counterparts a technicality? Not to mention the kidnapping of the leader of an independent system."

"By force?" Kumara's lips curled in a Klingon grin. "No one has touched anyone. As for the other, we'll argue about it later. I have no more time to waste on subtleties."

That casual comment was far more chilling than any direct threat could have been.

The elevator doors slid aside and they were ushered onto the bridge of Kumara's ship. Several Klingon officers looked back briefly from their respective stations. One called out urgently, "Honored Captain, the Briamosite security vessels are converging on your position."

"They have received word then that we've invited their Leader to be our guest," Kumara murmured.

A curt alien sound, midway between a cough and a grunt, came from the vicinity of the Briamosite leader. Translation was not necessary. Its meaning was abundantly clear.

Kumara made a gesture and two of the Klingon soldiers prodded the tall leader. He moved forward reluctantly. Kirk watched, thinking frantically, cradling the stasis box under one arm. It had been beamed aboard with him, and there was nothing more he could do beyond grabbing it before some Klingon plucked it from its resting place in the transporter alcove. He wondered how much longer it would be before Kumara's attention switched from the viewscreen forward and the closing Briamosite ships, to the softly pulsing box Kirk held tightly next to his left side.

"Give me an open channel," the Klingon commander instructed his communications operator, "to the Briamosite ships."

A few adjustments to his instrumentation and the Klingon nodded to his captain. Kumara indicated that the Briamosite leader was to come forward, where he would be within range of the bridge visual pickup. When the leader refused, he was "assisted." Not especially gently, Kirk noted tight-lipped.

"They're your ships," Kumara said, indicating the converging shapes on the main viewscreen. "Tell them that you're in good health and that as long as they keep their weapons quieted you will not be harmed."

"Why to my people should I lie?" The Leader stared over Kumara's head, entwined his flexible fingers in resignation.

"If you insist on playing the martyr, then naturally I can't stop you," said Kumara shrewdly. "You can always be one later. I think we can resolve our present situation, if you don't find our hospitality pleasing. So let's discuss before we come to any final, fatal decisions, shall we?" He indicated the viewscreen again. "They can attack any time. Why rush your death?"

Leader Sarvus looked uncertain. He glanced back at Kirk-uhura for advice.

Uhura grew frantic, tried to look at Kirk-sulu without looking at him. But they had several simple, prearranged signals for communicating in emergencies without giving their altered identities away. One tap on the floor would indicate a negative, two taps positive. Kirk-sulu's boot stamped twice, nervously it seemed to any onlooker, and Uhura hurried her reply.

"Go ahead and tell your ships to hold back, sir. Let's see what Kumara has in mind, first."

The Leader's ears twitched sharply. "It shall be as you say, Captain Kirk." He turned back toward the screen, his gaze passing over and utterly ignoring Kumara. "As we have little experience in dealing with the things of Klingon, we must rely on the advice of those who know them better."

Leaning forward over the pickup, he gave the order not to attack. There was a wait. A report came from the Klingon science station.

"Scanners show that all alien vessels continue to maintain their positions, Honored Captain."

Kumara looked up warningly at Sarvus. "Tell them to pull back. They can keep us within range if they like, but they're close enough to make me nervous."

The Briamosite leader spoke into the pickup once more. Then the viewscreen showed the warships, now numbering an impressive dozen, moving away from the Klingon cruiser.

Kumara appeared satisfied, and turned his attention to Uhura-kirk. "Now it's your turn, Jim. You'd better talk to your own people. As soon as they discover you're not down on the surface, and learn what happened, they're liable to panic instead of reacting sensibly."

"That'd be hard on you, wouldn't it?" a bitter Kirk-sulu said. Kumara ignored the lieutenant.

"Any attack would of course result in your death, Jim, and that of your companions. Needlessly, as you'll soon see. Either that or we'd destroy the *Enterprise*. Neither possibility can be to your liking." He barked an order at the communications officer, who promptly switched to standard Starfleet intership frequency.

Kirk-sulu's foot struck the deck twice again. Uhura-kirk didn't even look in his direction this time as she absorbed the instruction. *"Enterprise?"* she said into the aural pickup.

"Scott here. Is that you, Captain?" The chief engineer's worried voice gave no sign that he knew he was speaking to Lieutenant Uhura and not Kirk himself.

"Yes, Mr. Scott. We have been kidnapped by the Klingons."

Scott started to reply, sputtering, but Uhura-kirk cut him off quickly. "Remain calm, Mr. Scott." (How fortunate, Kirk mused, that Kumara wasn't aware Kirk commonly called his chief engineer Scotty.) "We have not been harmed. So far, it seems we are not going to be. We are going to . . . discuss the situation soon.

"Leader Sarvus of the United Systems of Briamos

has been abducted with us." She added, for good measure and for Kumara's edification, "If it was only myself involved I'd have you arm all weapons and engage, Mr. Scott. However," and she looked back at Sarvus, "with the Leader of our new allies on board, we cannot risk a confrontation."

Kirk mentally wrote out a commendation for Uhura. She had managed to confirm officially that the Briamosites had now formally joined themselves to the Federation.

"Are you certain, Captain?" Scott inquired, emphasizing the "Captain."

"Mr. Scott," Uhura-kirk replied, "Mr. Spock, Lieutenant Sulu, and Lieutenant Uhura are all here with me. If any of them could speak, I can assure you they would give exactly the same orders."

That satisfied Scott that Uhura was acting with Kirk's approval. "Verra well, sir. But tell the Klingons not to try movin' a single planetary diameter farther out than they are now. If they do, we're goin' to open their ship up like a pre-stressed package of carbonated beverage."

Kumara chuckled. "Such belligerence!" The amusement didn't last but a couple of seconds. "That's enough," he instructed his communications officer. "Keep monitoring both *Enterprise* and local frequencies. I want to know if and when any of the involved parties contemplates aggressive action."

"Yes, Honored Captain," the communications chief replied efficiently.

Another officer called out. "The *Enterprise* is raising defensive screens, sir. Energy readings indicate that she is activating her phasers!"

"Calm down, Kivord," the Klingon commander said. "They're just warning us not to do anything without informing them first of our intent." His gaze traveled to Uhura-kirk and Leader Sarvus. "We have no intentions of trying anything without your knowledge . . . and consent."

Leader Sarvus recognized a negotiating cue when it was offered to him. "You mentioned we might to an arrangement come," he murmured resignedly. "What sort of arrangement? You must know there is nothing I, a single individual, can do concerning the decision of the Council."

Kumara took his time, walked away from them and sat down in the command chair. "I realize that we cannot force Briamos to rescind its verbal agreement with the Federation, no matter how much more beneficial an alliance with Klingon would be."

This time Sarvus didn't bother to sneer. "Whatever chance the Klingon Empire might have retained for future assignations with Briamos has been obliterated forever by your actions this day of," the Leader said woodenly.

"I'm aware of that." Kumara sounded disgusted. "Those who are foolish enough to join themselves to the Federation rarely manage to extricate themselves from their entrapment. The Federation has numerous exceedingly devious methods for insuring that captive peoples never regain their independence of action. Once snared by Federation lies, a race can never free itself from that efficient network of agents, lies, and deceptions.

"However, we can do something else. If we cannot convince Briamos of the efficacy of aligning itself with the Empire, at least we can prevent you from making the fatal error of joining the Federation. You, Leader Sarvus, will sign treaty forms declaring yourselves to be permanent neutrals. You will make no alliance, mutual agreement of cooperation, or material exchange of any official sort with either the Federation *or* Klingon." Kumara leaned forward intently.

"Furthermore, Jim," he told Uhura-kirk, "you and your executive officer Spock will acknowledge witnessing this treaty. You will sign, in your official capacity as ambassadors-designate, treaty forms to the effect that the Federation will not violate Briamosite neutrality or attempt in any way to induce the Briamosites to ally themselves with the Federation any time in the future." He sat back in the command chair.

"I think that's a reasonable request, considering your present situation, Jim. If you consent to do this, then upon the signing and registering with relay stations of the treaty articles, you will all be permitted to return to your ship and you, Leader Sarvus, to your world, free and unharmed."

"I . . . I don't know what to do." Sarvus looked hopefully at Uhura-kirk.

She responded, staring straight at Kumara, with the same words she thought her captain would use. "You expect us to give in to political blackmail, Kumara? If you kill us, the *Enterprise* will take you apart deck by deck. If the *Enterprise* fails, the Briamosite fleet surely won't. The Briamosites will know what you've done because you'll have to kill Leader Sarvus also. Once that's done, their alliance with the Federation will become stronger than ever. And there will be trouble on a scale you can't begin to imagine."

"Oh, I can imagine it," Kumara responded, unperturbed by Uhura-kirk's stormy reply. "I just don't think what you postulate could happen."

"You seem to place a great deal of confidence in the Federation's unwillingness to go to war."

Kumara executed the Klingon equivalent of a shrug. "A few officers lost here, a couple kidnapped there. That's not sufficient grounds for intergalactic war. Besides," he continued, smiling humorlessly at each of them in turn, "future political possibilities and the legality of the treaties you sign need not overly concern us here. What is actually at stake, now, here, this moment, is far simpler to grasp and balance: your lives. But there's no need," he added more easily, "to consider such extreme possibilities." The smile returned. "I can see that in order to convince you to see clearly, some persuasion beyond mere logic is going to be necessary . . ."

XVI

The Klingon bridge was silent save for the steady thrumming of instruments as the prisoners considered that first direct, ominous threat.

"This is the so-called civilization you considered allying yourselves with," Uhura-kirk said sadly to the towering Briamosite leader.

"Forgive us," Sarvus replied. "We were ignorant of true facts. That has now changed."

"One of our respective moral codes is not necessarily better than the other," Kumara observed, "simply different." He turned his gaze on Uhura's form. Spock regarded the Klingon commander calmly out of Uhura's eyes.

"Say what you mean," snapped Uhura-kirk. "Your attempts at rationalizing criminal behavior aren't fooling anyone."

Kumara ignored her, glanced at the Briamosite leader. "I think we can demonstrate the sniveling sentimentality of the Federation races in the face of danger, Leader Sarvus. It will serve to illustrate the undependability of the Federation in difficult situations. For example, it is enlightening to know," he went on, his attention returning to Spock-uhura, "that humans are absurdly irrational when it comes to threats to females of their species. All I need to do is threaten one of them. That one," and he pointed suddenly at Spock-uhura, "with bodily harm, and they will rapidly capitulate to the most unreasonable demands. Are those the kind of people you wish as allies?"

Kumara looked around the bridge, beckoned to one of the guards standing near the elevator doors. "Kora. Present yourself."

A massive Klingon ensign left his station and marched over. He was a young, hugely muscled specimen and stood nearly as high as Leader Sarvus's shoulders, towering over everyone else on the bridge.

"A little demonstration can be entertaining as well as instructive," Kumara said easily.

Uhura-kirk looked outraged. "This is barbaric, Kumara!"

"Perhaps. Sometimes old methods are best, however." Kumara glanced up at the waiting, silent ensign, then pointed across the bridge. "That one, the female."

Kora nodded, grinning wickedly.

"Not too fast, mind you," Kumara instructed the

bulky soldier. "I have to give our guests plenty of time
to change their minds about my proposal."

Sulu-spock took a step in front of Uhura's body.
"You can't let this go further."

"Why not?" Kumara appeared to be enjoying himself thoroughly. "I see no one who is going to stop
me."

Several other guards now focused their weapons on
the other three officers.

"It's all right, sir," insisted Spock with Uhura's
voice, as he stepped out to confront the Klingon
fighter. He looked at Kumara. "Let us proceed."

"Brave lady," the Klingon commander said. Privately, he was disappointed. She should be cowering in
terror, as obviously outmatched as she was. Well, Kora
would change her attitude fast enough, and perhaps
her face as well.

"Don't try to interfere, Captain," said Spock-uhura
to the real owner of the body he was using. "I'll . . .
take care of things."

Kumara stepped down out of the command chair,
gave further instructions to his fighter. "Remember," he
whispered, "I don't want her killed. Rearranged convincingly, yes, but not killed."

"I will be careful, Honored Captain," the soldier insisted. Kumara nodded, then stepped out of the way.
The huge Klingon advanced on Uhura's body, arms
outstretched.

"You can stop this any time you wish, Jim," he told
Uhura-kirk, "by agreeing to my requests."

Uhura-kirk looked agonized over the situation. Actually, it was a cover to allow Uhura a covert glance at
Kirk-sulu. When the captain appeared content to let
events take their course, she wiped the concern from
her/his face and watched the open space in the middle
of the bridge.

The Klingon reached out with a long, thick arm.
Spock-uhura's leg whirled up and around in a peculiarly forceful kick that battered the grasping arm violently to one side. The kick was followed by a hand
that thrust straight at the Klingon's solar plexus. Even

with Uhura's lighter musculature behind it, the well-directed strike carried plenty of impact.

Kora *whooshed*, looked surprised, and backed away clutching at his middle.

"Don't fool around, Ensign," ordered an irritated Kumara.

"I was not, Honored Captain," Kora growled. Glowering ferociously at Uhura's form, he approached more cautiously. The combatants warily circled each other.

This time the Klingon feinted with a kick of his own. Before he could withdraw the feint, Spock-uhura's hands came up in a strange way and caught the leg. They twisted, applying leverage as well as force. With a crash the Klingon fighter tumbled to the deck. Several of the other Klingon crew members murmured in confusion among themselves.

Breathing hard, Spock-uhura stepped back as the ensign slowly climbed to his feet. If Spock had been using his own body, Kora would not be getting off the deck. He was trying to compensate for lack of strength with skill.

"Watch him, Uhura," Uhura-kirk warned.

It was a deserved warning. Doubly embarrassed now in front of his crewmates and captain, the ensign had turned an apparently routine assignment into a personal vendetta. He advanced carefully, giving Spock-uhura all the respect he would a Klingon male.

Spock-uhura thrust with an arm. A Vulcan arm would not have been blocked, but Kora just barely managed to deflect Uhura's slimmer limb. Forsaking any hint of subtlety, the much bigger, heavier Klingon rushed past the extended arm, charging blindly into the communications officer's body.

They fell to the deck. Powerful arms locked around Spock-uhura's waist and began to tighten. Spock knew he would have to do something fast or the body he was inhabiting would soon pass out.

Bending and moaning as if in dire distress, he reached back with one hand concealed beneath the two entwined bodies. It came up behind the Klingon soldier, caught at his neck in the difficult-to-duplicate fashion which only a born Vulcan could truly master, and pinched.

The massive shape of the ensign went suddenly limp. Spock extricated himself from beneath the Klingon bulk, stood up panting, and looked around.

Puzzled and angry mutterings came from the Klingon crew members. One, another guard, bent over the unconscious Kora's body, threw a bewildered look at Captain Kumara and an even more uncertain one at the retreating form of Spock-uhura, who had moved to stand alongside his companions.

"Well?" an angry yet confused Kumara said.

"Ensign Kora is alive but unmoving, Honored Captain," the inspecting guard declared. "If I did not know better, I would say he has been somehow paralyzed."

"Impossible!" Kumara gazed in disbelief at Spock-uhura. "He must have struck his head on the deck."

"Face up to it, Kumara," said Uhura-kirk, "our Lieutenant Uhura defeated your chosen fighter fairly by Klingon standards, and by Klingon law you can't force her to fight again."

"Yes, yes, I know." Kumara was desperately trying to salvage something of the disastrous situation. A glance at the Briamosite clearly showed that the honor of Klingon had suffered in the eyes of an inferior alien race. That was embarrassing.

Then he brightened, having thought of a way to turn a defeat into victory. "I have done what I really intended, Leader Sarvus, which was to fool these representatives of a heartless government into displaying their true inclinations. They are dedicated only to the arts of war, as their attitude just now proves."

"How can *you* say that?" interjected Sulu-spock, stepping forward. "You who are of Klingon, one of the most militaristic societies in galactic history. You have no room for honest feelings, for the good things of civilization such as art and poetry and song!"

This wholly impossible emotional outburst from the *Enterprise*'s executive officer left Kumara without words. "Poetry . . . Ah, you mean the coldly logical mathematical precision of rhymes."

"Oh no, no!" Sulu-spock protested vehemently.

"Members of all Federation races are sensitive to all aspects of creative endeavor. Myself, I often prefer free verse."

Spock-uhura shuddered at that, but no one noticed.

"From the heartrending strains of Szygenic music," Sulu-spock was saying passionately, "to the loose mind-stanzas of M'radd of Cait. Some of those sonnets are so . . . so . . ." Sulu-spock wiped away a tear. The unfamiliar precipitation burned, but Sulu bore it stoically. "You'll have to excuse me," he said, the tears flowing freely now. "The mere thought of his poetry causes me to lose all control."

If Kumara had been flabbergasted by the diminutive Lieutenant Uhura's prowess at hand-to-hand combat, the sight of a sobbing Vulcan was unreal enough to paralyze him almost as completely as was the still-unconscious Ensign Kora.

Uhura-kirk jumped into the silence. "You see, Kumara, you can't win. You can't threaten us into signing those treaty forms, and now you'll never convince this gentlebeing," and she indicated the Briamosite leader, "that everything you say isn't a lie."

"No doubt there is to that," Sarvus declared with finality.

No one could tell if Kumara heard any of this. He was in a state of shock, first from seeing one of his most powerful warriors knocked silly by a delicate human female, and second by the sight of an emotionally upset Vulcan.

Finally he blinked, seemed to see them clearly again. "There are a great many things in this universe I do not pretend to understand," he declared softly, with more modesty than the average Klingon fighter, "and today's events are among them."

He turned to face Uhura-kirk. "I concede this conference to you, Jim. I cannot continue playing the game while I doubt the evidence of my own eyes. You have won a round, not a war. But while I do not know how you have done what you have done here, I still can win a greater victory. You may return to the surface of Briamos," and he smiled mirthlessly, "but *that* remains aboard." He gestured at the glowing cube beneath Kirk-sulu's arm.

"That's not possible," insisted Uhura-kirk, playing her part to the hilt. "You know what the Federation's reaction would be if we turned over an unopened stasis box to you."

"My dear Jim, how outraged you can be. You have no choice in the matter. I am not a believer in useless causes, so I will not kill you when there is no benefit to it. Briamos has married itself, sadly for them, to the Federation. Similarly, it is useless for you to insist on retaining the stasis box. It is allied to no one. It remains here, with me. I would rather have it than Briamos anyway." He threw Sarvus a contemptuous look. The dignified Briamosite leader was not affected.

Uhura-kirk turned to Sulu-spock. "Mr. Spock, your opinion?"

"It is a risk, Captain. The box hopefully contains nothing dangerous to the Federation. Captain Kumara is correct when he says we have no choice. He risks a major diplomatic incident over the theft, but that is his problem. We can do nothing except refuse transport. By moving within the field, we could conceivably kill ourselves, thus inviting attack by the *Enterprise* and Briamosite ships. But we have someone besides ourselves to consider." He indicated the watching Leader. "We cannot ask him to risk his life."

"Don't for me worry, gentlebeings," Sarvus said. "If you believe that box would be so valuable to these . . . creatures"—and he gestured at Kumara, who bristled but did not reply—"then I am here quite prepared to die."

"No. It would be useless," Uhura-kirk said, seemingly despondent but actually trying hard not to laugh. "Kumara would still have the box." She composed herself, faced the Klingon commander.

"We accept your offer because we have no choice. I'm betting the box contains nothing the Empire can use."

"A wise choice, Jim." Kumara was feeling progressively better about things. What matter a few systems? They had gained a Slaver stasis box! "Naturally,

the box may be empty. Who knows?" He waved at the
guards. "Escort them all back to the transporter room
and have them beamed down to their previous positions."

The four Federation officers and Sarvus were herded
from the room, Kumara's attention turned to the box.
Walking over to where Kirk-sulu had placed it on the
deck, he picked it up. Turning it over and over in his
hands he finally placed it on the floor next to the command chair, basking in its strong azure glow.

"Klaythia," he called to his chief science officer, "set
up a field nullifier."

"Immediately, Honored Captain."

"Perhaps this will contain the final weapon,"
Kumara murmured as he stared at the metal cube.
"The device which will enable us to achieve our des-
tiny and wipe the decadent Federation from this part of
the galaxy, so that we may expand as was intended for
us in the Great Scheme of Things." He walked around
the box, inspecting it from all sides.

"And even if it is empty," he concluded with delight,
"Kirk will have no way of knowing that. It will always
prey on his thoughts that he might have given us an
all-powerful discovery. At least, if nothing else, I will
gain personal satisfaction from this unfortunate conference!"

The instant the five former prisoners had rematerialized on the surface of Briamos, before the startled gaze
of two guards in the otherwise empty conference chamber, Uhura-kirk turned to the Briamosite leader.

"I hope you'll excuse us if we depart quickly, sir.
There are reasons to think Captain Kumara might try
to go back on his decision letting us go. We'll be safely
out of the grip of the Klingon transporters back on the
Enterprise. And some simple adjustments in your own
communications equipment will prevent him from
beaming you aboard also."

"No need to worry about that." Sarvus's reply was
calm, but his ears were semaphoring like leaves in a
hurricane. Other excited Briamosites were entering the
room, having been called by the two guards. Several

turned as soon as they entered, departing on the run. "I have just given orders for our ships to attack, assuming the Klingon beast has been foolish enough to linger within range of our weapons." He sounded curious now. "But why should the Klingon risk waiting here to try and recapture you? He has gained the valuable box. Surely he should be speeding away from this spatial vicinity to avoid pursuit by your ship."

"He might try to come back," Uhura-kirk told the Leader.

"We'll beam a complete explanation to you, sir," Kirk-sulu said, unable to restrain himself any longer. Ignoring Leader Sarvus's increasingly confused expression, he flipped open his communicator. "Kirk to *Enterprise*."

"*Enterprise* here," came the prompt response. "Engineer Scott spea—" There was a pause, then Scott added excitedly, "Captain! You're back on the surface. What—?"

"Tell you soon, Scotty. Beam us up immediately and prepare to get underway."

"But I . . . Aye, Captain. Stand by."

Kirk flipped off the communicator. While he didn't think Kumara would return on discovering that the stasis box had been opened previously and that the instrument generating its "stasis field" was a fake of Federation manufacture, he did not want to linger around Briamos to find out. The Briamosites could take care of themselves. While he didn't necessarily relish the thought of someone else destroying Kumara, diplomatically it would be better if the Federation wasn't involved.

Four pillars of multicolored energy filled the conference chamber. Beyond, tall pleasure-seekers enjoyed the warm waters of the cliff-cupped bay and the white gypsum sands, ignorant of the drama that had been played out during their vacation times.

Before his vision faded, Kirk saw the Leader of the United Systems of Briamos waving to them. His perpetually frozen expression had finally shattered, and he was smiling with his face as well as his ears, as if to insure beyond a doubt that Briamos and its sister worlds would remain a staunch and valuable addition to the Federation civilization for many centuries to come.

Kirk was no more disoriented than usual when he rematerialized back on board the *Enterprise*. Scott was manning the transporter console himself. When Kirk took a step toward the engineer, out of the alcove, he nearly stumbled awkwardly. It was an awkwardness, however, born of renewed familiarity. At the same instant he was looking down at himself, there came a startled exclamation from behind him.

"Captain!"

The voice and form were those of his helmsman, Lieutenant Sulu. But *he* had been occupying Sulu's body! And if Sulu was standing there, healthy and composed *behind* him, that meant that he—

Sulu finished the thought for him. "Captain, we're back in our own bodies!"

"So it would appear, Lieutenant." Spock stepped out of the alcove, looking expectantly toward the transporter console.

Scott trotted around to greet them, beaming with personal as well as professional satisfaction. "I tried to tell you, Captain, but you told me to beam you up *fast*. I figured that explanations weren't necessary anyhow. Besides, there was a *chance* it wouldn't work, that I hadn't made the repairs completely or properly."

"Unlikely, Mr. Scott, if you felt confident enough to beam us back up without warning us first."

Spock's comment was delivered with his usual seeming indifference, but Scott knew the first officer well enough to recognize a supreme compliment when he heard one. Spock's seemingly unconcerned statement meant more to the chief engineer than a fistful of written commendations.

He accepted it as matter-of-factly, however, as it had been given—one professional, high-ranking officer to another.

"I don't know about the rest of you," Sulu said, "but I feel like I'd been wearing the same set of clothes for twenty years and just had them cleaned for the first time."

"It's strange," Kirk agreed, "to be back in something you never imagined being without." He smiled tightly at his chief engineer. "Thanks, Scotty. Ship's status?"

"Ready to leave Briamos orbit, Captain. All stations alerted and waiting."

"Then we'd better get underway." He moved to the nearest intercom, flipped it to open mode.

"Bridge, this is the captain speaking," he said forcefully, thoroughly enjoying the sound of his own voice inside his head.

"Is it really the captain?" came the uncertain reply. Kirk recognized the gentle voice of Lieutenant Arex.

"It is, Lieutenant. We're all back in our own homes again. Warp-factor three, set course for Starbase Twenty-Five. I'll be up in a second."

"Very good, sir. And sir?"

"Yes, Lieutenant?"

"It's great to have you back where you belong."

"Thanks, Mr. Arex." Kirk grinned at the ancient snatch of song. "We feel the same. Kirk out."

Uhura stepped down out of the alcove, still a little dizzy from reintegration, in more sense than one. "You can go now, Mr. Scott."

The chief eyed her oddly. "I beg your pardon, Lieutenant?"

She looked abruptly embarrassed. "I'm sorry, sir. I was still playing the captain."

"And you did a conference-saving job of it, too, Lieutenant Uhura." Kirk eyed each one of them in turn. "That's something which will go into everyone's records. Let's go."

As they stepped into the waiting turbolift car, Kirk noticed that the communications officer was limping. Old fears came back. Perhaps Scott's rectifier hadn't been one hundred percent corrected. "What's the trouble, Lieutenant?" he inquired uneasily.

"I've got a bruise that feels like it covers the whole back of my right leg, sir," she replied feelingly, "and both my arms weigh about twice normal."

"I am sorry about that, Lieutenant Uhura." Spock sounded apologetic. "It was difficult enough for me to counter the size and strength of the Klingon soldier

Captain Kumara pitted against me. I'm afraid I was
forced to employ muscular arrangements which your
body is not familiar with, as well as blocking off certain
neural responses in order to shut off pain so I could remain functioning."

Uhura winced, rubbed at the back of her injured leg.
"I wish you'd been a little more careful, Mr. Spock.
I'm pretty proud of this body myself and I don't like
having it banged up."

"Truly, I'm sorry, Lieutenant. If there had been another way of avoiding the damage, I assure you I
would have employed it."

They emerged on the bridge to be greeted by a number of uncertain stares. As soon as it was made abundantly clear to all that the four officers were back in
their original selves, the bridge personnel relaxed.

One who was waiting to greet them on their return
strolled over to the command chair as soon as Kirk
had seated himself.

"If you've no objection, Jim, there's something I'd
like to request of you." McCoy indicated Uhura, Sulu,
and Spock. "Of all of you."

"What is it, Bones?"

"When we're well on our way, I'd like to interview
you four and record the interviews. I think the results
would make an excellent monograph, one I'd like to
submit for publication in the *Journal of Starfleet Physi-
cians*. Mind-to-body transposition has been accomplished surgically, via transplant, but never before by
transporter. If we could determine how to do it safely
and repeatedly, there could be enormous potential benefits for—"

Sulu glanced back over a shoulder from his position
at the helm-navigation console. "Just as long as I don't
have to go through it again, Doctor."

"Nor I, Lieutenant," added Spock from behind the
science console, in a tone that was not truly emotion-
laden but that carried plenty of impact.

Kirk checked the main viewscreen. Stars showed
brilliant against the velvet blanket of space where Briamos had recently rode. They were well on their way.

"The Klingons should be opening the stasis box about now. Don't you think so, Mr. Spock?"

"Yes, Captain."

Kirk was unable to suppress a sly smile. "Wonder what they're going to say when they find nothing inside except a small generator projecting a simulated stasis field?"

Spock sounded unexpectedly uncertain. "The scenario you envision is not entirely in keeping with the facts, Captain."

Frowning in puzzlement, Kirk turned in the command chair, stared at his first officer. "What do you mean, Spock?"

"It was not my idea, Captain." Spock almost sounded embarrassed. "It was done at Chief Scott's insistence. I remonstrated with him, insisting that it was a juvenile notion, but the chief can be difficult to dissuade when he fixes on a particular idea. Also, he has less tolerance for the Klingons than most of us. I could, despite my personal position, see no harm in allowing him to proceed."

"Proceed? Proceed with what? Spock, what are you talking about?" Kirk didn't know whether to be upset or consoling. Here he was sure the entire Briamos incident was behind him, and now Spock seemed to be hinting that something had been done without his, Kirk's, knowledge. The first officer's comment about Scotty's well-known dislike for the Klingons only made him more nervous. They had escaped Briamos with a solid commitment from its inhabitants, while avoiding any dangerous encounter with the Klingons. But now—

What had Scott done . . . ?

Kumara and his science staff had adjourned to a sealed, double-walled room. They stood behind a portable shield, watching through the superdense but transparent plate as the field nullifier continued to hum at the stasis box.

"Something's wrong," Kumara muttered uneasily. The nullifier had been operating for several long moments, yet the blue aura surrounding the box had not disappeared as it should have.

"I do not understand, Honored Captain," his equally concerned science chief said. "All settings and power levels are correct. The instrumentation is not complex and follows precisely the schematics set down in the manuals for such a nullifier. The aura should vanish. It should have vanished long before now."

"Try successively lower power settings, Klaythia," the Klingon commander suggested.

"I will try, sir." Klaythia adjusted controls on the remote he held. The third setting he tried produced an audible click. The blue halo vanished instantly. Everyone in the room was satisfied, except Klaythia.

"I don't understand, sir," he murmured uncertainly. "This stasis-field generator is operating at a much lower output than any previously recorded level for a Slaver box.

"There's a first time even for stasis boxes, Klaythia. Since the box itself generates the field, anything is possible. Maybe this box is especially old and its power has failed." He sounded pleased. "It may contain a particularly valuable device, to have been sealed for so long."

He was leading the assembled science officers toward the box, which sat on a low table in the center of the otherwise empty room. This was a great moment for the Empire!

A low whine sounded from within the box, rising rapidly in volume to a dangerous howling. The party of Klingons froze.

"Is that normal, Honored Captain?" asked one of the lower-ranking specialists.

"No. No, I've never heard of it happening before," declared Kumara, taking a cautious step backward.

The whining increased. Powerful lights began to glow, pulsing unevenly from the slowly opening top of the box. The whine became a scream and the box started to quiver and bounce on the table.

Kumara and the other Klingons continued their steady retreat, eyes glued in fascination to the dancing box. "Something went wrong with the nullifier, Klaythia. We've set off some kind of previously unknown type of Slaver self-protection device."

"No . . . Honored Captain." Even now Klaythia was more afraid of his commander's wrath than of what the increasingly energetic box might do. "I assure you, all was checked and rechecked before the nullifier was activated. It is operating properly. I admit I cannot account for the way the top of the box is opening without manual assistance but—"

There was a loud *bang* from within the box and several howls of despair from the assembled officers and specialists. The box jumped several meters, hit the right-side wall, leaped to the ceiling, then fell to the deck again, while the Klingons scrambled to open the sealed door.

The box lay still. Two officers paused, half in, half out the opened doorway.

A violent explosion blew the top of the box roofward. Most of the Klingons broke and ran in terror, shoving each other aside in their haste to escape. More colored lights shone from the box's interior. Flashes of bright, colored smoke appeared, formed glowing symbols in the smoky air of the chamber.

Kumara squinted, coughing in the haze. He discovered he recognized the symbols. They were Federation script and spelled out:

FEDERATION FOREVER!

And below that:

DOWN KLINGON!

Now the noises from inside the box organized themselves into a coherent pattern. Klaythia, who had flattened himself to the deck at the initial violent explosion, looked up thoughtfully. Kumara lay next to him and was climbing to his feet.

"I believe, Honored Captain, that those sounds are an electronic rendition of the Federation Interstellar Anthem."

"Imbecile!" Kumara belted his science chief hard

across the mouth, even as he was drawing his sidearm. "I am all too familiar with the insulting propaganda contained in that wailing that passes for music among humans!"

Aiming the sidearm at the cheerfully tooting box, he fired. There was a small *ke-rummp* as the box blew apart. The music died out slowly and rather pitiably. Kumara fired again, at the glowing words floating in the atmosphere of the chamber. The burst passed through the letters, blew a smoking hole in the far wall. He could only hope the infuriating words would fade before anyone else saw them. He turned away, confronted the face of a security officer who had gathered enough courage to peek back into the room.

"No one," he said angrily to the soldier, "is to enter this room until those obscene symbols have been cleansed from the air, and this debris disposed of. Is that understood?"

"Yes, Honored Captain." The security officer withdrew hurriedly.

Walking back into the room, he holstered his sidearm and kicked contemptuously at the shattered rubble of the box. Most of the container had been vaporized or melted by his weapon.

"Let this remain always in your memory, Klaythia," he told his science chief, "as an indication of the fiendish way in which the human mind works."

"It will, sir," said the subdued Klaythia. He stared mournfully at the remnants of the box. "What a shame, sir. . . . All that valuable Slaver metal, gone."

Kumara let those words sink home. Realization filled him.

Kirk was just a light-minute too far away to hear the stream of curses that filled the chamber on board the Klingon cruiser.